COMPROMISED

COMPROMISED
HEIDI AYARBE

HARPERTEEN
An Imprint of HarperCollinsPublishers

HarperTeen is an imprint of HarperCollins Publishers.

Library of Congress Cataloging-in-Publication Data
Ayarbe, Heidi.
  Compromised / Heidi Ayarbe. — 1st ed.
      p.   cm.
  Summary: With her con-man father in prison, fifteen-year-old
Maya sets out from Reno, Nevada, for Boise, Idaho, hoping to stay
out of foster care by finding an aunt she never knew existed, but a
fellow runaway complicates all of her scientifically devised plans.
  ISBN 978-0-06-172849-5 (trade bdg.)
  [1. Runaways—Fiction.   2. Voyages and travels—Fiction.
3. Family problems—Fiction.   4. Foster home care—Fiction.
5. Tourette syndrome—Fiction.]   I. Title.
PZ7.A9618Com 2010
[Fic]—dc22   2009023545
                                                                   CIP
                                                                    AC

Typography by Mischa Shoni Rosenberg
    10 11 12 13 14 CG/RRDB   10 9 8 7 6 5 4 3 2 1

First Edition

For my dad and mom, Gil and Twylah Ayarbe,
with love and admiration.

COMPROMISED

CHAPTER
ONE

First they take our flat screen.

And the computers, all of Dad's satellite equipment, stereos, DVDs. Even the George Foreman grill.

I watch from down the street as they pile our things in the rusty trailer. I steady my breathing and walk up the driveway.

Dad sits on the front steps, head leaning against the brick porch. Icy beads of water drip off his beer can.

"You're home early," I say, walking up the driveway.

He nods. "I'm sorry, Maya," and motions to the house.

I pause at the front door, running my hand over the smooth oak. I grasp the brass doorknob before entering, then wander through the stripped rooms—naked

1

sockets, way pre–Best Buy.

The only thing they left is that garage sale microwave that whistles when it's on. I haven't used it for about a year, though, since I don't want to grow an extra ear from electromagnetic waves. Not scientifically viable, but I'm not taking any chances.

I slump next to Dad on the porch. It's not like I'm surprised. We're all creatures of habit and this was bound to happen. But I can't help feeling disappointed. I guess things had been going too well for too long. My chest tightens.

Dad shakes his head. I smell beer on his stale breath.

"It's okay," I say.

He pulls me in close. "That's my girl." Dad pushes my hair back behind my ears and wraps his arm around my shoulders. "You look a lot like her, you know. You have her eyes. Gray."

Yeah. Storm clouds. Sadness. Thanks for comparing me to the chemically imbalanced family member. Who would want to be anything like her? I shrug, pushing the knot from my throat. "Who cares about all that stuff? We'll be fine." We always are.

He smiles. Tired. He always looks tired just before a move.

I scan the block, taking in the variety of decorative flags:

everything from cutesy pumpkins to ladybugs. Manicured lawns, ceramic house numbers—it'll be a while before we live in another neighborhood like this.

Dad leaves after I go to bed—like I'm not gonna know. He probably has some loose ends to tie up. I always picture Dad's bungles like a tangled-up small intestine—twenty-odd feet of knots and feces.

After I hear the clatter of the garage door shutting, I raid the dwindling supply of Pepto-Bismol to coat the burn in my stomach.

Hypothesis: If they've taken our TVs, DVDs, and stuff, they'll come back for more.

I just hope we won't be here when they do.

Next they take our car.

They drive up in a mud-caked truck that has ROY'S REPO painted on the side in faded red letters. It actually says ROY' R PO. And they have one of those bullet-hole stickers on the side.

Different guys from the ones before.

The short guy wears army boots, tight jeans, and a tighter T-shirt that says HAVE A BALL AT LEE'S 12TH ANNUAL

3

TESTICLE FESTIVAL. Sheep nuts for dinner. Yum.

The big guy wears jeans and a shirt that rides up his stomach. A sweat-stained baseball cap sits crooked on his head. He scratches his gut and stretches his faded T-shirt down. I watch them through the laundry room window.

"Roy's Repo!" The big guy raps on the door with raw knuckles. "We know you're in there."

I hold my breath, hoping they'll go away. Hoping they'll hop back into their truck and drive away. But I know that's dumb. Hope isn't real—just a circuitry problem in my head.

He bellows, "Mr. Sorenson. We need to talk to you, and we're not going to wait all day."

I duck to keep away from the windows and crouch behind the kitchen counter to phone Dad. The line's dead. My cell service had been "discontinued" too. It's not like I was text queen, anyway. I don't think the only message I got—the one from Genevieve Dodge when I went to one of the science club's lunch meetings that said SCI BTCH GO HOME—justified Dad paying my unlimited texting plan. I think she was miffed that I figured out the joke: What's the chemical name of CH_2O? Seawater. Like who couldn't figure that one out? I stare at the useless phone. I might as well have had two cups with string attached to them.

I slip out the back door and jump the fence to call Dad from Mrs. Velasquez's house. "I think we're having trouble with our phone line," I tell her.

Mrs. Velasquez's eyes narrow. She crosses her arms—that perfect I-told-you-so stance only nags can pull off. She stopped bringing us her homemade flan and sopapillas when Dad made a business deal with her brother. The guy probably should've checked out the nice beachfront property at Lahontan before he went for it. Maybe he didn't have Google Earth or something. Anyway, she's pretty bitter now.

I dial, trying to keep my hand from shaking too much. "They're here."

"I'll be right there." I listen to the click and hum of the line.

Dad drives up in his Beemer. The latest model. He swings open the door and steps into the dry October heat. We're having a weird heat wave in Reno. Last year at this time Dad was all psyched about getting me into skiing. I shade my eyes and watch them talk. The tears are probably just from the glare of the sun. Definitely global warming. But the end of the earth doesn't seem all that important right now.

Dad looks handsome in his pressed suit and starched shirt. He loosens his Italian silk tie and faces the repo guys. As soon as Dad starts to talk, the red splotches on the big guy's face fade. He looks almost apologetic. Dad's got big-time attractive genetics. Some people are genetically more attractive than others. It's their smell, their chemistry—something inherent in that double helix, twenty-three pairs of chromosomes. Most people call it charisma. Whatever you want to call it, Dad has it.

The big guy tugs at his shirt. The short guy turns to the house, eyes me, and winks. He flexes and flares his nostrils.

Dad points to the house. "Misunderstanding, I'm sure," he's saying as he passes me on the porch. "Maya, honey, can you get these gentlemen something cold to drink?"

I nod and go to the kitchen, fishing out two of the coldest Cokes I can find in the cooler. The ice has melted. A piece of lactose-free Velveeta cheese floats and bobs. I give them the Cokes, making sure there's no skin-to-skin contact. The last thing I need is scabies or some other kind of communicable disease repo guys have buried under their skin.

The big guy hands Dad a letter. "Here's the information,

if you want to try to get your car back."

Dad flashes me a look. Panic. Funny. I still don't get how he doesn't see this stuff coming. Supposedly we use about ten percent of our brain capacity. But since the brain's hard drive is never full—with an infinite capacity to learn, taking ten percent of infinity is impossible. Pretty arbitrary, really. The brain's potential, with ten billion neurons and one hundred and twenty billion glial cells, is staggering. Potential, however, is the key word.

Sometimes Dad doesn't seem to reach that potential.

It's out of his hands now.

The repo guys leave dusty footprints all over the carpet. The engine of the truck sputters, then roars to life. We watch as they tow away the car. Dad flinches.

"It's just a car, Dad. Whatever." I try to hide my anger and throw the letter on the table, turning my back to him. I know he's sorry. But sometimes . . . sometimes sorry isn't good enough.

"It's a setback, baby. Nothing more." He moves to me and puts his arm around my shoulder. "Let's go out to dinner."

We don't even have money to pay our phone bill— where will we get the money for dinner? I look down at my designer jeans and trendy shoes. It's not rational to get upset over *things*, but my throat feels like somebody has wedged a grapefruit in it.

"How about going to that steak house we like so much?" Dad pulls out his wallet and flips through his credit cards.

I pry open the lid of the cooler. "Let's just eat grilled cheese sandwiches." I do a mental inventory of the things I can sell. We just need enough to get us a couple of bus tickets to Nowhere, U.S.A.

Dad sits slumped over the kitchen table, his head cradled in his hands. The sandwiches sizzle in the fry pan. At least they haven't cut the gas line. Yet. I pass a sandwich to him on our last Chinet plate and hold mine in a napkin. It'll pass. We'll be okay. We just need about a thousand miles between Dad's latest scam and us.

Before bed, I make the plan. It's always worked before.

Purpose: Keep Dad out of trouble

Hypothesis: If I get all of our money together and get us on a bus ASAP, Dad and I will make it out of Reno safely.

Materials: Money from cache, materials to sell, bus tickets, me, Dad

Procedure:

1) Get money from the cache

2) See how much we need to sell to get to price of tickets

3) Sell necessary items

4) Buy tickets

5) Convince Dad to go with me

6) Get on bus

Variable: Time: How quickly can I do this? How quickly will the cops get here?

Constants: Me and Dad—we never change. He never changes.

F inally, they take Dad.

They drive up early in the morning just as I'm leaving for school. It's not a regular police car with sirens and horns. It's a brown Buick. And the officers looked like insurance salesmen. A beige lady follows behind in her cardboard suit and soft-soled shoes.

"Tax evasion."

"Embezzlement."

"Fraud."

Lots of other phrases fly through the air.

Dad hasn't shaved yet and wears a shirt that smells like yesterday. He drops his head as they cuff him. Then the lady comes to me and tells me to pack a bag. That's when I hear "foster care."

Foster care.

Dad speaks. He's probably saying something like "It'll be okay. I promise, baby. It'll be okay."

But all I can hear is "foster care."

The cardboard suit follows me upstairs. She has a tedious name—Beulah—and is a droopy woman with transparent skin—way vitamin D deficient. Clearly too many hours spent sitting under the glare of fluorescent eco-saver bulbs.

"I'm your caseworker," she says.

"Can I have a sec?" I ask. She steps out of my room. I sit down and lay my head on my knees. My heart drums in my chest, my throat tightens, sweat trickles down my back.

Foster care.

It's as if those two words are being drilled into my skull.

I slow my breathing.

"You okay in there?" Beulah asks.

No.

My whole world has just crumbled to pieces.

My stomach is on fire.

I take another breath and a swig of Pepto-Bismol. I've

been sleeping with the stuff for a few weeks now—easier than getting up every couple of hours at night.

I revert to the scientific method. Anything can be explained and sorted by looking at it objectively. Take out the emotion, and things tend to make more sense.

I lick the chalky pink liquid off my lips and try to ignore the cramping in my stomach.

Purpose. I need a purpose.

"You okay?" Beulah hollers.

"Yep," I manage. "Just need a minute." And a purpose— a plan.

A plan. Order. There's a science to everything—even something as absurd-sounding as foster care.

My purpose: Get dad out of jail? Get out of foster care? I can't figure it out. Too many variables. I breathe in again.

Purpose: Get Dad and me back together again.

Okay. Not the most scientific of purposes. But it's a start. Step one.

I exhale.

Beulah clears her throat and raps on the door. "Maya? I need to come in now, okay?"

She probably thinks I'm gonna do something a

melodramatic pubescent fifteen-year-old normally does, like drink nail polish or something.

"Yeah. Come in," I say, steadying my voice.

She peeks her head in the door. "We need to get going. You should pack some things."

I grab my favorite jeans and sweater and pack them in a backpack and head toward the door.

"You might want more," Beulah says, and clears her throat.

I shrug and throw more clothes in the pack until it bulges. Beulah leads me out to her car.

I turn back and see a man lock our front door and stick some paper up. There's already a sign on the lawn: BANK OWNED PROPERTY.

That didn't take long.

Beulah drives me to Kids Place—a "middle ground shelter," as she calls it. We coast through the gate and park between small square houses painted yellow with white trim. A heavy woman with bread-kneading hands meets us on the walk. She takes my backpack and grips my hand in hers. "I'm Rose. Welcome."

She strides ahead of us, her hips swaying back and forth. "Beulah's your social worker," she turns to say, "and

I'm the one in charge here. We'll check you in and take you around so you can get more comfortable."

Beulah and I follow Rose into a colorful office. Finger paintings are pasted on the walls and her bookshelves are covered in dioramas and toilet-paper-roll art projects. I sit next to Rose, across from Beulah.

Rose hands me a peanut butter and jelly sandwich and an apple.

"That's okay. I had breakfast." I push them back. That burning feeling that started in my stomach spreads until it feels like all of my organs are on fire. Classic gastritis attack caused by stress. I hope they won't take away the Pepto-Bismol I packed. That's as much a staple in my diet as protein.

Rose smiles and says, "I'll leave you two for now," and hands me an instruction manual. "Rules and Regulations of Kids Place."

Beulah registers my bag and takes out the Pepto-Bismol. "No medication here."

"But," I start to say, and then think better of it. I have a bottle in my locker at school.

She hands me a pile of stiff clothes. "These are for you."

"I have clothes."

She purses her lips. "It's procedure."

Procedure.

She has her scientific method, too, I guess.

"This isn't . . . ," She flips open a file that says AMAYA SORENSON and jots something down. "Amaya, this isn't going to be an overnight thing."

AMAYA SORENSON. I have a file. She puts my name and case number in her computer.

I clench my jaw and try to focus on the dinosaur dioramas—one of which is totally off since some kid put a Triassic dinosaur next to a Late Jurassic dinosaur, only the Triassic was extinct by then. Sloppy work.

Beulah's tapping on the keyboard brings me back to the room. "There," she says. "Just need to get the basic information down. Your family doctor should be able to provide us with medical information we might need."

We have no family doctor, I think. I've never actually been to a real doctor, except for emergency rooms.

I'm officially in "the system."

"We're trying to contact family." Beulah clears her throat. "Do you, um, know where your mother is?"

I nod. "Dead."

❄   ❄   ❄

When I came home from kindergarten, her lips were blue, her hands cold. I covered her with a blanket and waited for the doctors to come. Doctors are magicians. They had gotten her to come back before. I knew I just had to wait for them to turn Mama's blue lips pink.

Then we'd find a way to make her happy again. She wouldn't want to go away. I'd be a really good girl.

They drove up with flashing lights and a blaring siren. But the machines didn't work. Or the pumping. Or the fluids they shot through her body.

"Five minutes. If only we had gotten here five minutes ago," I heard one of them say under his breath. Another one shook her head and pulled me away from Mama, covering her face with my soft pink sheet.

Five minutes doesn't sound like much. But five minutes is time enough to run through the big pile of raked leaves at the schoolyard three times, get a hair ribbon back from Jimmy Sanchez, sneak an Oreo from the cookie jar, or turn on the TV, the volume off, to see if the grown-up kissy shows are on.

Five minutes is a lifetime.

Dad ran through the door just as they were wheeling her into the back of the ambulance.

"Ahem." Beulah swallows and blushes. "Dead mother" is always something that gets people squirming. They want to know how, when, why. A kind of morbid curiosity. Some things, I've learned, are okay. *She died of a terminal illness. She was in a car accident and slipped into a coma. She had a heart condition.* People like those explanations.

I usually say, "She had a neurotransmitter imbalance with deficiencies in seratonin and norepinephrine." Most people don't know what I'm talking about and just figure it's some rare virus. Better that than telling someone that your mom downed a bottle of pills with a bottle of whiskey. That makes for some pretty awkward moments.

People don't "get" suicide. Who can blame them? It's against nature considering we're born with the instinct to strive for survival—it's our biological inheritance. Think concentration camps, famine, slavery, and the will to live all those people had. All animals are wired to strive to survive. Humans, though, are the only animals that commit suicide; it's like some people's survival instinct gets all tweaked.

Major evolutionary flaw.

Beulah gives me one of those horrible pity looks. One I don't need. I kind of figure if I'm over it, the rest of the world can find a way to deal with it. She leans forward and a crease forms between her eyes. Her cardboard suit crumples at the armpits and hips.

"And, um, other relatives? That you know of?"

I shake my head. The branches on my family tree are pretty bare. Dad and I have spent every Thanksgiving and Christmas at Denny's or the local diner since Mom died. People think that's sad. But it's not. It's just our way—our tradition. And it's always been fine by me.

"When can I talk to my dad?" I ask, staring at the phone.

Beulah taps her pencil on the desk in a rat-a-tat-tat. "Right now"—she clears her throat—"right now your dad can't talk to anyone except for his lawyers."

"Doesn't he get a phone call? Isn't that standard?"

"It's a pretty big federal investigation, and your dad has been put in isolation until things get weeded out. And—" She pauses.

"And they need to weed me out."

She nods. "Something like that. But it won't take long."

"Sure. Quick and fair trial."

The point of her pencil snaps off during her last rat-a-tat-tat. "Maybe, um, you can get settled in. I should have a clearer picture of what's happening later today or tomorrow."

We leave the office and walk down the concrete path to one of the yellow houses. She opens the door and I gag on that industrial-clean smell. I look down the blindingly white hall. Colorful bulletin boards announce activities, birthdays, tutoring. I'd like to call somebody—anybody. But after two years in Reno, I haven't made one close friend. Unless you count Eileen Jones, my chemistry lab partner.

Eileen's not really a reliable lab partner. Last week, for example, she got sick and blacked out when we were testing the oxidative rancidity of food. I missed out on a cool lab because I spent the rest of class with her at the nurse's office. She brought me a thank-you card the next day.

Friendship has always been a waste of time since I never know when Dad and I will be leaving with new identities and lives. And I definitely didn't inherit Dad's attractive genetics. I sigh.

"This is your room and bunk. For now. Until we find appropriate placement."

I freeze in the doorframe, then exhale and throw my stuff on the top bunk Beulah assigns me.

She clicks her pen in and out and clips some papers together. "Tomorrow things will look a little brighter." Even Beulah's smile is cardboard.

It feels like I've swallowed a thousand cotton balls. It's never gotten this bad. Sure, there was the time we had to sneak out the bathroom window of our apartment, scramble down the fire escape, and leave town. But that was more like an adventure. Dad was with me. And we always made it. Together.

The last two years have been too good—like an NBC Family Channel sitcom without the token, politically correct minority character. I should've known it wouldn't last. The nice car, nicer house. Suburbia in all its glory. I remember driving up that first day, not believing what I was seeing. After years of apartments, trailer houses, and seedy motels, Dad drove up to American suburbia.

Our neighborhood looked like one of those model cities you see at science fairs. All the houses were that same Popsicle-stick color. Every yard followed regulation landscape rules with decorative rocks and desert plants. And an obligatory status SUV filled every driveway. American flags flapped in the wind.

At first I thought I'd get lost in all the sameness. Like if Dad dropped me off, stripped the house of its number and streets of their signs, I'd never find it. It could be a new reality show: *Suburban Survivor.*

You've got ten minutes to find your own home. Go!

We pulled up to a house that looked like every other house.

"What do you think?" Dad grinned. "I've got a great job now, honey. All those other things are behind us."

I looked at Dad and back at the cream-colored house. I blinked. I wouldn't have believed it if I hadn't seen it. The next-door neighbor waved enthusiastically. "Hey there! Welcome to the neighborhood!"

I wasn't ever allowed to talk to our neighbors. Not in our old places, anyway. Dad was already waving. He winked at me and grinned.

"Why don't you go and pick out your room?"

I walked into the empty house that smelled like fresh paint and lemon wood polish. I sniffed. Not a trace of backed up sewers, urine, or greasy pizza. Almost too clean. The back windows faced mountains with blooming yellow sagebrush—not a dump or a back alley. Open Nevada-desert space.

"Come on. Let's check out the house."

The narrow entryway opened up to one of those great rooms, combining the living room, family room, dining room, and kitchen. In the back, a narrow staircase led upstairs.

We walked up. I chose the first room on the left, with a view of the mountains. "How are we going to fill all the space?" I asked.

Dad flashed his smile. "I guess we'd better go shopping."

I believed him. The human mind is funny like that because even if we stack up the evidence that shows life will go a certain way, we ignore the evidence and "believe"— deceiving ourselves. But I fell for it—that sense of normal. How stupid.

"We've already called your school. They know you won't be coming in today."

I hold my stomach and think about the half-full pink bottle stuck in my locker. "I can go. I don't mind."

Beulah pats my shoulder. "You're a great student. One day won't interfere with your school performance."

I sigh.

Beulah points to the rec room on my personalized orphanage tour. "You can play cards, read, just take it easy. Tomorrow we'll have some answers—or some direction, at least."

She slips a gnawed pencil behind her ear. Her nails are ragged, chewed down to the skin. It has to be a really hard job, taking kids away from their parents. She leads me back to my room.

I lie down on my bunk. Midday light glints off the polished floors.

Dad's in jail. I'm stuck at some orphanage. And for the first time in my life, everything has spiraled out of control. There isn't going to be a nighttime "escape" or frantic rush to the train station. Dad isn't going to surprise me at school midday to pick me up because we were going on an "adventure."

I'm screwed.

I clutch my stomach and wonder how hard it would be to stage a prison break. Step one: State your purpose.

Purpose: Break Dad out of prison.

Yeah. Like that's a normal thing for a fifteen-year-old to be considering.

CHAPTER THREE

Step two: Hypothesis. The hypothesis, though, is based on prior knowledge and observations. It's not just some random shot in the dark.

I try to think about ways to research prison and orphanage breaks—neither of which seem plausible outside the realm of Hollywood and Charles Dickens's novels.

I'm not a big fan of either.

Hydrogen, helium, lithium, beryllium, boron . . . I finally fall asleep when I get to the Lanthanide series.

"The freak's back," a husky voice rasps. The room smells like cheap perfume. "And we're stuck with her in here."

The bedsprings groan as somebody flops onto the bottom bunk. She sniffles to the count of five. One, two,

24

three, four, sniffle. One, two, three, four, sniffle. "They say she went on a hunger strike and they had to force food into her. *Sniff.*"

"Fucking cracked. And the worst part is she never shuts up."

"I know. Her mouth is on total rerun mode."

"Just blow her off. Everyone else does."

I peel my eyes open and turn over on my side. "Hi," I venture. "I'm Maya." I'm not what you would call socially gifted to begin with, and have no idea how one goes about introducing herself in an orphanage.

Two girls stare at me. The one bathed in drugstore perfume wears tight black jeans and a leather dog collar. I refrain from telling her that our noses are always homing in on potential mates, and with her stench, her breeding possibilities are slimmer than mine. (My lessened reproductive chances are due to the fact that my hair looks like a Brillo pad and I have way underdeveloped mammary glands.) The one on the bunk below me blows her nose on a ragged Kleenex stuffed in pudgy hands. Folds of milk-blue skin stick out from the top of her jeans.

Just then a girl walks into the room and the other two get real quiet, looking right through her, like she's invisible.

I recognize that look.

Dark circles ring the girl's black eyes. Her arms are scarred and bruised. She stares at me, then turns her attention to the dog collar and Sniffles.

"I'm back!" Her face transforms, and she cracks a smile, throwing her bag on the bottom bunk. "Move your shit, Jess. I get the bottom."

Jess glares and climbs up to the top bunk.

The girl stares at the poster on the wall and rips it off; Sniffles winces. "What is this, Shelly? Another one of your 'Dream Big' posters?" She shakes her head. "Fucking psychobabble bullshit."

"Yeah. You'd know about that, Nicole," Jess says.

"Sure thing. I'm just a regular Vincent Gigante. This time they declared me depressive with thought disorder." She laughs. "Last time it was manic depression. I have a list a mile long of cool diagnoses." And she goes on about this guy Gigante—aka The Chin—and how he snowed over thirty-four psychiatrists over the years. She's on number eight.

Jess flips open a book and puts in earphones, cranking up music on an MP3. Shelly noisily rolls up the poster Nicole took off the wall, smoothing it out where it was torn.

And Nicole keeps talking, taping up a poster of Marlon Brando. "Now that's style. He didn't do motivational speaker crap—he fucking lived."

I clear my throat. But nobody pays attention. Finally I say again, "Hi. I'm Maya."

The three turn to me and Jess flicks out her earphones. "Fuck," she says. "We've got ourselves a greeter here."

Shelly says, "Oh. I'm Shelly. This is Jess"—she points to the one with a dog collar—"and Nicole," motioning to the girl who just walked in. "Nicole just got back."

"Yep, from the loony bin," Nicole says, and laughs—forced. Hollow.

"Good thing we got the introductions out of the way, Shelly. Maybe you can show her where we play shuffleboard on the Aloha Deck," Jess sneers. She looks me up and down. "Why don't you just go back to your sweet dreams about designer jeans? Nobody here gives a rat's ass who you are."

Shelly blushes and mouths, "Sorry." She blows her nose.

I feel an urge to mark my space and half wait for their claws to come out and tear me to shreds. That's something I really like about the animal kingdom. It's direct. Every animal knows the rules. They're genetically designed to know the rules.

Humans change the rules.

I stare Jess down and sit cross-legged on the bed. I've had a pretty crap day so far and am not in the mood for a territorial war in some dorm room.

Jess glares and turns to Nicole. "So? You done with that Gandhi shit?"

Nicole pulls herself up on the windowsill and takes out a clove cigarette, inhaling the sickly-sweet smoke and blowing it out the crack in the window. She wears a T-shirt with some guy's mug shot. LUCKY LUCIANO is written in bold letters below his picture.

"I mean, you eating now?"

"No, Sherlock, I'm just here on fumes. What do you think?" She looks at a trash can filled with little candy papers and sighs. "Dude, Shelly, what's with that? You hoarding again?"

"No," Shelly says.

"Fuck, Shelly." Nicole shakes her head. "Who's your shrink now?"

Shelly shrugs. "I'm back with Dr. Jenkins."

"Figures. Fucking 'Dream Big' poster." Nicole turns to

Jess. "And where have you been the last nine months?"

"Fuck you. You think you're the only one with problems? Your biggest problem is not going through with it."

Shelly blanches. "Jess," she whispers.

Jess hugs a pillow and mutters, "I hate it here."

"Then leave." Nicole inhales. Smoke curls up from her cigarette.

Jess turns, staring straight through Nicole. "Why don't you? Oh yeah. I forgot. You can't even read where the buses are going." She lowers her voice. "You can't even kill yourself."

Nicole tenses. Nobody speaks. I can almost smell the alarm pheromones.

Jess and Shelly won't even look at her.

Nicole faces me. "What are you looking at?"

"You," I say.

She flinches, then glares at me, her eyes narrowing. Then she smiles again. But it's not real.

I hate when that happens, when the observer becomes the prey. I wonder how I'll deflect the attack when I blurt out, "This is definitely an issue of territorialism."

The three of them stare.

"You know," I say. "When an animal stakes its claim to

an area. It has to suss out its possibilities to win the battle, depending on the size of the other animal, maturity, which one already possesses the territory, and value of the territory in relation to other available locations." They continue to stare, so I continue to talk, never taking my eyes from Nicole. It's like we're in some kind of staring contest.

I won't lose.

So I talk. This has often been a problem of mine in social situations—either I talk too much or not enough. And when I talk, I spew out scientific facts that most people really don't care about. Most people don't get the beauty of science. "The classic scientific example to illustrate territorial possession is the hawk and the dove." I clear my throat. "Humans aren't all that different."

Nicole's eyes come to life for just a second before they turn off again. "What? If you can't beat 'em, bore 'em, Jeopardy? Jesus, where did you come from?" She finally looks away. I win.

Jess mutters. "Why don't you just stay at the bus depot with the street trash where you belong? Or better yet—" Jess motions to the scars on Nicole's arms.

All I can think about is Mom. And my stomach gets that achy burn feeling.

Nicole turns and flicks her cigarette butt at Jess, grazing her ear.

I cringe, afraid the whole place will go up in flames from Jess's generous use of flammable hair products.

Nicole jumps from the windowsill and brushes past Jess, pausing for just a second to stare her down. Jess turns away.

Nicole leaves the room. And I don't say anything. I just slink back into the corner.

Nobody breathes.

"Jess." Shelly sniffles when the silence gets too heavy to bear. "How could you? I feel so bad."

Jess rolls her eyes. "Jesus, Shelly. She's a freak. She's a total waste of oxygen. And Christ, what do you have to feel bad about? You'd probably take the blame for the next fucking world war. Stop saying sorry for shit you don't have anything to do with. It bugs the hell out of me."

"I'm sorry," Shelly says, pulling out more tissues.

Guilt. That's one of the easiest human emotions to play on. A dirty trick, really. But if you find somebody like Shelly—someone who feels permanently responsible for global warming and other apocalyptic stuff, you have the perfect target. I hate watching people with a hyper sense of guilt squirm around like Shelly. Dad says those who feel guilty about something are the first to confess, then, more importantly, pay. That was during his Preacher Tent Days—before he went white-collar.

Once, after a heated revival in some dusty old town, Dad came up to me and said, "Religion is based on one thing. What do you think that is?"

"God," I said, happy to know the answer. That day I had seen no fewer than eighty-seven miracles performed by my daddy's own hands. I studied them, soft and manicured, not understanding why he couldn't have done the same for Mama.

He cupped my face in his miracle hands and grinned. "Even better. Guilt."

What about God? What about all those people who believe? I wanted to ask him but couldn't say the words. (Later I learned about neurotheology.) I couldn't let him know that I had believed, too.

I don't anymore. Not unless it's written up in some science journal with facts to back it.

The last day of the revival, he winked and said, "It's time to ease these people's minds and give them a chance to mend their ways. Ready for some miracles?"

We left Arizona thousands of dollars richer and ate dinner at the Sizzler buffet instead of Denny's. But I lost some part of Dad in Arizona. That part that all kids worship. Dads are heroes, right? But do heroes steal? Do heroes lie?

I don't think so.

Shelly looks up at me apologetically. Dad could easily clear her life savings, though I'm quite sure it wouldn't be worth the effort. Shelly sniffles. Major postnasal drip. Probably chronic rhinitis. She rubs a near-disintegrated Kleenex on her raw nose. "I have a runny nose," she apologizes.

Yeah. It is pretty annoying having somebody always apologizing for stuff.

Shelly slumps back onto the bed, rocking the frame. "I was kinda hoping she wouldn't come back."

"Major Spam," mutters Jess.

"Spam?" I ask. "As in computer crap?"

"No. As in unidentifiable meatlike substance crap. She's been in the system so long now that she's been here more than in regular foster care. Long shelf life. Nobody wants her."

"Oh," I say. "*That* spam."

"Yeah, she's had a couple of good shots with good families, but she blew it." Shelly shrugs. "Anyway, she's just got Kids Place now. She runs away every other month, but she never really leaves." Shelly wipes her hands on her jeans. "They had her on suicide watch a couple weeks in the hospital when she did that hunger strike thing. She does that."

"Does what?"

"You know. Try to kill herself. Freaked out one of her foster moms a few years ago. Slit her wrists. Almost died."

I nod.

Jess glares. "She's wacked. Like this bigger-than-life person who doesn't even want to live. She'd probably be better off dead."

I wait for Shelly to apologize again. But this time she sucks in her breath and lies down. She pauses, then says, "Nicole's just kind of, um, different, you know?"

What's wrong with different? I wonder. But it's not like I'm on any homecoming court, either. Different doesn't work in high school. If I can make it to college, then things will be okay.

Maybe that's all Nicole needs, too. Get to the magic number and be whoever you want. It's like we're all stuck in Cloneville until we're eighteen.

Shelly rubs some Vicks on her nose. "First time?" she asks.

"First time what?"

Jess turns over on her bunk. "First time at Girl Scout camp, genius."

I nod. "Yeah. First time."

"Well, you won't want to miss the evening bonfire and marshmallow roast."

"Have you lived here for a long time?" I ask both of them.

Shelly blushes and gnaws on her fingernails. "Kinda."

Jess pulls a history textbook out of her backpack. "What's it matter to you?"

"It doesn't," I say, and I mean it. I won't be like them.

For the first time all day it really registers that I'm in a children's home. I swallow and take a deep breath.

"You got a mom?" Shelly asks.

We buried her in a lonely cemetery. I remember the day as if it were a drawing—a Crayola-blue sky with cutout construction paper clouds. I looked up at the cold December sun, pasted on the blue sky. Just like Wild Blue Yonder—my favorite crayon color, only a nub left. A spindly tree threw off a sad shadow. Dad shivered and we watched the men pile frozen clumps of dirt on the pine box. Their rusty shovels pierced the frozen ground, a tip snapped off, ringing, falling on Mom. I clapped my hands over my ears. Nobody came. Just Dad and me.

I threw away Wild Blue Yonder that afternoon, crushing it under my polished black shoes. I still hate the color blue.

I shake my head. "Just my dad," I say.

"He a good guy?"

"He's not the president of the PTA or anything. But we do okay, you know?"

"So where is he?"

"Jail." I sigh. "He always manages to talk his way out of stuff, though. So I kinda figure he'll either be set free or made warden by the end of the week." I try to laugh and ignore the acid that works its way up my esophagus. I wish I had my Pepto.

"Probably," Shelly agrees. But I don't like the tone in her voice. That I've-heard-it-all-before-know-it-all tone. One, two, three, four, sniffle. She blows her nose and wipes her watery eyes. She's pretty leaky.

We sit in silence for a while. A bell rings and kids shuffle down the hall past our room.

"Ready for dinner?" Shelly asks. "You can sit with us, if you want."

"Sure." I follow them out the door. The hallway fills with other teenagers. Abandoned. Orphans.

I feel relieved knowing that I'm not one of them—Spam.

I just need to wait it out for a while. Do my time. Thanks to Dad.

CHAPTER
FOUR

We walk into the cafeteria, and I head to where Nicole is sitting. Shelly grabs my elbow and veers me to the next table. We scoot onto the benches, leaving Shelly a spot on the end. She can't fit between the bench and the table. The cafeteria fills up. A couple of young kids run and give Nicole a hug, but nobody sits with her.

And I think about all of those first days I had at new schools during lunch sitting alone in the cafeteria hoping my sandwich looked like everyone else's. I wonder if that feeling ever goes away.

"Um, do you want to eat here?" I ask Nicole. "With us?"

Our table goes silent and Nicole looks at me. "Why would I want to do some dumb-ass thing like that?"

38

There's a collective exhale at the table. Then everybody starts to eat, heavy plastic forks clanging on the plastic tray. They talk about their days—like this is the most normal place in the world. Finally Shelly introduces me. Nobody's asked, though. We're just all stuck—in transit—homeless. Children of the state. Shelly says, "It gets easier, okay?"

I nod. "We're brood parasites." I say it a little too loud.

A couple of kids look up from their dinner trays. Jess rolls her eyes and mutters, "Shit. Here we go."

Nicole raises an eyebrow and faces us, saddling the bench. "I've gotta hear this."

"Um. You know. It's when the biological mother leaves her eggs in the nest of another and splits. So all the biological mother has to do is conceive and not worry about the actual parenting. The brown-headed cowbird has two hundred and twenty-one known hosts; it can even lay eggs the same color as the unsuspecting host. Sometimes the host doesn't even realize it's raising the young of another."

Nicole shakes her head. "Fucking name-that-useless-science-fact. Do you have a name for that?"

"Brood parasitism," I repeat.

"Not that. I mean the academic bulimia that you spew. Jesus." Nicole picks up her tray and walks by me.

She whispers, "You're not gonna last."

I feel my face get hot. The table is quiet. *Why,* I want to ask.

Shelly pats my hand.

"Hey, Jess knows all about that parasite thing," some kid with black greasy hair and acne says, elbowing the guy next to him. He talks too loud, like that's going to erase Nicole's words. "You never told us about the nice family that got your little"—he sneers at Jess—"parasite." The two of them snicker.

"Fuck you, Keith," Jess says.

Keith and his friend laugh. Shelly leans into me. "Jess just got back from City of Refuge. She doesn't talk much about it. Gave the baby up. She's been pretty cranky since—"

"Shut up, Shelly. Like anybody really needs you to do the ongoing commentary here. Brainiac can probably pick up on a few things without you spelling them out for her."

"I just—" Shelly starts to say.

"Christ." Jess stands up and leaves, banging her tray on the kitchen counter. The rest of us finish our dinner in silence, then return to our rooms.

Ten o'clock: lights-out. A sliver of light beams across

the ceiling whenever the motion detector goes on outside. I listen to Shelly's snores, Jess's crying, and Nicole's silence. It's as if she doesn't even breathe. I listen to the other sounds of Kids Place—the shuffle of security guards pacing up and down the halls, the ticks of clocks, one of the faucets leaking. I don't know if I'll ever fall asleep again.

Unfortunately, I do.

"Get up." A clammy hand covers my mouth. "Now." Somebody drags me off the bed. Piercing pain shoots up my legs when my feet hit the cold linoleum floor. "Hurry up," he whispers.

Two guys and a girl pull me out into the hallway. They drag me through the kitchen, out into the alleyway. I rub my arms in the chill night air.

"What the?" I say.

"Shut up," the girl snaps. "Parasite," she sneers. "What the fuck."

I think my scientific method for surviving orphanhood should probably include not opening my mouth. Not speaking. That's probably a better approach to this situation.

The girl nods at the guys and they throw me in the Dumpster. The hinges creak before the metal lid slams in a clamor. I listen as a latch clicks into place.

Blackness envelopes me. I jerk my knees to my chest and flick a monstrous cockroach off my neck. I retch and tremble, pounding on the lid of the Dumpster. "Please! Please!" I scream between gags. "Please let me out."

"Let's go," the girl says.

I pound on the Dumpster. "Please. Please," I whimper.

"What? No Animal Planet fact?" she asks. "Snot-nosed bitch."

I listen, horrified, as they walk away. "Don't panic," I whisper. "Don't panic. Panicking is not rational. I'm just in a Dumpster. I'm okay. There's space. Somebody will find me in the morning." I squeeze my eyes shut and pretend I'm somewhere else—like that apartment we had in downtown Sacramento. It smelled like sewer and garbage and had tons of roaches. But I make the mistake of opening my eyes for just a second and feel the wave of terror build up inside me.

So I begin to scream. And scream. And pound on the Dumpster. My chest feels tight; I gasp for breath until every bit of air in my body is squeezed out of my chest, and as hard as I try to gulp air, nothing enters. I don't remember passing out. When I wake up, I'm being pulled out of the

Dumpster and dropped on the pavement. Jess and Shelly stand over me.

"Welcome to Kids Place," Jess says. "You really pissed off the wrong people today. The Triad doesn't usually come down this hard this soon."

"C'mon." Shelly lets me lean on her and leads me to our room.

Nicole is lying in bed. "Looks like you were the dove tonight, Jeops. Gotta watch that territorialism. Maybe you should pee around your bed." She rolls on her side.

I spend the rest of the night trembling, waiting for them to come again. I'm the new Kids Place prey.

CHAPTER FIVE

At breakfast the girl is wearing my clothes. My favorite sweater and jeans. The jeans are as soft as flannel, almost worn through the knees. And I've had that sweater since before we moved to Reno. It was the only thing I took with me from New Mexico. Rosa, our next-door neighbor, gave it to me the day we left.

It's just a sweater, I tell myself. But for some reason it feels like more.

"It's just a stupid sweater," I mutter.

The girl looks up at me and smirks. Like she knows.

I look around. Lots of girls have pieces of me. Sweatshirts, pants, a belt. Even Jess has a scarf of mine, and Shelly's trying to hide her socks. Nobody looks me in the eyes. I'm see-through—a glasswing butterfly. Last night my life was spread around, leaving me with nothing.

I smell like Kids Place soap—kind of detergenty lemon. Cheap. I smooth out the stiff clothes Kids Place gave me—a boxy pair of khaki pants and too-big sweatshirt. They probably don't use fabric softener or anything. The clothes smell like plastic.

I go to the room and rifle through the drawers looking for a piece of me. Anything me.

Jess comes back in from the bathroom, my scarf wrapped around her neck. I stare at her.

"Get over it, Maya." She wraps the scarf around again. "It's just the initiation thing the Triad does. You're obviously new. Just don't *act* so new. It's like you walk around here looking at everybody like we're from the zoo. Brood parasites. God."

I open my mouth to protest but nothing comes out. Don't speak, I think. Just don't speak. I've become one of those lab rats, trying to make my way through the maze to find the cheese. I'm not the scientist but the experiment. My stomach cramps and I fight back the tears.

Jess shrugs. "That's nothing compared to what you'll

see in some of the foster families. Better get a backbone." She clears her throat and laughs. "Actually, a vertebra." She looks over at me. "You think you're the only one who knows how to read around here." She leaves the room.

Shelly comes over. "We've gotta wear the stuff. All of us are, um. Well, we've gotta wear it. You have to understand."

I nod. It's a brilliant crime. I watch as all my clothes walk by the room in some in-your-face kind of parade and do everything I can to keep from crying. Stay rational. Come up with a hypothesis. They're just stupid clothes.

I look over at Nicole. She doesn't have anything of mine on. She looks at me—the only one who looks me in the eye all morning. "They have no code," she says.

"Huh?" I ask.

She walks by, swinging her backpack over her bony shoulders. "Those animals—the ones that follow each other and all commit suicide together—what're they called?"

"Lemmings," I say. But I don't bother to tell her the suicide part is a myth. *Keep mouth shut,* I think.

"Yeah. Lemmings." She leaves the room.

Maybe she's wearing a pair of my underwear. Why would she be different from anybody else?

The next few days I just go through the motions. At school I watch everybody walk down the hall as if nothing has changed in the world. For them it hasn't. Or maybe it has. But who knows? It's like each person in this world is totally alone. I think knowing that humans are the most social animals makes everything even lonelier.

If there is a God, he must be a scientist and we're lab rats. I look up. What if the sky is the lens of God's monocle? And nighttime is the blink of His eye? "The data has been compromised!" I want to shout.

But there's no God. Dad taught me that.

I look down the hallway and watch as life unfolds: Kids group together according to attire and hairstyle; they cluster together for protection, only separating to go to their respective classes. Occasionally, the species mingle. Like when they have to do book reports together. Survival. Nothing more. Then they revert back to the safety of their groups—their own likenesses.

The social committee is in a huff about the Halloween dance since Principal Kinne won't approve the Playboy Bunny party idea. Apparently having a bunch of libidinous teenage guys dressed in silk bathrobes ogling girls with bunny costumes is "inappropriate." Go figure.

The science club's suggestion of Forces of Nature has been ignored. As usual. As well as the debate team's. The social committee didn't take their Dead Presidents idea to heart.

Today when Mr. Hunter pulls out the hot chili peppers for chemistry lab, Eileen hands him a note. I'll work alone while she does worksheets. She's allergic to peppers . . . or something. I think Eileen should be exempt from taking science even if she's the only one who talks to me at school, text messages aside.

After school I slip into the office where all the school counselors and Beulah are sitting around Principal Kinne's conference table. I bite down on a nail. My finger still burns from the spill in chemistry. I was helping Mr. Hunter organize the lab and dropped some nasty bhut jolokia pepper oil on my hand. I had to run my fingers under water and milk, but the tingling is still there. Now my lip hurts from where I bit down on my nail. Stupid. And I ran out of milk.

This time Beulah looks gray. Not beige. She sucks in her sallow cheeks when she sees me. One of Principal Kinne's fluorescent lights sputters and dies. We sit in the shadows while the janitor works to replace the bulb.

Beulah hands me a piece of paper. "The State of Nevada is beginning the process to terminate your father's parental rights based on the long-term deficiency of his parental duties."

No one speaks.

The school counselors squirm in their chairs. Awkward, really. Star student. Felon father. Definitely a conversation stopper.

I look up at the picture hanging behind Principal Kinne. They wear matchy-matchy clothes—he, his wife, and three kids. Two big dogs with shiny fur lie in the shot. They all sit in front of a tree. It's fall and the leaves are bright orange, red, and yellow. The frame is engraved: A FAMILY IS A LITTLE WORLD CREATED BY LOVE.

I look back at the piece of paper. *Termination of parental rights.* I read the words over and try to say them. Everybody stares at me. Waiting.

In order to speak, the brain has to create an idea of what it wants to communicate to somebody else. But what am I supposed to say when there's *nothing* to say?

How could I have messed this all up? I think back to

my first plan. The money from the cache was gone. So I just thought I'd sell my things. But time. It just was too late, and now—

And now.

I need a purpose.

The words blur on the page. So we don't have the matching sweaters or the picture, but Dad is my family. I don't know if our "little world" is created by love or necessity or obligation. But it's ours. I take a big gulp of air and look up at Beulah. "You can't do this. My dad not my dad? He'll never let this happen."

Beulah scowls. "It's not personal, Maya. This is in your best interest."

Not personal?

Ripping my family apart?

I concentrate on a water stain on the ceiling. One of the counselors pats my shoulder. "Maya, we're so sorry," she says. "We had no idea."

Beulah clears her throat. "In the meantime, we'll be looking for appropriate foster-care placement."

"What about bail?" I ask.

Beulah blushes, her cardboard face turning blotchy. "All of your assets have been seized."

"Can't I just stay at Kids Place until Dad gets out? How long could that be, anyway?"

"We're not sure." Beulah's face has gone back to that beige color. "And it's not realistic to wait around until he does, uh"—she coughs—"get out." She pauses, then says, "For the time being, we believe it would be healthier to place you in a foster home." Beulah flips through her file. "With a family."

I think about what Jess said about freak foster families.

Family.

So now I'm going to live the two-parents-and-two-point-zero-nine-children American dream mandated by the State of Nevada. Whoopee.

"Your father has mentioned some relative, but he's pretty vague." Beulah gnaws on her pencil.

What relative?

I sigh. I figure there has to be someone. It's not like Dad and Mom were bizarre results of asexual reproduction. Jesus, even if they were test-tube babies, some woman had to have given birth to them and some guy's lucky sperm was involved. Maybe Dad's been checking out Genealogy.com or something.

Probably not. It's not like there's WiFi in prison.

I look at everybody in the room and try to deflect their pity stares. Maybe I have a seventh cousin four times removed or something. Somewhere.

Honestly, I've never thought about other relatives. It's always just been Dad and me. But now it's just me. Just me.

The rest of the meeting passes in a blur. One of the counselors wants to make sure I'm still eligible for advanced placement classes. Wow. Great priorities there.

"Maya? Are you listening?" Mrs. Peters is definitely the nicest school counselor. She's one of those people who look distraught about the downfall of today's youth. Her hand is cupped on mine. "Maya, you don't have to go through this alone. I'm sure that Beulah will work hard to find you a good family—in this area. So you don't have to change schools. It's such a shame about your father," she says.

I nod.

So Dad's a crook. But I didn't think anybody could say, "Hey, you're not a parent anymore. Give her back." Kids don't come with a return policy. Do they? On a scale of one to ten, Dad's probably a high five, sometimes six. A ton better than lots of deadbeats out there.

I've lost my home and everything in it. I'm losing Dad. And I feel like I'm becoming a blank slate—generic. I need to come up with a procedure. I sigh. At least I still have science.

CHAPTER
SIX

When we get back to Kids Place, I head for the bathroom. The only good thing about school is that I now have my coveted bottle of Pepto-Bismol in hand. I sit in a bathroom stall—my feet up so nobody can see me—and take a swig. A couple of girls come in, zip open makeup cases, spritz on perfume, and talk about going to some school dance. I hold back a sneeze and slip out of the stall.

And there's Nicole sitting in the corner stall, its door ajar. She's flipping through a pile of postcards, a prescription pill bottle next to her.

I leave before she sees me but pause in the hallway, thinking about those pills. *Nah,* I think. She probably just has allergies or some kind of prescription meds for a cold.

Or maybe they prescribed her something while she was in the psychiatric ward.

But what if that's not true? If it's not, what could I possibly say to her? It's her life. If she wants to kick it, that's her deal, not mine.

But I always dream of saying these perfect words to Mom—to make her want to stay. Some stupid Einstein quote. But what would Nicole think if I just went up to her and said it?

Academic bulimia.

I go to our room and wait, holding my breath until Nicole walks in. I sigh, exhaling for the first time all afternoon, and just watch her.

"What?" she asks, and tucks her pack of cloves and bottle behind Marlon Brando.

"Nothing," I say. "Just, um, kinda glad you're here."

"Wish I could say the same, Jeopardy." She glares.

Jess and Shelly give me weird looks.

But late that night, I can't help it. I slip down off the bed and pull up the corner of Nicole's Brando poster to find where she hides her cigarettes in a crack in the drywall. Right next to them is the bottle. I take it out and read the prescription: Fluoxetine. I count the pills and slip a note into the bottle. Maybe those words do matter. I don't know.

The next morning, getting ready for school, I watch Nicole sweep her hand behind the poster and pull out the bottle. She stares at the note and puts it back in the bottle, carefully covering the hole with her Brando poster. She doesn't say anything. She just throws her pack on and leaves.

"Oxygen waster," Jess sneers.

I sigh. And things go back to normal.

The monotony continues; the experiment is repeated. And every night I count those stupid pills—she never takes one. That's weird. I watch her. Waiting for the signs. But she's always bigger than life with a huge smile glued to her face. She sometimes hangs out with the younger kids. And she's always talking. Talking, talking, talking. Liborio Bellomo, the Genovese family, the Gambinos. It's like listening to a direct feed of the True Crime radio station. That or some waiter in an Italian restaurant with those tacky checkered tablecloths telling you the day's special. *Today we have Lucchese linguine with some garlic Gotti bread on the side.*

But nobody listens.

And she still talks. And talks. Maybe to fill up the

emptiness. I don't know.

Every day is the same: school; meetings with counselors and Beulah and the DA; eating tasteless food off heavy plastic trays; avoiding the Triad. I start to mark days off the calendar so I won't lose track.

Then he comes. I see Beulah and Rose bring him in. He's young—ten at the most. And we can all smell his fear. I wonder if I looked that scared.

He sits at a table across the room, not looking up from his food. Nobody at his table talks to him. Talking is a risk. Because if you can just hold it all in until lights-out, you'll be okay. Nobody cares if you cry at night.

I sigh and look over at the Triad. They whisper and stare at the boy. They're planning something—something bad. Probably one of their typical pranks. Shelly's told me all about them: feces on your bed or other even more disgusting bodily fluids, the icy shower, the Dumpster, all followed by getting everything you bring with you stolen.

I hate the Triad. The more often I see them, the angrier I feel. My body turns to ice; my tongue feels like sandpaper; my stomach clenches. It's like my amygdala goes into hyperdrive at dinnertime.

I hate feeling helpless even more. *Weak*. Maybe I am weak. I feel like I play a part in keeping this whole messed-up place in order. I look back at the boy, his bangs flopping in his eyes. Nicole stands up from her table and walks by the Triad staring them all in the eyes.

They laugh at her. The girl smirks and says, "Oh, real tough. Like you can do anything?"

Nicole sits next to the boy, banging her tray on the table. He still doesn't look up. He's probably gotten the tour already—been assigned his locker with generic soap, sandpaper towels, and dollar-store shampoo.

Everybody here at Kids Place has a locker for their bathroom stuff—toothpaste, toothbrushes, those kinds of things. We have shifts for showering and getting ready. We have shifts for cleaning. There's a bathroom schedule, cleaning schedule, everything's pasted in the hallway. Basically, we all know what everybody else is doing from sunup to sundown.

Routine can be tedious. But it can also be advantageous. I watch as the Triad huddles together, eyeing their new prey.

I finally feel like I might have a little control over something in life.

And I have a purpose.

CHAPTER SEVEN

Purpose: Keep the new boy safe. Regain self-dignity

Hypothesis: If I can send a message strong enough to freak out the Triad, they'll back off.

Materials: Bhut jolokia pepper oil, a medicine dropper, plastic gloves, flathead screwdriver, safety pins or paper clips, flashlight, Triad's toothbrushes

Procedure:

1) Get the pepper oil, medicine dropper, and gloves from Mr. Hunter's supply room

2) Borrow the screwdriver and flashlight from Mr. Hunter's top right-hand desk corner

3) Get paper clips from Beulah

4) Find the Triad's lockers

5) Look up the bathroom schedule

6) Pick the locks

7) Drop oil on toothbrushes

8) Sit back and enjoy the show

Variables: Time: How quickly can I do this? What are

the bathroom schedules this week? Locks: Will they all be pin-and-tumbler locks? They're the only kind I know how to pick.

Constant: Me

I decide I need to do it tomorrow night. I just hope the boy is safe until then.

Another plus to this whole thing is my Pepto-Bismol supply might not dwindle so fast. If I stop hating the Triad, then my gastritis won't be as bad. If my gastritis is better, I won't need so much Pepto-Bismol. If I don't need so much Pepto-Bismol, I won't have to worry about finding a way to get my next bottle. Science experiments come with all sorts of bonus results.

Now it's time to put things to the test. A perfect pre-Halloween prank.

I smile. Supposedly every scientist should do the test several times, but I don't really think I'll need more than one.

There's nothing like trust. That's how Dad screws people over. I hate using Mr. Hunter's keys to get into the science supplies. He gave them to me so I could open early in case I wanted to study in the mornings before he got there. But I just need a few things—things he probably won't even notice are gone. And one day I'll replace them. It's not like I'm becoming my dad.

I search the shelves of the supply closet and find the one labeled bhut jolokia. Mr. Hunter ordered it from a supply shop in India. We saw how long it took different hot sauces to corrode iron. Not long. Same day I got it on my finger.

With just a few drops, the Triad will be done.

That afternoon Kids Place is like any other day. Nothing has happened. I can tell. There's no buzz. The boy eats dinner at the same table, bangs covering his eyes.

I wait until lights-out and listen as the last shift of security guards locks up. I slip into the boys' locker room first—two locks to pick there—and find the lockers. It doesn't take long to get them open and get a few drops out of the vial onto their brushes. I worry for a second. What if they don't brush their teeth every morning? That's a variable I hadn't thought of before.

I push the thought away. With all the information out there on dental hygiene, I can't imagine anybody *not* brushing.

I repeat the same thing in the girls' locker room.

Then I lie on the bunk and wait for morning. Odd-numbered rooms have the second bathroom shift today. Luckily the Triad all bunk in even-numbered rooms. That really worked to my advantage. Hey. I never said luck wasn't a little part of science. Think penicillin.

When the sun comes up, I pretend to read. Kids shuffle down the hallway in bathrobes. The water pipes whine awake.

Then we hear the first shriek, followed by two more. Rose's heavy footsteps pound down the hallway, followed by more screams and chaos. Shelly and Jess run out the doorway. Everybody floods the halls, wondering what's happening.

"Hey, Jeops, don't you want to know what's going on?" Nicole eyes me.

I shrug. "Answer in the category Kids Place: This is the region that grows bhut jolokia, the hottest pepper in the world." I force a smile and go back to reading *Nobel Prize Women in Science: Their Lives, Struggles, and Momentous Discoveries.* Dad bought it for me the week before the repo guys came. It was like he had finally paid attention to what I liked, not what he thought I should like. Too little, too late. I close the book.

Kids Place staff sweep the three of them down the hall. I watch them suffer. And in a horrible way, I feel glad, glad that they hurt as much as I did when they stuffed me in the Dumpster—glad that they're the prey and I'm the predator.

Shelly returns, breathless. Her eyes bulge so much it looks like she has developed a major thyroid problem. "Oh. My. God. You won't believe what has happened," she says between sniffles, then tells us a pretty blown-up version of what happened, including some kind of explosive device in lockers.

Jess rolls her eyes and says, "It was just Tabasco sauce or something. Anybody could've done that." Then she says, "But I don't know who would've had the nads to do it. I mean messing with the Triad is suicide." Then she looks at Nicole.

I jump off my bunk and get ready for school. We're all corralled into the cafeteria for breakfast. A kind of electric expectation fills the air. Everybody's a lot quieter than normal.

My stomach still hurts, though. The oatmeal tastes like sawdust. I choke it down with overfluorinated water, counting the minutes before I can go back to the room for a swig of Pepto before school. I look at the Triad's empty seats and feel the oatmeal work its way back up my system.

But they don't load us onto the buses. We listen to the

phones ring in the offices and watch as the buses idle in the parking lot.

Rose returns after what seems like an eternity. She stands at the front of the cafeteria, hands on heavy hips. "Kelly, Jared, and Wyatt all have blistered tongues and lips— second-degree burns. And their fingers have burns on them as well. This was a serious, brutal attack, and none of us are leaving this room until someone tells me who did this."

Beulah stands behind Rose in a skirt that sticks to her nylons, making a fizzly sound whenever she moves and tries to unstick the skirt. Major static cling. The skirt is that salmon color you see old ladies wearing at retirement centers in Florida.

"I'm waiting," Rose says, shifting her weight.

We search one anothers' faces for the truth. Even the new boy looks bright-eyed. Maybe they warned him. Maybe he's been waiting for something bad to happen to him, only to be relieved to see it happened to someone else.

Before Rose can say anything else, I stand up. "I did."

Silence.

Nobody congratulates me.

Why would they?

You can't congratulate cruelty.

They send everybody off to school and Rose yanks me into her office. I don't even hear what she says. It's like I'm in some kind of bell jar, Rose's words all muted and soft. Phone calls. Reports. Anger management. Therapy. Consequences.

"There will be consequences," she says, her words ringing clear as her pudgy hand squeezes my shoulder.

I sigh and feel relieved that I've confessed. I wonder if that's how Dad feels. Like all these years of running are done. Behind him. He's free.

"You of all people," she says. "Why would you do such a thing?"

It seemed so clear before. It made sense. I wanted me back, but what I did to the Triad doesn't change anything. It just changes me. So I can't get me back. She's gone.

In the end, my dad's still in jail and I'll be shipped off with an unknown to who-knows-where. Unless Dad stops being so vague about that mystery relative.

End of experiment.

CHAPTER
EIGHT

After a day of talking to counselors and meetings with lots of other random people, they all decide that my punishment is to become a pseudo-indentured servant for Kids Place as well as take anger management classes. That and I've been banned from the Halloween social this weekend. Whoopee.

The plus of orphanages? There're no parents to press charges.

The Triad returns with bandaged tongues and swollen lips. At dinner they stand up in front of everybody and Rose pulls me to face them. She wants to make an example of me so others will be shamed into being good. "Do you have anything to say?" she asks.

"Repent!" I can hear my dad's voice at those tent revivals. Maybe I spent too much time listening to his sermons instead of counting the cash.

You know, lots of people think blind people have a

heightened sense of sound, touch, taste, and smell. But we're all born with the same "sensory" capacities, so to speak. A blind person seemingly has heightened other senses because a blind person uses them more.

I wonder if Dad's conscience is turned off. Maybe he was born conscience-impaired, and mine is heightened because I use mine for both of us. It doesn't matter much.

I stare at the Triad—weeping blisters caked with shiny salve.

"Well?" Rose nudges me half a step closer. In her thousand-page manual of rules and regulations for Kids Place, she doesn't once touch on the rules of survival. She doesn't know them. Rose clears her throat. "Maya has something to say."

I nod and look each one in the eyes. "I will not be generic." Then I turn on my heels and go to my room.

The next morning, getting ready for school, I open my drawer and find my favorite jeans and sweater. There's a note with scrawly kid handwriting on it. "You aren't generic."

I pull the sweater over my head and slip on my jeans. I sigh, relieved. Shelly, Jess, and Nicole are gone, so I hug myself and feel strong.

I am not weak.

And the Triad has disbanded. At least for now. Everybody just ignores them. And over the course of the next couple of weeks, I get most of my clothes back. Except for the scarf Jess wears. I say to her one day, "Why don't you just keep it?"

She blushes and mumbles something about me being a rich snot.

But I'm not too at ease. I kind of think the Triad's planning a nasty and painful revenge. Nature is nature. Just ask Roy Horn or Grizzly Man.

Tonight Nicole and I have kitchen duty together. I've had kitchen duty ever since I burned the lips off the Triad.

Nicole hardly looks strong enough to scrub the dinner trays—her arms spindly with blue veins running through tissue-paper skin. She looks up at me and strips off the yellow kitchen gloves. "Brutal stuff."

"Huh?"

"Bhut jolokia."

"Yeah." I'm impressed she remembers the name. "Like that Mafia guy you talked about—the acid guy who threw finger bones in soup," I say, and wince at the reference, but that's how I've felt. I finish wiping off the tables and go into the kitchen.

"Carneglia?"

I shrug. "Yeah. I guess. They all have the same-sounding last names to me. With all your Mafia stories, it's hard to keep them straight."

Nicole scrubs the dishes harder, a line forming between her brows. She looks up. "Easier than listening to your science spew." She pauses, looking through the steam from the hot water rinsing the dishes. "Why do you go through my stuff?" she asks. "My pills?"

I shrug.

"Don't. Okay?"

I nod. "I, um, tried to disguise my handwriting. On the note."

Nicole scowls. "You're so absolutely random."

I guess that does it for my stellar don't-kill-yourself note. It's good to know that it's not as great as I thought it was. Maybe it wouldn't have made a difference with Mom after all. Not like that matters to me anyway.

Nicole dries her hands on a dingy towel.

"Nicole?"

"What?"

"I mean it. What I wrote. Really."

"Why do you give a shit? I didn't care when they threw

you in a Dumpster and took your stuff. I didn't care when you walked around feeling sorry for yourself all those weeks. I don't care now."

"Yeah. But you didn't wear my stuff."

She shrugs. "You have no style. Don't think it was anything more."

"And why did everybody give me back my favorite jeans, sweater? The rest of my clothes?"

Nicole smirks. "Carneglia. They don't want to be an ingredient in finger soup. You're scary!" She makes a phantom noise and laughs.

But I know it's more than that. It's like Nicole has some power in this place. The Triad never touched her. Even though the only ones who talk to her are the little kids, others do what she wants them to.

One day Shelly told me it was because of the crazy look. "Her eyes," she said. "They have that crazy thing to them. Like she could snap at any time."

I never see that, though. I just see sadness.

Nicole cocks her head to the side and stares at me for a long time. "I'm going for a smoke." She walks out. Before leaving, she turns back. "The clothes are yours. You earned them. Not a lot of kids here have a vertebra, you know." I watch her and look out at the empty cafeteria. I feel better about cleaning up the rest of the kitchen alone. It's nice to be alone here, because it almost never happens.

I watch as Nicole paces outside and blows puffs of smoke into the autumn air.

In the meantime, the pepper incident doesn't do anything but make me some kind of underdog hero. Weird. I don't want that, though. I just want things to be back to the way they were. I have these fantasies that Dad gets out of prison; that they aren't processing me into orphanhood; that Oprah's Angel Network will find reason to bail us out.

I think back to all those promises he's made. He's kept some. Okay, a few. But he always found a way to put food on the table and keep me in school.

We were having a picnic at a park near our trailer home in El Paso. Yellow tumbleweeds tripped over our blanket; dust pelted my bare legs. Dad wrapped me in his Windbreaker, his heart pounding next to my ear. His cheeks were sandpaper rough. His shirt smelled like smoke and French fry grease. But when I moved in closer, I could smell the tangy soap he used before working the night shift at the bar.

"I'm going to buy a beautiful home one day, Maya. You'll go to the best schools. There's nothing you won't be able to do."

I tried to smile. But tent revivals and Arizona were too fresh on my mind. I hated feeling bad for those people. I wondered, though: If they really believed, did Dad do any harm?

Dad said, "What is the easiest human trait to play on?"

"Guilt," I answered. I had learned well.

He ruffled my hair, then leaned back against the lone tree at the park, his eyes heavy from having spent the entire night feeding drunks. "Greed. Greed beats them all," he murmured, a smile on his lips.

I let him fall asleep, not wanting to bug him even though I so much wanted to swing. He was so tired all the time. Even then I was trying to take care of him.

The next week Dad took out a simple ad in the *Pennysaver*. And before long, we bought a house. And a swing set.

CHAPTER NINE

Beulah sits next to me in her polyethylene terephthalate suit. She wears a watered-down blue one that matches the vein in her temple. We pull up to the jail in silence. It'll be the first time I've seen him in almost a month. Corroded iron gates screech open to let the bus drive through. We get off and brace ourselves against the icy morning air. I don't think I ever stared so hard at my shoes in my entire life. A square box houses a couple of guards who watch us through barred windows. The generic clock hangs crooked on the wall behind them. Eight fifty-three.

It reeks. I turn and see that the jail is located right in front of the city sewage treatment plant. Appropriate.

Everybody wears their Sunday best. A few babies cry. The guard standing at the box house looks bored. He snaps his gum and glances at his watch. At nine A.M. he opens a gate that leads us to a metal door. We walk down a long corridor through airport-security–like devices. Mustard walls and dingy linoleum. There are no leering prisoners screaming vile things at us. It just looks like a school I went to in downtown Sacramento for a few months—minus the nervous-looking teachers.

I check in my bag and give my name to the clerk at the end of the hall. He nods and motions for me to take a seat. "It'll be a few minutes. You can go in round two."

I inhale the heavy smells of metal and floor polish and scuff my shoe on the floor. Everybody whispers. I watch the first group of people trickle into a room. Some come out crying. Most leave stone-faced.

The guard motions for me to go in. "I'll wait here," Beulah says, scratching her gnawed-off nails across her polyester pants.

This line of work really doesn't suit her.

I walk into the small room and my stomach knots. He sits behind one of those Plexiglas barriers. He hasn't shaved and his beard has grown thick and wiry on his broad chin. He looks off into space, dark circles under his eyes. There is no spark anymore.

He forces a smile and puts his hand up to the glass. I match my palm to his and swallow back tears. He motions for me to pick up the phone.

"Hey, Maya. It looks like I've made quite a mess this time."

"It's okay," I say.

He grins. "That's my girl."

I feel more at ease. We're back to us. Just a little, anyway. "I'll take care of things, Dad. Really. I'll figure something out."

He winks and whispers. "A prison break?"

"If I pass you hot sauce and a radio, you could make a break for it in about, hmmm, fifteen years. I saw it on *MythBusters*." For just a second I fantasize about Dad slipping between his cell bars and running away. But on *MythBusters* the prisoner was in Mexico. Under the hot sun. Maybe I could slip Dad a heat lamp, too. I'd pick him up in a run-down car, and we'd head to Canada.

Then I'll be a felon, just like Dad.

"How's school, baby?"

"Dad—"

"How's school? You have any projects coming up?"

I shake my head. "Same old stuff, Dad."

Then we just sit and stare at each other through the smudged glass. I put my cheek to the glass, and he does the same. I can almost feel his scratchy beard.

"You are so much like her."

I shake my head. "I'm nothing like her."

"Do me a favor."

I nod.

"Get the box of her things out of the house." He has a shoe box of Mom's stuff. I never look at it. I can't. She *chose* to leave. What mom does that to her daughter?

"No," I say. "*That* I won't do."

"Your mom has a sister, Maya. I told them about her, but they said nobody by her name lives in Rugby. The authorities haven't been able to find her." He clears his throat again. "I'm having, um, credibility problems here."

I push my hair back behind my ears and try to control my voice. "An aunt?"

He nods.

"For real?"

He nods.

I feel like I've been bulldozed. "An aunt? After all these years—"

"It's just—" He clears his throat. "When your mom died, things were pretty bad between us. And we just drifted. She wanted to get custody of you back then, but I couldn't let that happen. So I left. We left."

I stare at him through the smudged glass and try to retrieve a memory of this aunt, but I come up blank. I don't remember anybody but Dad and me at that cemetery. Where was she?

Beulah said Dad had been pretty vague about the relative thing. I don't think an aunt is anywhere near as vague as what I imagined, say the cousin of a third cousin twice removed. How is an aunt vague?

Why can't they believe him?

Then I think about the other shoe boxes Dad has stashed, full of the Social Security cards, bank statements, checks, credit cards, and histories of all of those people Dad created—none of them real.

An aunt.

"She'll take you now. She's a good woman," Dad says.

Everything has been a huge lie. Everything. We could've had a family. We could've had normal.

"I'm sorry, baby."

I blink back the tears that burn my eyes.

"In the shoe box, there's information. Her name is, was, I don't know—Sarah Brandt. But she could've gotten married, divorced, remarried. You've got to get into the house. Find the spare key."

"So I get to find the long-lost aunt." A few people look over at us, and I lower my voice. "Why didn't she try to at least keep in touch all these years? Why did she just let you leave like that? Why didn't she care enough—" Why am I surprised?

Dad shakes his head. "Look in the shoe box."

"I don't care about Mom and her things and her family," I whisper.

He leans in closer. "Mom's more than a bottle of pills, Maya."

A bell rings and a guard shouts, "Two minutes!"

"Maya, listen to me."

I close my eyes.

"I signed some papers."

"What papers, Dad?"

"It's for the best, Maya. It's for you. Things are pretty complicated."

"What papers, Dad?" I shake my head and don't even try to stop the tears that spill down my cheeks. "No, Dad."

"I have no choice. It's done."

We all have choices. We *all* do. Mom did. Dad did. Mystery Aunt Sarah did. They chose wrong.

"But—" I protest.

"Look at me." I stare into Dad's iceberg eyes. I've always wished I had his eyes and not Mom's gray, dreary eyes. I push the thought away. He clears his throat. "It's for the best."

Leaving me. Abandoning me. That's the best? How is that any different from Mom?

"Get her things from the house," he says. "Find Sarah. They won't."

The guards start to shuffle everybody out of the room. One taps Dad on the shoulder. He hangs up the phone.

Click.

So that's it. After all these years, he gives up.

We've never given up.

He stands and pauses, like he's going to say something— something to make it all okay. "I love you, Maya," he mouths. "I love you."

I watch as he walks away. He doesn't turn around. He just leaves, and I sit there with the telephone stuck to my ear.

CHAPTER
TEN

Pressure is an easy scientific equation that measures the force on an object spread over the surface area. So the definition of pressure is force divided by the area where the force is applied. When too much force is applied to a surface area, watch out.

I'm pretty sure my head's going to explode. Or maybe it already did. That's why my thoughts are fuzzy and my days seem to last forever. I know that the world is about four and a half billion years old and humans have been around for only two hundred thousand years of it. But this past week has felt like an entire Proterozoic Eon.

The method, I sigh. This can work. I take the aspirin the school nurse gave me. Think. Think.

Purpose: Find Mystery Aunt Sarah

Hypothesis: If I find my only other known living genetic link on earth, assuming she's still alive, then . . . what? I'll live happily ever after?

I scribble out the method and crumple up the page. I can't even figure out a decent hypothesis. This will never work.

"Sorry to interrupt." Beulah peeks her head into the room.

We all look up at her. Nicole stops talking long enough for Beulah to say, "Maya, can you come with me?"

"Looks like you're getting the call," Jess sneers.

Shelly clasps her hands. "Oh, I hope they're nice."

Nicole turns away and stares out the window.

I follow Beulah out to the conference room.

"We are thrilled you're going to be part of this family." The woman holds out a porcelain hand. Her eyes dart between her husband and me. He holds out his hand as well; it's waxy with manicured nails. He has beady eyes and wears a starched white shirt and too-skinny blue tie. He sits back in his chair and puts his arm around the lady, squeezing her shoulder.

She winces and shifts in her seat. "It's been a while since we've opened our home to a—"

Orphan. Stray. Urchin. I'm about to fill in her sentence but decide I'd better keep quiet to spare her the embarrassment.

"A teenager," the man finishes. "We had a couple of bad experiences." He looks at me with little brown eyes, heavy pouches underneath. "But your case interests us." He tsks. "Unfortunate circumstances."

Having your dad sign you away is "unfortunate"?

"Anyway," the man continues, "my name is Donovan, and this is Cherise."

"Cherry." She blushes. "You can call me Cherry."

Donovan nods. "We're God-fearing folk at our home and expect you to attend services with us. You'll get baptized right away, of course."

I feel my jaw tense. Who are they to tell me who I'll pray to? I'll pray to a freaking McDonald's arch if I want. I open my mouth to protest and look over at Beulah.

This is an argument I can't win.

I have no choices. My family made theirs and left me with none. Nice.

Donovan goes on and on about devotion and God and prayer. I listen when he starts talking about tithing and duty to church.

Cherry nods enthusiastically.

Maybe they're part of a freak cult and are looking for

virgin sacrifices. That's why they want me. It's not likely Beulah will buy into my theory.

For being so God-fearing, Donovan doesn't seem to worry about staring at my chest. I want to tell him that as much as he stares, they're not going to grow any bigger. I know. I've tried.

I look at Beulah. She has pasted a grin on her face from her box of expressions. "We wanted to place you, Maya, before . . ." She pauses and takes out a damp handkerchief. "We just think it's better to get you into a nice family home as soon as possible to avoid any further, um, incidents."

I clench my jaw. So I just sped up the process by standing up for myself. Maybe the wallflower thing would've been a better way to go. It always worked for me before. But things are different now.

"It says here your full name is Amaya Terese Sorenson." Cherry looks at my file. "What an interesting name."

I nod. They stare at me.

"What kind of name is that?" Cherry asks.

"It's Basque."

"Basque, huh? What kind of people are those?" Donovan asks suspiciously. He's probably one of those camouflage-wearing militia guys—you know, the kind who'll have a ham radio in his garage to report suspicious ethnic activities to his grand wizard. He apparently hasn't ever eaten lamb stew at Louis's Basque Corner.

"Honey, you know the Basque people! We saw on Discovery they live in the mountains over in Europe." Cherry claps. "I never realized Sorenson was a Basque name."

God, she makes us sound like cavemen.

Actually, my last name is Aguirre. But that was about six last names and Social Security cards ago. Another great way for Dad to make a buck. He'd read the obituaries, then kind of reassign Social Security numbers for those who needed them. It was a popular business in New Mexico. Dad always said it was his way of opening up the borders— being a cultural attaché between the United States and Latin America. I always thought of it as recycling lives— administrative reincarnation, so to speak.

"So it looks like we're your family now. You can be relieved you've been placed in such a loving home. With role models that you can look up to." Donovan leers.

As much as I hate it, he has a point. Dad's a federal prisoner who signed me away as if I were a piece of real estate. Knowing Dad, he would've liked to auction me on eBay, sell me to the highest bidder. But that's probably illegal.

Whatever.

Dad'd be the one to find the loophole to pull it off.

No one says anything. The windows bulge from the silence.

Beulah titters nervously and hands out stale cookies with Hawaiian Punch. "It'll just take some time to get to know each other." She turns to me. "The Nicholsons have received countless children into their home. We are so grateful," she coos. She lowers her voice and turns to me. "You have no family, Maya. And these people want to make you part of theirs."

No family. That again.

The other day when I asked about Aunt Sarah, Beulah told me that Dad had been lying. "Aunt Sarah doesn't exist," she said. "We looked."

This is not how I imagined things going. Dad wasn't supposed to sign those papers. He was supposed to fight for me; get a lawyer; make us a family again. I'd stay at Kids Place until the state came to some kind of settlement and he'd have litter duty or something. Whatever those white-collar criminals get. Even Martha Stewart got to go home and plant potatoes. Okay. After nine months in jail.

But still, nine months is nothing. Anybody can hold out for nine months.

"What about contact with my dad? Can I talk to him?" I'm sure I'll want to. Sometime. When the anger goes away.

I wonder if it will go away.

It never has for my mom.

But he's all I've had all these years. It's not as easy as signing a piece of paper for me.

Donovan shakes his head. "Now that I'm your interim guardian, I think it would be best for you not to see him."

"Excuse me?"

"Your dad is in federal prison. Outside Elko."

No more Carson City minimum security jail for Dad.

My stomach flip-flops. It's okay not to talk to him when I don't want to, but when somebody else mandates that, it's not.

Donovan continues, "You need to be steered away from those kinds of people—away from the influence of such a sinful man."

And into the arms of the creepiest family in Reno.

Jess wasn't kidding about foster homes. No wonder Nicole runs away.

"He's my dad," I finally manage to say. So he signed a

piece of paper. Maybe he was forced to. Maybe. I think of a hypothesis that would work with that scenario. There are too many maybes, but none of them take me where I need to go. I feel like I'm hitting dead ends in my lab rat maze.

I scan the faces sitting at the table and can feel the gastric fluids bubbling in my intestines. It's as if they all got together and decided that there was a right kind of dad, and mine wasn't it.

"Evolve!" I want to shout. But Cherry probably thinks she comes from a rib and the word *evolution* is blasphemous.

"Right now, your father is just another man in prison." He does that annoying quote thing with his fingers when he says "father." Donovan has cold eyes. Cherry blushes again.

I cross my arms and look away.

He mutters something under his breath, then half smiles. "So we'll be back on Wednesday to take you home." They get up and embrace Beulah. I'm afraid they'll wrinkle her, but she springs back, her suit as pressed as before.

They move toward me, but I shove my hands into my pockets and turn away.

I fight back tears. October drizzle blurs the window-pane. I watch as they pile into a two-tone station wagon plastered with bumper stickers: a glowing Guadalupe; WHO WOULD JESUS BOMB?; THIS fiSH WON'T FRY. WILL YOU?; ARE YOU FOLLOWING JESUS THIS CLOSE?; and, my personal favorite, DARWIN IS DEAD. JESUS IS ALIVE. WHICH ONE DO YOU TRUST WITH YOUR ETERNAL SOUL?

It's Monday. I have two days.

I lay my head in my arms and cry.

CHAPTER ELEVEN

Purpose: Find Aunt Sarah.

Hypothesis: If I can find Aunt Sarah, I can avoid being sent to the Holy Rollers' house.

Materials: Mom's box, a backpack, any cash I can find in the house that I might've missed, a couple changes of clothes, Pepto-Bismol, food, water, me

Procedure:

1) Get a Citifare Bus schedule

2) Sneak out of Kids Place

3) Take the bus and get to our old house

4) Look for the spare key under the address stone in the garden and get into the house

5) Get Mom's box

6) Pack a backpack of things

7) Search the box for clues to find Aunt Sarah

8) Never look back

Variables: Time: I have two days. So I need to go. Today. Dad: Does Aunt Sarah really exist or is she a figment of his con-man imagination? Box: Will it have any clues as to where I can find Aunt Sarah?

Constants: Me, Dad's word

I look at my purpose and wonder if Dad would lie about somebody like a long-lost aunt. He's many things: a con man, crook, thief, and at the best of times a businessman with less-than-ethical practices. But he's never lied to me. Plus, why would he invent an aunt at the last minute?

The material list bugs me. The box. I have to get Mom's box. My stomach tightens. I hate thinking about that box and Mom's things all stored away. Dad taught me to never look back. Even though he did. Prime example? The box. I watched as they piled the last of that frozen dirt on her grave. She's buried.

Gone.

And now I have to go start digging things up again. I've never been into forensics.

I get the Citifare schedule from the Kids Place rec room. The last bus home leaves downtown Reno at 10:45 P.M., and Kids Place last rounds are at eleven P.M. The only way to get out of Kids Place and gain some time is to take the first bus in the morning, at 5:45 A.M.

I wait until Kids Place has a shift change—at three A.M. I listen to Shelly's soft snore and Jess's deep breathing. The only time Nicole never makes a sound is when she sleeps. It's like her body shuts down after being on "play" all day. That's a problem, though, because it's impossible to tell if she's asleep or not. It's sometimes hard to tell if she's alive.

I check Nicole's pills one more time. Habit. I exhale— all there.

At four A.M. I leave, doing that pillow thing everybody does in the movies so that people think there's actually a human body. Given more time, I could definitely have come up with something better.

I walk through the dark streets, avoiding lights and cars, dodging in and out of shadows. I've done this walk about ten times in my head. Today I can't afford to get lost.

The RTC Citicenter isn't that far, but it feels a lot farther in the dark. And I can't shake the feeling somebody's following me. It can't be Beulah. Her suits make too much noise. I hear a twig snap behind me and spin around to an empty street.

I'm definitely paranoid.

But paranoia is actually a necessity—a normal human defense mechanism designed to protect us from harm. It becomes problematic, though, when the paranoia evolves into a constant delusional state in which the person truly believes, and reacts to the belief, that some harm will come to him or her at all times. Considering the fact that this is the first time I've been on the lam, so to speak, by myself, I don't think my paranoia is delusional. Just precaution.

Downtown's practically empty. All the drunken gamblers have probably already gone home. I watch some old grandmas feed the nickel slots, bloodshot eyes, hoping for the big win. Shocks of sprayed blue hair stick to glistening foreheads. It makes me sad to watch them like that. Reno can be a pretty sad place.

I make my way to the bus station and sit down on a bench outside. I have forty minutes to go. A guy who smells like pee sits next to me, moons of dirt under long fingernails; matted, greasy hair; a gaunt face caked with grime. He shivers and talks to himself. I move to the edge of the bench and watch, embarrassed for him.

When I take a closer look, I realize he's not much older than me.

Now the place is crowded with casino workers who just got off the night shift. The bus finally comes, and I rush on with the jostling crowd. I keep my head down, avoiding eye contact with everybody. When we get to my stop, at 6:10 A.M., I clamber off and turn around in time to see a thin figure slip out of the dim light of a streetlamp into the shadows. I shiver and rub my hands up and down my arms, heading toward home. This morning everything seems too dark—too cold.

When I look back at the streetlamp, the figure is gone.

Paranoia.

Now I'm getting into the certifiable wacko paranoia stuff.

I run down the block, white puffs of breath trailing behind me. So much for global warming. It's really cold for November.

The neighborhood looks the same. I run up to the address stone and pull it up out of the half-frozen ground. The key is gone.

Way flawed planning. I didn't count on having to break into the stupid house. I circle around, looking for an open window. Finally, the laundry room window cracks open when I push, but I can't pull myself up. I plop down and rest my head on the frosted ground trying to think of what to do next.

My stomach burns, and I dig through my backpack for Pepto-Bismol.

"Breaking and entering? That's a felony." A shadow emerges.

My heart lodges in my throat and I scramble to my feet.

"What're you doing?" she asks.

"God, I just about had a heart attack. You . . . God." I lean against the side of the house, trying to catch my breath.

"So," she repeats, "what're you doing?"

"Nothing."

"Nothing looks like it's pretty important to me." Nicole stands in the slanted moonlight, a bag slung over her shoulder.

I turn back to the house and jump up, trying to get a hold of the windowsill.

"This doesn't look good, and it would be terrible if the police came, wouldn't it?" Nicole takes out her cell phone. "Plus it'll be light soon."

"Go ahead. Call. I don't care," I say.

Nicole pauses, then puts the phone away. "Where are you going?"

"Nowhere," I say.

"I guess I'll go nowhere with you."

"You can't."

"Why not?"

"I just have stuff I've gotta do."

"You met the Nicholsons, huh? They're a real piece of work."

I jump up again, my fingers slipping off the windowsill. "What do you know about them?" I ask, dropping to the ground.

"Just that they're nutcases you definitely don't want to live with. And if I call Kids Place right now, it won't be long before they come for you and send you off with Cherry and Don. Nice guy, isn't he? Real nice."

"Okay." I motion to the house. "I need to get inside."

"What's in it for me?"

I shrug. "I don't know."

Nicole cups her hands and heaves me up. I squeeze through the window and tumble onto the floor where the clothes drier used to be, banging my elbow. "Damn," I mutter. I had forgotten it was repossessed with the rest of our stuff.

I run upstairs and grab a couple of warm sweaters and jackets. In the junk drawer in the kitchen, I find a fuzzy twenty-dollar bill. I double-check to make sure it's not one of the counterfeits. Nope. It's real.

Twenty bucks. Whoopee.

Finally, I go to Dad's closet. The shoe box is tucked behind some of his old high-school yearbooks. The edges are bent in, the top tattered; an old rubber band keeps the lid on.

I shove it in my backpack and make one last sweep of the house, packing the half-empty bottle of Pepto-Bismol. I'm not a half-empty kind of person, but it just stands to reason that if you start with a full bottle and use the contents, soon the full bottle will become half empty because every time you use it, you empty some more out. The opposite goes for a glass—an empty glass filled halfway with milk is half full, not half empty, because it began empty.

I stare at the Pepto-Bismol and wonder why I have these stupid debates in my head. Better in my head than out loud, I guess.

I take one last look at the house and realize I won't miss it all that much, with its catalog furniture and polished-wood banisters. It's a house—a place where Dad and I crashed for a couple of years. No family pictures are up. I don't even remember the last time I saw a picture of me—except for my school pictures. Dad's not the video-cam-toting kind of dad. He has other priorities. And let's face it, I don't have lots of cool moments to film, anyway.

When I return, Nicole is sitting on her duffel smoking. In a weird way, she looks relaxed. Her eyes actually have some light.

I toss her a coat. "I thought you could use it."

"I don't need your fucking charity."

"I don't need your company—minus the expletive."

"God, you're such a geek," Nicole says.

We walk in silence.

"Where to?" she asks.

"I go my way; you go yours."

"And if your way is my way?"

"I doubt that."

She takes out her cell phone.

"I need to work some things out." I eye her phone. I highly doubt she has Kids Place on speed dial. She probably doesn't even have any minutes.

"So?"

"I don't even know where I'm going."

"Wherever I'm going," she says.

"I don't have any money, Nicole. It's not like this is going to be a first-class trip. So why don't you just go back to Kids Place?"

"With your clothes," She looks me up and down. "You expect me to believe that you don't have any money?"

I pull out the crumpled twenty-dollar bill. "That's all I've got."

"Yeah, right." Nicole shakes her head.

"Oh yeah. I forgot. I have a million buried underneath the neighbor's award-winning rosebushes." I roll my eyes and walk past her, trying to get as much distance between us as I can. Plus I'm not going to fork out the cash to pay for another bus ride, now that the important stuff is taken care of.

"You going to California or something?"

I shake my head. "Downtown. I need to sort some things out."

Nicole laughs. "Turn around then. Downtown is that way."

I look down the street and back toward where Nicole is pointing. "Oh. Yeah."

She whistles. "You're ass-backwards at directions, huh?"

I shake my head. "Just tired." I walk past her.

Nicole follows. We walk in silence for over an hour, the soles of our shoes slapping the cold pavement. My feet ache and toes feel numb. I wiggle them in my shoes to get some warmth going. Another flaw in my experiment: running away in Rocket Dogs. God, I hate the fact this is a one-time kind of experiment. I know already I'd be a much better runaway the second go.

I look at Nicole's shoes. They aren't any better. I guess she didn't learn from her earlier experiments on the streets.

I tighten the straps on my backpack. It feels like the shoe box of Mom's stuff—her memories and who-knows-what-else Dad has kept of her—weighs me down even more. God, I hope I don't find a lock of hair or something creepy like that.

I stop when we reach a neighborhood park and sit on the damp swings. The sun has crept from behind the mountains, though its light brings no warmth. They must know I'm gone. And Nicole. And they'll be looking for us.

The fact that there are two of us now irritates me. Nicole's dead weight. Not planned. Not part of my materials list. I sigh.

She sits next to me on the swings. The cracked plastic seat creaks. For once, she's quiet. Maybe her mouth doesn't work until the sun is high in the sky. I laugh to myself thinking of the "solar mouth" concept. That would suck during summer up in Alaska.

I pull out the box and sift through the contents. I wipe a layer of dust off a picture of Dad, Mom, and me. I was probably two years old. We look happy in the picture. We look like a family.

There are other pictures, some letters, paycheck stubs, papers, and shoved at the bottom of the box, a locket on a chain. I open the locket and stare at the faded photo. Two girls hug each other. You can tell they're sisters: gray eyes, curly hair, and the same dimples. They're about my age in the picture—fifteen years old or so. They look like me.

I look like them.

Dad always says I look like Mom. I hold the locket in my hand and rub off some of the tarnish.

Aunt Sarah. He wasn't lying.

I look closer. Is Aunt Sarah dead, too? Does suicide run in the family? If I bring this "proof of relative" to Kids Place, will they try to find her? I think about the piles of files on Beulah's desk, and all those kids she has to process through the system. She hardly has time to pee, much less go on some wild aunt chase.

If I show up at Aunt Sarah's door with this locket to prove I'm her niece, will she take me in?

I sigh.

"You really don't know where you're going, do you?"

For just a second, I forget that Nicole is sitting next to me. She's a new variable. Maybe not, though. Maybe she'll just stay in Reno. I don't know. I put the locket on. "I'm going to the library."

CHAPTER TWELVE

"The library? You run away to go to the library?"

"And I suppose you have a better place to go?"

Nicole shrugs.

We walk to the downtown library, but it doesn't open until ten o'clock, so I sit on one of the benches outside, trying to pound some feeling back into my toes. Nicole sits next to me and pulls out a cigarette, blowing a stream of smoke into the air. I move away.

"What?"

I shrug. "Secondhand smoke. It's been classified by the EPA as a known cause of cancer in humans. And I don't fancy going bald and throwing up my intestines because you choose to cut your life short."

Nicole rolls her eyes. "Have you ever done anything fun?"

"Waiting for a premature, painful death isn't fun."

"Yeah. Like you really live now. Whoopee. One fucking Discovery special after another. I just don't know how you contain yourself."

In Maryland Dad and I didn't have cable, so he jimmied something to hook up to Mrs. Carlotta's dish. Everything was fuzzy except for Das Erste, some German news channel, and Science Channel, the British version of Discovery. Dad had to work every afternoon, so I'd come home from first grade and watch TV. I had stopped playing in leaves and chasing boys for my ribbons. I remember I'd time myself, trying to get home as fast as I could after school—the faster the better. I loved these shows.

There was one about making time machines. When Dad got home, I told him that all I needed was a jar, atoms, a worm hole, negative energy, and to travel at the speed of light. And we could change things.

That's when Dad bought me a bicycle and unplugged our connection to Mrs. Carlotta's dish.

I spent years trying to take back those five minutes. And since then, I've learned that everybody looks into the past every second of every day. It takes eight minutes for sunlight to reach the earth.

But seeing into the past isn't the same as traveling there.

"Yeah. You're a model of fun living a life at the Reno bus station," I say, biting down on my lower lip to stop from mentioning pill bottles and suicide attempts.

Nicole blows a puff of smoke in my face and snuffs out the cigarette.

Thankfully, the library doors open, so I go into the library and find a corner table where I have space to sort through the box. I pull out all the papers and organize the letters from the most recent date to the oldest date.

Nicole sits next to me and picks at her hangnails, peering over my shoulder.

"Do you have to do that?" I ask.

"What?"

"Hover."

"I'm not hovering."

"Yes, you are. Go read a magazine or something."

She yawns. "Boring."

"Then just move a foot back, please."

"Touchy," she says.

All the letters are addressed to Mom but none have the return address stickers on them. They've all fallen off. I can see where the envelope is darker there. She must've used those freebie address stickers you get from charities.

Dad and I had one of those businesses once. We posed as a foundation for homeless cats. I asked Dad why we didn't pose as a foundation for homeless people, and he said people are nicer to animals. Anyway, we printed out cheesy address labels, asking for donations, and we didn't do too bad.

The stationery is brittle and yellowed by time. I gently open the letters and read each word. Weather, health, school, blah blah blah. For all Aunt Sarah writes, she doesn't say a whole lot. I wonder if I have a cousin. Or two. I wonder what Mom wrote Aunt Sarah. Did she write about me? Dad? What would Mom have said?

I smell the paper. Strange. Letters. I don't think I've ever gotten one. A real letter. In a way I'm lucky Mom and Aunt Sarah didn't get swept away by the world of the internet.

I open the last letter. A pressed flower falls from the pages—its delicate reddish petals like rice paper in my fingers.

"Can I see?" Nicole holds out her hand.

"Be careful."

Nicole holds the flower in the palm of her hand. "That's cool. Sending a flower in a letter." She hands it back to me. "Kind of like something you'd see in the movies."

I nod. It is. I hold the faded flower in my hand, then carefully tuck it back in the envelope. A piece of Sarah's home? It's a puzzle. Everything about Mom and her life is that way. Dad never talks about her. We buried everything with her that day in the cemetery—her memory, her past, her entire existence.

But she had a sister.

She *has* a sister. And it makes me feel sad to think that Mom might have had three people who loved her so much but still swallowed it all away.

In with the other papers in the box, there're four paycheck stubs—all dated more recently than any of the letters—one with a note on the back. "Hope this helps. More on the way. Sarah." They're from some restaurant in Boise, and have the name Sarah Jones printed on them. Great. She married some guy with the last name of Jones. That's real helpful.

I can't make out the first word of the restaurant on the stubs, but it's Something Grill. Its address is faded, too, but I can read Main Street. I go to the media lab and look for restaurants on Main Street in Boise, Idaho. There are nine restaurants with Grill as part of their name.

Okay. Somebody there has to know her. Who she was. Maybe they have an old manager who remembers all the people who passed through—even someone with as generic a name as Sarah Jones.

I consider calling all of them but change my mind. I'd probably end up talking to some gum-chomping waitress fresh out of high school. Pass. Things are usually better done in person.

Nicole taps on my shoulder. "What are we gonna do now?"

"*I'm* going to Boise, Idaho. I think," I say.

It's a start.

In Mr. Hunter's class we're going to start unknowns after we're done with the science of food. Aunt Sarah is about as big an unknown as there is. If I can find her, I can do anything.

I print out the MapQuest directions and tuck them under my shirt, clicking off the computer. I pay for my copies and ask the librarian which way Boise is.

"Northeast," he says.

Like that's a lot of help. "So I walk out these doors and take a right," I say jokingly. "School scavenger hunt."

"Left, then left," he says with a furrowed brow. "Highway Eighty east. Why," he starts to say when he's distracted by some girl spilling coffee all over a computer keyboard. I didn't know librarians said *those* words.

I escape toward the entrance. I'm leaving. I'm not going to look back. Dad died the moment he signed those papers.

He's as dead as Mom. But maybe Mom's stupid box has answers.

"You walk fast." Nicole trots to keep up, practically toppling over the new-releases display.

I push through the doors out into the bright afternoon sunlight, Nicole on my heels. I look at the clock before leaving: one thirty.

Crap.

I didn't realize we'd spent so much time there.

"Boise, huh? Cool. I've always wanted to go there," Nicole says.

"Whatever," I say.

"Why wouldn't I want to go there? Maybe it's a great place to visit." We leave the library. She pulls out another cigarette and curls the edges of her mouth up. But her eyes never smile. "Road trip!" she says.

I leave the building. "Left, then left," I mutter. "Eighty east. I need to go east." I glare at her. "*I*, singular. Goodbye. Have a good afternoon at the bus station." My stomach growls.

I turn my back to the mountains and walk east along the river. After an hour or so, I turn around. "I know you're there. Quit stalking."

She catches up. "Good. It was hard to be stealth. I was

trying to be like Hill when he staked out JFK airport and stole five million dollars. I need to work on that. Stealth, you know."

I sit down and rub my foot, tuning out Nicole's voice. I don't know why I'm so tired. My head hurts and my stomach roars.

"Hey!" Nicole taps my shoulder. "To run away, we actually need to, um, *run*."

I glare at her and we walk down Fourth Street—probably the dodgiest street in the entire state—following it until we get to The Nugget. My feet are pounding, like the bones are poking through the soles of my shoes. After another hour of walking, Nicole stops and sits on a curb. "I'm tired. Are you planning on walking all the way to Boise?"

"You have a better plan?" I hope so.

"Take a bus."

"Do you have any idea how far twenty bucks will get us?" I ask.

Nicole shakes her head. "Not far."

"That's why I walk. This is emergency funding."

"Well, fuck. Is Boise far?"

I stare at her. "It's in Idaho. Yes. It's far."

"How far is that?"

"Have you ever had a geography class?" I snap.

Nicole raises her eyebrow. "You're such a snob. Sorry, Jeopardy, if I'm not exactly sure where we're heading. I didn't get my map and briefing notes. At least I know where to find fucking downtown."

She has a point. "So you have a better idea."

She taps her temple. "I just *might* have a brain in here. We hitch."

"We?"

"I'm coming along." She crosses her arms and stares at a patrol car pulling up. The chill of late afternoon has set in.

"Why? Why do you want to go?"

"I don't ask you why you need to go to Boise. So you don't ask me."

"I don't get it. Why would you even bother coming along? We're nothing alike."

"Except for the fact our parents are shit so we're orphans?"

"Dad's not shit. It's complicated," I say lamely.

Nicole pulls out a cigarette and lights up. "Yeah. Real complicated."

God, I wish she'd just go away. Like I really need to spend the most important trip of my life on suicide watch.

Been there. Done that. Blew it.

"Trust me," she says. "I'm better company than the Nicholsons—unless you're into late-night Bible readings with Donovan so he can cleanse you of your sins."

My stomach lurches.

"Hitching alone is dangerous—especially for girls, you know. Not to disrespect that feminism shit." Nicole puffs out O-shaped rings..

Running away has a lot more variables than I accounted for when I wrote out the plan. In fact, "Find Aunt Sarah" barely touched on the technicalities of the actual running-away part. And I never imagined Nicole as the biggest variable in the whole thing. I sigh. "Okay. We stick together. But only until Boise. Then we each go where we need to go. Separately."

She nods. "Tomorrow we'll get a ride. Better earlier in the day. Safer."

"What's wrong with hitching now?"

"We have about one hour, tops, left of light."

"So?"

"So vampires come out at night. Jesus, Jeopardy. Night is bad, okay? That's when the crazies come."

"So you've done this before?"

She shrugs. "Nope."

"Then how do you know?"

"You're supposed to be the smart one? Common sense." She sighs. "You've got a lot to learn, Jeops."

"Okay. So where do we spend the night?"

I follow Nicole through the labyrinth of streets in downtown Sparks until she slips into an alley where she points out an abandoned warehouse. "This'll do. Let's go hang out at Victoria Square, though, until it gets dark."

We wander around the streets, looking in the shop windows. It almost feels like we're on vacation. When we see the sprinkle of stars through the casino-light haze, we head back to the warehouse.

We duck inside and set some loose boards up over the entrance, leaving a slight opening. "I don't like the dark so much," she says.

"Me, neither," I admit. It's early. Only seven o'clock or so. But the night is black with a sliver of a new moon. I sigh. It's going to be a long one.

Nicole flicks on her watch light and we make our way to the far corner, where she sets up some cardboard boxes for us to hide behind.

I'm kind of glad she's here.

CHAPTER THIRTEEN

Rats scratch and scuffle in the walls. Paws patter across my toes, and a thick tail slides over my ankles. I shudder. "The rats are the least of our worries," whispers Nicole. "Listen."

We huddle closer together. Someone stands outside the loose boards Nicole placed in front of the doorway. It reeks like decomposed bodies. I choke back the acid that works its way up my throat and wish I had easy access to my Pepto-Bismol.

"Home sweet home," a thick voice slurs. Heavy boots break down the boards—a dim light filters into the warehouse. "What's up with the boards here?"

"What a fucking dump," says another.

"You want the Holiday Inn, asshole?"

Four figures stumble into the warehouse. They work their way to a pile of cardboard boxes in the far corner, sitting between the door and us.

Nicole's fingers encircle my wrist and squeeze. I hardly notice the legs and feelers that crawl up my pant leg. The four guys light up and pass around something that pops and crackles in the silent warehouse.

The dim light that burns casts weird shadows on the walls. Dark clothes drape thin frames; matted greasy hair is tucked behind pierced ears. Hollow laughs echo in the warehouse.

I never believed in monsters before.

"Shit," Nicole moves closer to me. "I didn't notice their stuff there."

The warehouse is big. It isn't like they need the whole area. But I know we're in trouble. I can feel it in my gut. Instinct—as basic as it is—is the strongest thing we've got going for us. That "feeling" that spreads through my body is telling me to run, hide, do anything I can to get away.

"Crack," Nicole whispers.

"Crack? As in crack cocaine?" I ask.

"Jesus, Jeopardy, yes. This isn't some after-school special. Those guys are jacked up high. Bad news."

"How do you know?"

"Smell it. Listen to the sound. And watch them. They could blast off, and we're fucked if they do."

Her hands are clammy on my wrist. She digs her fingernails into me, and I bite my lip to keep from shouting out.

"What do we do?" I ask.

Nicole scoots closer to me and we hunch down. She's actually trembling.

"What's your problem?" I whisper.

"Fucking junkies," Nicole whispers, and rubs her arms. "They do anything for a hit."

I try to make out her expression in the gray light but see only shadows. One takes out a syringe and shoves it into his arm. Two start to fight and throw each other against the wall. The last lies on the ground convulsing in his vomit.

Nicole and I wait for dawn—the obsidian night turning Nevada purple. Soon the warehouse will fill with light streaming through its cracks. And they will see us. But now they don't move, and I worry the one with seizures is dead. He hasn't moved for hours.

Nicole nods to me and we slip out of the warehouse into the cold November air. The only sound is our feet pounding the pavement. Sirens blare in the distance. I just follow Nicole, not knowing which way we're running or if we'll ever get away from the warehouse and this neighborhood.

We don't stop until we collapse. I catch up to Nicole and hold my side. My lungs burn, and I gasp for breath. "H-how did you know what they were doing?"

Nicole shrugs. "It's not like something I've studied for my SATs: Topic: Identifying crack cocaine in an abandoned warehouse."

I stare at her.

"Let's just say my mom taught me well."

I open my mouth.

"Drop it, Jeopardy."

I sit down and lean my head on my knees. "Do you, umm?" I start to ask, but then feel really parochial.

Nicole sits on the curb pinching her side. "Nope. Fucking users." She walks away from me.

"But they said—" I stutter. Shelly had told me Nicole got kicked out of her last family because she stole pills. "What about the pharms?" I ask, grabbing her elbow.

Nicole pushes my hand off her arm. "It's not like doing real drugs or anything. Shit, they're all advertised just as much as cough drops."

I raise my eyebrows.

"So Nadia had a prescription. She was a user just like anybody else. She and Martin got pretty freaked out when I took a few pills from her bottles and brought me straight back to Kids Place. They were 'antidrugs.' But I don't see the difference between her and me."

"Maybe she *needed* them." I think about the prescription bottle Nicole had at Kids Place. But she never took the pills. I don't get it.

"Maybe *I* needed them, Jeopardy. Whatever." Nicole scowls.

"But you don't take them," I blurt out.

Nicole stares at me. "I told you to stop going through my shit."

"So why do you have them? Why don't you take them?" I ask.

"I don't need them."

"So what did you do with them?" I ask. "Did you bring them?" I look at her bag. Why would anybody want a whole bottle of pills?

I know the answer and it makes me mad. I don't want to do this again.

"Jesus, Jeops, can you lay off the inquisition here? Plus, I don't think this is best place to give you the D.A.R.E. talk. Let's go find a Denny's or something."

We drag ourselves toward Highway 80 and find a strip of restaurants. A small casino-restaurant's parking lot is filled with eighteen-wheelers. Chunky silverware scrapes across ceramic plates. Endless cups of steaming coffee are being served. The restaurant buzzes with heavy predawn voices.

We scoot into a booth, and I shake my pant leg hoping I haven't become some kind of bug-infested human petri dish.

"You've got that twenty bucks, right?" Nicole asks.

"Eighteen ninety-five," I say. "Photocopies at the library."

She pulls out a wadded-up five-dollar bill. "Twenty-three ninety-five."

I stare at the crumpled bills and change.

"How far is it?" Nicole asks. "To Boise?"

I pull out the MapQuest map. "Uff. Four hundred twenty-three miles," I say. "More or less." And I have zero sense of direction, but I'm not about to tell Nicole even though she's probably already figured that one out.

She shrugs. "How much is that per mile? How much can we spend?"

"Over five cents a mile," I say.

"And it's worth it?"

"What?"

"Going where we're going?"

"I don't know." I'm chasing a ghost. I'm chasing hope. And I don't believe in either.

The waitress brings the truckers sitting across from us piles of steaming pancakes with thick pats of butter melting down the sides.

"A nickel a mile?"

"Yeah." I sigh. My stomach growls.

"Fuck it," Nicole says. "Let's order pancakes."

CHAPTER FOURTEEN

"I just want to know why you have the bottle," I say, and pour a spoonful of Pepto-Bismol. "If you don't take your medicine."

We're quiet. It's like the question hangs in the air. "Insurance," Nicole finally says. "Always have backup, right? Plan B. And that bottle can get us out of a tight spot—" She shifts her gaze from me when she says that.

"Insurance," I mutter, and down my second dose of Pepto. That's one way of putting it.

"You've got yourself a pretty little habit there, Jeops." Nicole points to the pink goo that drips down the side of the bottle. She smiles.

"Pepto-Bismol? Pepto-Bismol isn't a habit. It's not an

illicit drug that people make in their garages out of laundry detergent. It's . . . it's Pepto-Bismol."

She's grinning now. "Aw, c'mon. What's the diff between pharms and your Pepto? Tomorrow it'll be on the DEA's most dangerous drug list. Who knows? You're still an addict."

"I happen to have chronic gastritis, okay?" I say, and take another swig. "And if we're going to do this runaway thing together, it's good to put all the variables on the table."

"Variables on the table?" Nicole slurps more coffee. "Okay, Brainzilla, let's get this straight: We're using each other."

"Okay, then. What do you add to any of this?" I ask. "How can *I* possibly have use for you?"

"Someone here has to have common sense."

"And that is common sense?" I point to her wrists. "Not eating is common sense? Suicide is common sense?" It's like she never even read the note I had written. Wasted words.

Her eyes turn black. "Fuck you, Jeops." She shovels handfuls of sugar, Sweet'n Low, and grape jelly into her backpack.

"Don't take them all." I slump down in the booth.

"Trust me. You'll be grateful for this later on."

My head spins from the seven cups of coffee Nicole insisted I drink. "We have to be alert," she said. I don't think a caffeine buzz is equivalent to alert. I lean back in the booth. Major gastric suicide.

"You'll remember this breakfast," Nicole says.

"How will I forget?" I unbutton my jeans. We've been eating for about three hours.

"You girls need anything else?" The waitress snaps on a piece of gum, pushing greasy bangs off her forehead. A thick layer of foundation covers up acne. She eyes the empty sugar and jelly baskets and motions to the clock. "Our pancake special ends at ten thirty." She snaps her gum. "Shouldn't you girls be in school now, anyway?"

It's ten nineteen. I've been a runaway for more than twenty-four hours and still haven't gotten out of Reno.

"And what's with the luggage?" she asks.

Nicole looks up casually. "Honors classes. Big books."

I shove my backpack under the table. My cheeks burn. Nicole kicks me and mouths, "Be cool, Jeopardy."

Yeah. Cool.

The waitress nods and clears our plates. "I'll bring your bill, then." I watch as she heads back to the kitchen.

"We've gotta split," Nicole says. "We shouldn't have

brought our packs in with us."

"She's just going to get our bill. No big deal." My stomach feels like I swallowed wet cement. Five pancakes. Seven cups of coffee. I fumble for my last spoonful of Pepto-Bismol. "We're in a casino-restaurant. This is the least likely place anybody's going to care about two teens with overpacked schoolbags," I say. "We're chameleons— just a little entry-level cell manipulation, changing our melanocyte cells, so to speak. We're blending." I just want to sit for about seven hours until I can digest the concrete ball in my stomach.

Nicole arches her eyebrows and shakes her head. "Just don't *talk* when the waitress comes back with our bill. Cut the science shit, okay?"

Some man with a button-down shirt and standard casino tie comes to the table holding the bill in his hands. "It looks like you girls really enjoyed our all-you-can-eat special."

I open my mouth and snap it shut when I feel Nicole's heel grinding into my foot. I bite my lip to keep from yelping.

Nicole glares at me.

"Are you on vacation or something? You look like you're packed and ready to go somewhere."

Nicole smiles. "Like we said. Honors classes. Lots of books. Lots of homework."

How lame does that sound? Taking a look around the restaurant, I can see that maybe we're not blending. Nobody else our age sits around the tables. It's filled with truckers and middle-aged people with bloodshot eyes and stringy hair. We even stick out in a roadside diner—the literal melting pot of America. We might as well have posted "hungry runaways" on our foreheads.

I try to think of something to say, but my tongue feels sticky. I down a glass of water and cross my legs. God, I wish I had gone to the bathroom earlier.

A couple of security guards walk toward our table. The manager nods at them and smiles. "Why don't we just call your folks now? Time to go home, girls." He looks proud. His good deed of the day: Returning the two damsels to their rightful owners.

Nicole stands up and I follow. She says, "Sure. Maybe we can just use your phone?"

"Definitely," he says. "My office is right this way."

Nicole grabs my arm and pushes past him. We rush out of the restaurant into the smoky casino lounge, zigzagging between the slot machines, out a side door.

"Run!" she hollers.

We run away from the highway toward the underpass. I look back and see the security guards standing in the parking lot—arms crossed in front of their steroid-enhanced chests. They hardly followed us. They probably don't get paid enough to chase after a couple of runaways.

When we stop, I kneel over and throw up.

"What a waste," says Nicole. "Don't piss and moan when you get hungry. That was our meal of the day. Maybe week," she mutters.

I just want to sleep—to be somewhere else. Somewhere where I can invent a new name, new family history, and reason why my dad and I moved there. And then I'll blend. Nobody will notice me for a year or so except for the nerdy science teacher. Then we'll leave again. There's something oddly comforting about how Dad and I live.

Lived.

I take in a deep breath of air and wipe off my chin. Dad and I always do things alone. Did. Alone.

Nicole slumps next to me, tapping her forefinger on a clove cigarette pack; its crinkly outer paper slips off.

I grab it from the gutter and stick it in my pocket, glaring at her. I can feel the acid burbling in my stomach lining. I watch as she twirls a cigarette in her fingers, then taps *rat-a-tat-tat, rat-a-tat-tat* on the stupid box some more.

Sit still, I scream in my head. Just. Sit. Still. This is all wrong. She's not part of the purpose or procedure—just an erratic variable that messes everything up.

I lean on my backpack. Heavy trucks thunder on the highway above. I stare at the graffiti on the overpass. "Candice is a pretty popular girl."

"And flexible from the looks of it." We crane our necks to the side. "Holy shit. Way flexible." Nicole whistles.

I stand up and walk back to Highway 80, stopping at the first gas station we find to use the bathroom.

Nicole shakes her head. "What a waste of a good meal, Jeopardy."

I take a long look at Nicole. Her hair looks limp; dark rings circle her eyes. She hugs herself with thin arms. I put my hand to my hair and realize that it will take two bottles of conditioner to get through the knots. But I don't really have the time to worry about conditioner.

We are runaways. But that's not anything new to me, I realize.

I've been a runaway my entire life.

CHAPTER FIFTEEN

Nicole is still with me. I never really thought she'd actually go through with it—running away for real. It's unlike her previous patterns of sticking around and waiting to be found. That's the thing about humans—highly unpredictable variables.

I have to construct a new hypothesis, change the materials and variables. And that irritates me, because even my purpose has to change.

Purpose: Find Aunt Sarah. Convince her to take me in. And maybe Nicole?

Hypothesis: If I show up to Aunt Sarah's house, locket in hand that proves I'm her niece, with "the system's"

127

Spam, Aunt Sarah will invite us in for tea and call social services and send us on our way. (Why would she keep two runaways? What's in it for her besides catching up with a niece she apparently didn't care enough to send birthday cards to in the first place?)

Materials: Box of Mom's things (most importantly the paycheck stub for a "Grill" in downtown Boise, Idaho), Nicole, me

Procedure:

1) Get to Boise—somehow (This could use more detail, but I'm tired.)

2) Find the restaurant

3) Find Aunt Sarah

4) Convince her to take me in

5) Convince her to take Nicole in, too?

6) Never look back

Variables: Time: It's getting cold. So we don't have a lot. Walking takes too much time. Hitching: Who picks up hitchers? Isn't it dangerous? Nicole: How do I know she won't mess things up? Restaurant: Will it have the same manager? Owner? Will anyone know Aunt Sarah?

Constant: Me

Lately it seems I have more questions than answers. My variables pretty much suck.

I sigh.

I like the first hypothesis I constructed—the one with the new family and being invited to stay and all. That's the hypothesis I want. That's what I'll do even if I have to dabble in a little data manipulation. At this stage in the procedure, things are getting pretty desperate.

It's all about looking at things objectively. I don't have to care what happens to Nicole. She's not part of it. She isn't a variable that's ever been part of the procedure.

I turn to her. "I don't want you coming with me. You go your way, I'll go mine."

"You need me."

"I need you? So far I've spent the night in a rat-infested warehouse with some whacked-out druggies, almost got caught at a café because we ate pancakes for three hours, have my stomach in some kind of flaming inferno because you insisted that we need to drink all the coffee we can, have thrown up among other disagreeable bodily functions, and just feel downright rotten. You add nothing. Zero. I. *Don't. Need. You.*" I hold out my hand. "Good-bye."

Nicole tsks and shakes my hand. "Fine. Go ahead."

"Fine." I start to walk when Nicole whistles. I turn back. "What?"

"You're going the wrong way," she says.

"I am—" I look up. I'm heading toward the mountains. "Crap." I walk past her. "Good-bye."

"Bye," she says, and walks after me.

I turn around. "Go away."

"Free country. I'll go where I want."

I listen to her scuffle her feet behind me. She's one of those walkers who don't pick up their feet but drag them. She probably doesn't even unlace her shoes to put them on. I hate that. It's irritating. Scuffle. Scuffle.

And she talks.

Nonstop. To herself. To me. I don't know. But I really wish she hadn't had those cups of coffee. Then she sings. She must know the word to every top 40 single on the *Billboard* charts from the past fifteen years.

Mom used to watch this old show, *Name That Tune.* If it were still on, we could go on it to make the money to get to Boise. Nicole'd rake in the cash.

I stop to rest. It's been a couple of hours and nobody's picked me up yet. Probably because I haven't got the courage to stick out my thumb. And Nicole's right behind me. It's like she knows I'm too scared to hitch on my own. I walk off the highway and sit on the embankment, leaning against my pack. My stomach growls.

Nicole sits a few yards away, slurping down some grape jelly. I turn away and massage my stomach.

Then I get up, walk to the highway, and stick out my thumb. Within seconds an SUV veers over to the side of the road, coming to a screeching halt, kicking up dust in my eyes. "Hey, Little Miss, you need a ride?"

I look in the rear window and see a couple of guys leering at me. "We've got room," they holler. One of them throws a beer can out the window. Another opens the passenger door of the car and throws up.

"Come on." The guy takes a step forward. "Don't waste my time. You need a ride or not?"

I shake my head. "No, thank you."

"No thank you?" He turns around. "Hey boys. This little lady doesn't want a ride anymore? We're not good enough for ya?" He walks toward me, and I walk back until I almost bowl over Nicole.

She pushes me aside and pulls out her cell phone. "One more step, asshole, and I call nine-one-one." I look over and see her phone is dead. Dear God, I say before I remember that I don't believe in God.

The guy steps forward. Nicole dials and puts the phone to her ear. "Yes. Um, about ten miles past the last exit on I-80," she says.

The guy turns pasty white.

"C'mon, Mike. Let's go," one of them yells. "We need to get to the Old Bridge. Dude, if my balls get any bluer—"

The guy spits a glob of chew at me—it streams in the air and spatters all over my face. "Stupid bitch." He jumps into the SUV; it leaves skid marks on the side of the road, pelting us with asphalt and stones.

Nicole puts her cell phone away. Her hand is trembling.

My heart thunders in my ears. When I can finally hear over the din, I whisper, "Um. Thanks." Then I drag my sleeve across my face trying to wipe away the billions of germs that probably have landed on me and now are infesting my being: glandular fever, hepatitis B, swine influenza. I already can feel my lymph nodes swelling.

"What a total MRSA," I mutter.

"Mersah?" Nicole asks, and hands me a couple of napkins.

"Flesh-eating bacteria. Nothing. Thanks." I take the napkins and try to control my voice. Then I pick up the cans they threw out on the side of the road and shove them into my backpack.

"What're you doing that for?"

I shrug. "Habit. Um, 'Keep America Clean.'"

She rolls her eyes but comes forward and dabs off some more spit from the side of my head. "Nasty stuff," she says.

"Yeah." I rub and rub, keeping my mind off anaerobic bacteria. I shiver.

Nicole holds her hand out and touches my arm. "It's okay."

I exhale and rub my hands on my jeans, hoping she doesn't notice how scared I am.

"It's dangerous alone," she says.

I nod.

"Let me come along."

I look up at her. "What's in it for you? Why don't you just stay at Kids Place?"

"Why do you need to know?"

I pause. "Because it's a long way. And it doesn't make sense to me, okay? I don't get the feeling that you like me all that much. And personally I think you're pretty much the most irritating human being on the face of the planet."

"Thanks."

"I'm just being honest."

"Honest, huh?" Nicole asks. "That's something you don't get much."

I shrug. "I don't have the energy to put on a front. So why? What's in it for you?"

"I can't be there"—she points to Reno—"anymore. And I can't be on the streets. I've done that." Nicole takes out a cigarette and lights up. "Shelly's been in the system for four years; Jess, six."

"And you?" I ask.

"Nine."

"So?"

"Have you ever just thought if you could start all over again, things would be okay?"

Who could argue with that? That was the story of my life. "Yeah."

"I just need a clean slate. And you're it."

CHAPTER SIXTEEN

Nicole hands me some jelly and I slurp it down. I'm glad she swiped it. And she starts to talk. And talk. And talk. Another hour goes by when she says, "We've gotta lay down a few ground rules."

"Fine." Maybe if we get her ground rules out of the way, she'll shut up for a while. I need time to think.

Now the method has to include Nicole. She's not a variable anymore. She's a constant. But maybe the purpose and my hypothesis can stay the same. Aunt Sarah and me as a family and Nicole doing whatever she wants to do.

But part of me doesn't think so.

"Are you listening?" she asks.

"Do I have a choice?" I say.

"These are the ground rules. They're important, so listen up. One: We never give anyone our real names."

"Since you don't even know my real name, I hardly think that'll be a problem."

Nicole glares. "Two: We never fall asleep in anyone's car. Or if we're real tired, we take turns sleeping. Okay?"

"Okay."

Nicole sits down on the shoulder of the road. "Let's take a break. You got any rules?"

I think about it. "Not really."

She nods. "Fair enough. And three: Loyalty. Like Cosa Nostra."

"Cosa Nostra? The mob?"

"Listen, Jeops. We just stick together. However you want to call it."

I've heard that one before.

We both lean back on our packs. Comfy enough for a rest. "How's your stomach feeling?" she asks.

"Okay."

"Okay." She inhales. "Shit." She brushes off her pants. "There's so much fucking dust in this dump."

"Could be from Chad," I say. "The Bodele Depression. You know billions of grains of sand are moved by the wind all around the world, blown across the Atlantic on trade winds—and most come from there. It's like a hub—you know. A place where all travel begins." I like that, thinking that the dust that lands on me isn't just Reno dust. I just hope these dust particles haven't given any unwanted microbes or bacteria a free transatlantic ride. "It's kind of like hitchhiking—what we're doing."

"The only time you talk is when you're vomiting science facts and shit." She takes a drag. "Jesus, Jeopardy, can you turn off the Discovery Channel and be a person for once?"

I shrug. It's better not to talk at all, I remind myself.

"Total academic diarrhea," she mutters. "You might want to keep that science shit down to a minimum out here. People on the streets don't like that, you know, being talked down to all the time like they're stupid or something."

"Sure," I say, "and you're real different with all of your Mafia stuff and nonstop talking. At least I do turn it off." I close my eyes. I can't believe I thought I wanted her along. Theory is always different from practice.

"I talk that much?" she asks.

"Nonstop."

She offers me a drag.

"No thanks."

She stares at the cigarette and flicks the butt on the road.

"Can you not do that?" I ask.

"What?"

"Throw your garbage out like that. Here," I hold out a plastic bag. "Go pick it up and we'll throw it away when we find a garbage can."

Nicole glares.

"Go on."

"Jesus, Jeops. It's just one cigarette butt."

"Well, cigarette butts account for twenty percent of all litter items found. And there are a hundred and seventy-six million pounds of cigarette butts thrown out each year in the States. You are contributing to that."

Nicole goes and picks up the butt and flicks it in the plastic bag. "Happy?"

"No."

"Je-sus," Nicole mopes. We sit quietly until she says, "This is my first time out of Reno. It's like breathing for the first time."

"You've never been anywhere besides Reno?"

"Yerington. But Yerington doesn't count."

"Why not?"

"Have you ever been?"

"No."

"Well if you had, you'd know that Yerington is a pit. Shithole, Nevada."

"So why'd you go there?"

"You can't help where you're born. I'd bet half the people in Africa wish they weren't born in some mucky desert with no water, either."

"Well, I hardly think Yerington can be compared to the most impoverished continent in the world."

Nicole glares at me. "Have you been to Africa?"

"No."

"Seen some kind of Discovery special about Yerington or Africa?"

I shake my head. "Not that I remember."

"Well, then, how would you know? Sometimes it's not about a book or sci channel documentary. Sometimes just living it is good enough to know, okay?"

I shake my head. There's no reasoning with someone like Nicole.

"It's good to leave, you know. Start over," Nicole says. "Breathe."

"Yeah. It is, I guess." It feels really familiar, in a weird way. This is the only thing I really know how to do. Leave. Reinvent. But it leaves me more tired than happy. Maybe Nicole has a lot more to run away from.

"Hippie van!" Nicole jumps up. "It's a sure thing."

This rattletrap of a van chugs down the highway, other cars racing past it. I can practically see the cloud of marijuana smoke encircling it. Nicole and I stick out our thumbs, and it pulls over to the side of the road just as she predicted.

"Where're you heading?" The guy is major retro: long hair, Lennon glasses, flip-flops, and a McShit T-shirt.

"That way." I point down Highway 80 east.

He laughs. He looks harmless enough. A bit like he walked off the timeline about forty years too late, but that works, too. "Hop in. I'm going to Winnemucca."

Nicole and I jump in. "Logan," he says, holding his hand out.

"Capone." Nicole shakes it and motions at me. "That's Jeopardy."

"Capone and Jeopardy?" I mouth.

She nods.

"That's cool. I don't need to know your names," he says.

"Doing the Kerouac thing?" he asks.

Nicole and I exchange a look. Whatever that means.

"Never mind." He laughs and pulls back onto the highway. I'm smooshed between the two of them. He hands Nicole a piece of paper. "I've got satellite radio. What do you want to listen to?" He looks at her. "That's the programming."

"That's obvious." She clears her throat and squints at the paper, finally passing it to me. "You pick. I get first sleep shift, okay?" she whispers.

"Okay." I look at the list. Everything is blurry and I realize how tired I am. "Anything," I say.

"Right on," Logan says. He turns on NPR. Talk radio. That's all I need. More talk. Blah blah blah blah. He finally turns to a station that's playing the Velvet Underground's "Run Run Run." It's a nice change and I lean my head against the back of the seat, humming along.

"Groovy that you're into the music." He's the encapsulation of the 1970s.

He rests his hand on my thigh and I squirm closer to Nicole, who appears unconscious. I kind of want to flick it off—like a fly or something. God, I bet he's totally into free love and stuff. I mentally tick off the diseases he probably has—chlamydia, herpes, hepatitis B, HIV—when he pulls his hand away and stares at me. I feel like a specimen stuck under a microscope. Figures the only guys I'd attract were ones who forgot the century had changed. My face feels hot.

"Just trying to go with the vibe. Boomshanka, right?"

I glare at him. The only vibe going on is the one in his pants. I pull my leg away. Creep.

"We're cool, Jeopardy," he says, "You look like you're smart—like you come from a nice home. Is it worth running from?"

"I'm not running from anything," I say. Not technically. I'm actually running to a place. It seems to make it okay that way.

"Groovy. Just trying to keep it real."

"Can I turn up the radio?" My hand accidentally brushes his arm when I do and I jerk it back.

"It's cool," he says. He turns the radio up and keeps his hands on the wheel.

When we get to Winnemucca, it's late afternoon. The sky looks gloomy—threatening to snow. Logan pulls over. "Peace."

"Yeah, yeah," says Nicole. "Peace. Love. Boomshanka.

Whatever. Thanks for the ride."

We tumble out of the van and watch it chug down the highway.

"What a piece of work," Nicole says.

"Boom-what?" I ask.

"Beats me. Boomshanka. Must be some rock band or something."

"Or something is more like it." And the two of us laugh. It's fun. Laughing.

We walk down a side street. Some of the houses are empty; one has a FORECLOSURE, BANK OWNED sign up.

"Wanna sleep inside tonight?" Nicole asks.

I nod. I stare at the black house. It's a pretty shabby neighborhood, so the likelihood of tripping an alarm is nil. We find an open window, pull off the screen, and slip in.

We use the bathroom—though it has no running water. It just feels good to sit on a semi-clean toilet. Though it can't be any later than six or six-thirty, we fall asleep, curled in the living room. My last thought is that the carpet smells like smoke and cat pee.

CHAPTER SEVENTEEN

Nicole says, "Are you finally awake?"

"Yeah. What time is it?"

"It's after three A.M."

"Have you been up long?"

"No. Just since the house next door started their own nightclub. They're smoking enough fatties to get the entire state high." Nicole and I peer out the window at the people gathered outside. "Fuck. Figures we'd have to crash next to a party house."

I inhale and cough. My eyes burn and I cough some more. "It's like they're right here. In the house."

Nicole moves toward a door and puts her ear to it. "Shit. They *are* in the house. In the garage. No wonder it's so fucking loud."

I sigh. It's like we're doomed to share our sleeping arrangements with druggies. From the smell of things, we might as well have been lying on a bed of smoldering pot. I clear my throat, peering out the window. "It looks like some more people are on their way to party. Probably already stoned."

"Why?"

"They don't even have their headlights on."

"That's weird," Nicole says.

Weird is becoming a new normal for me. My stomach growls. "I'm hungry."

"That's because you puked up your breakfast." Nicole pulls away from the window. "You probably just have secondhand munchies, anyway."

Just as she says that, there's a heavy bang on the garage door. It sounds like metal clanging against metal. "Police!"

Nicole and I freeze.

There's a moment of silence, then the sound of a door crashing in. "Everybody down. Nobody move. You move, you die!"

I hear scrambling, glass shattering. "Fuck! Oh fuck!" somebody shouts.

Nicole and I run to the back bedroom. I manage to get

the window open and rip off the screen. A blast of icy air hits me. It smells like snow.

Heavy boots clomp down the hallway; doors are being kicked open; "Clear! Clear!" the police holler.

"Move!" Nicole throws our backpacks out the window and we climb into the black night, landing on the new-fallen snow. The cold bites through our clothes and snow reaches past our ankles. We run, scrambling over two neighboring fences, lucky there aren't any dogs, and run some more, heading toward the highway.

My throat and ears burn. But we keep running until we see the sporadic glow of headlights from the highway, blinking like fireflies in the night. Then we walk in silence, not stopping, not until the first rays of light shine down on the glistening asphalt—drifts of snow sweeping across the wet pavement.

"What are the odds we'd crash at a house used by mobsters?"

"Mobsters? More like second-rate dealers, I'd say."

Nicole hugs her arms to her sides. "True. I mean, it wasn't even a Joey Lombardo–worthy arrest. Did you hear some of those guys? They cried like babies. Today's dealers have no style."

All I could hear was the thrum of my heartbeat in my ears, so I wasn't too concerned about whether it was a what's-his-name–worthy arrest. Sometimes I have no idea what Nicole is talking about. "Yeah," I finally say, and start to recite the periodic table to unravel the gnarl of anxiety in my stomach. When I get through it twice, I exhale. "This isn't going as planned," I mutter.

"Jesus, Jeops, it's not like all of life has a plan. Today I didn't wake up and say, 'Oh. I think I'm going to crash in the house where there's going to be a huge police raid.' You can't plan life. Shit happens."

"Yeah. And your Plan B?" I ask.

Nicole shrugs. "That's Plan B. Plan A is the way life goes."

She makes no sense. There's always Plan A. At least for me. I always know what I'm doing every day. I realize I've made a mistake in my other write-ups because they were too global. I need to do micro-experiments—just take it one day at a time to work toward the big happily-ever-after purpose.

So today my purpose is to find another library. Do more research, because I'm tired of the runaway part of looking for Aunt Sarah. Maybe I can get some phone numbers to the restaurants or something instead. Risk it with the waitress. See if they'll put a manager on the line.

I look at Nicole. Now she has to be part of the purpose, too. That bugs me. I watch Nicole and wonder again if I have to worry about pills and suicide. She drums her fingers on her thighs and peels the dried skin off her lower lip until it bleeds.

Snow dusts my shoes. "You, um, okay?" I ask.

"Yeah. Just cold." She claps her hands on her arms. "What? Why are you looking at me so weird?" She wipes off the blood. "Habit."

"Yeah. Habit." I'm just not wanting her to do the forever-escape thing Mom-style. "Just wondering if you're okay. That's all, I guess."

"I guess." Nicole sighs. "Goddamn, it's cold for November. Your lips are blue. Let's get some coffee," Nicole says. She points to a clump of restaurants on the freeway exit. "Wherever they'll have free refills."

"Yeah."

We walk toward the neon signs blinking in generic restaurant windows to start off day three.

CHAPTER EIGHTEEN

"I think from now on, we might have to steer clear of empty houses. No more Motel 6 stuff." Nicole slurps down her fourth cup of coffee. "Goddamn, my feet are cold."

I swirl my spoon around the thick cup. It feels good to hold it in my hands and warm up even though everything in my intestines is screaming, "No! No!" I stare at the black liquid. "You know that caffeine is the most widely used psychostimulant in the world? It enters the body and is absorbed by the stomach and small intestine within forty-five minutes."

"No shit. So as we speak we're getting high." Nicole stares at her coffee for a while. "Yippeeee," she says.

"Kind of."

The waitress comes back. "You sure you only want coffee."

Nicole holds her cup out. "We're sure. Gimme another hit." I think she thinks she's being funny.

Nicole and I take turns going to the bathroom to clean up. I forgot to pack a toothbrush and toothpaste, and my teeth feel way past fuzzy. I look in the mirror and realize I look as bad as I smell.

When I get back to the table, our coffee cups are full. My head spins, but I slurp it down. It's like this weird take-it-when-you-can-get-it instinct has set in. "Next round, let's ask for decaf," I say. "Maybe it won't make me feel so sick."

Nicole nods. I pretend not to notice that all the baskets of jams and butters are conspicuously empty. In a way I'm glad Nicole takes care of the pseudodelinquency stuff. I go to pay for the coffee when the waitress says, "This one's on me, sweetie."

"Thanks." I shove the crumpled bills back in my pocket.

"Go home," she says, and slips me some saltines.

That's what I'm doing. I'm going home. At least that's what this whole plan is about. I rub the locket between my thumb and forefinger. Nicole and I grab our backpacks and leave the restaurant, heading down the highway.

"Well, we can at least talk to pass the time," Nicole says. Saltine crumbs gather in the corners of her mouth. Another hour has passed without us getting picked up. "Are you peeing again?"

I squat behind some shrubs. "It's a diuretic."

"It's a what?"

"Caffeine. It makes you pee."

"Well you don't see me peeing every ten minutes."

"I dunno. Maybe I'm more sensitive."

"Yeah. I'm sure I've built up a high tolerance to caffeine." Nicole sighs.

"I hate drip drying."

"Well, it's not like we can afford three-ply Charmin. Just shake a little."

I air dry as long as I can stand the cold down there and join her on the side of the road.

"So?" Nicole asks. "Let's talk."

"I'm listening."

Nicole stops. "Jesus, Jeopardy. We have a billion miles plus to go and I'm not going to do it in silence. The days are long enough as is." She glares at me. "If you're not spouting science facts, you don't say anything. At all. Fuck, it's annoying."

"I just don't talk a lot. Not about the stuff you'd be interested in, anyway." Plus it's only a little over two hundred fifty miles. A billion is a bit hyperbolic.

"Like you would know what I'd be interested in." Nicole bites her lower lip and mutters, "I'm not stupid. I can actually hold a decent conversation." She turns and keeps walking. She is so exhausting.

"Okay, okay. Sorry. It's just I've never been one of those best-friends-forever people, you know?" Most people don't get that it's nice to be quiet—that every second doesn't have to be filled with hot air.

I listen to the crunch of our shoes on the gravel. "I've never actually had a best friend," Nicole finally says. "I mean, how do people get to be best friends, anyway? You know all those BFF necklaces and shit like that? I never got it."

I puff on my cold fingers. "It's actually under debate."

"What?" Nicole asks.

"Friendship," I say. "Darwin said it had to do with self-interest. People are attracted to each other based on what they can get out of each other. A scientist named George Williams, though, came up with the theory that friendship in the most genuine sense aids in the process of natural selection because it makes people healthier and all that stuff. I think it's probably a little bit of both, you know?" I clap my hands on my thighs, trying to get my legs to warm up, too. "And all those friendship gimmicks—well, that's pretty much marketing. Personally, I think it's pretty crappy to make people feel obligated to express friendship with things. It doesn't seem congruent with the essence of the idea."

Nicole pulls out a cigarette and laughs. "You're about as big a geek as they come."

I swallow and walk ahead. For some reason that really stung.

Nicole follows me, puffing and inhaling carcinogens until the butt almost singes her skin. "C'mon, Jeopardy. I didn't really mean it in a bad way. It was actually pretty cool to hear about friendship like that." Nicole flicks her cigarette onto the highway. Orange ashes die and dance on the snow.

"Hey!" I say.

"Ah shit," she says, and scoops up the butt from the snow. "I guess it just takes getting used to you. The way you talk. Really."

I'll give her that. I've always been good at science, bad at people.

"So," Nicole says, "we don't have to be BFf or anything. But maybe we can talk a little more. Just to pass the time. It's colder than fuck out here and it'd be nice to have a distraction."

We walk down the road for about twenty minutes before Nicole stops. She turns to me. "So here are the rules: No questions. We pick a theme of the day and just tell what we want or think about it."

"Fine by me." I keep walking. "What's today's theme?" I feel like we're in kindergarten.

"I dunno. You pick. I'll pick tomorrow."

I pause and think about kindergarten. "How about like doing a show-and-tell. We can talk about something we have with us. That's easy enough."

Nicole nods. "Sounds good."

"You go first. Whoever picks the theme goes second."

"Good rule." Nicole pulls out a ratty map of the United States from her coat pocket—kept in a tattered plastic bag. It's on top of a pile of postcards, a playing card, and the prescription pill bottle. At least now I know where she keeps the pills. Plan B. I shake the thought away and look at the map that Nicole shows me; the creases are paper thin and some spots have been taped up. The edges are curled in and fuzzy.

Nicole smiles. A real smile. Her eyes, too.

I hold out my hand, and Nicole hands me the map. I'm careful not to pull on it, sure it'll disintegrate. There are green dots on different cities.

"What are the dots?" I ask.

She points to the postcards. "They're places my dad's lived and traveled. Here's Chicago." She points to a green dot. "That's where he is now. See?" She points to the postcard that says "You'd love it here" in scrawled man writing.

"Why don't you go live with him?"

She shrugs. "He's kind of hiding, I think. He works for some people, you know?" She smiles, emphasizing the "some people."

"Sure," I guess. I look at the postcard. "It's dated last week."

She nods. "Just got it. It's like a sign I got this just when you—"

"Is that where you want to go? Chicago?" I ask.

"Anywhere's better than Reno," she says. "But, yeah, Chicago's good."

"Is this place better than Reno?" I look down the highway and its scattered cars and trucks. Black exhaust billows from the tailpipe of an old Chevy. We cough.

"Even here," she says, looking around.

I motion to the postcards in the bag. "They're all from your dad?"

"Yep." She seems proud about it. I would be, too, I guess. Real letters from somebody who cares.

"What do they say?"

"Postcard stuff," she says.

Pretty vague.

"What about your mom?" I ask.

"No questions," she says, her eyes getting dark. "What's your thing?"

"Okay." I think for a bit, then unclasp the locket and open it up. "That's my mom," I say, pointing to the girl on the right. "And that's my aunt. Her name's Sarah. I don't know if she's alive or dead. I don't remember her. I don't know if she even cares about me. But the only way to find out is by following this stupid box of clues, starting with Boise."

"Wouldn't it just be easier to call?"

"Complicated. That's what I was looking up at the

library. She's got a different last name—Jones. About as generic in the name department as they come. So . . . until I figure out a better way to find her via the net, Boise's my best shot. At least somebody there will know her. Plus I needed to get away."

"Don and Cherry?" Nicole asks.

"Yeah. They kinda freaked me out."

Nicole laughs. "They're not really so bad. Just a bit over the top when it comes to God, Jesus, and all that salvation shit."

"Did you live with them?"

"Nah. But I know a couple of kids who did. One got sent back to Kids Place because she peed on their family Bible."

"Oooh," I say.

Nicole shrugs and looks at the picture again. "You look a lot like her—like both of them. So what happened to your mom?"

I close the locket and put it back around my neck. "No questions. Your rule." I don't feel like playing the 101-ways-your-mom-can-die game. My head feels fuzzy and throbs from the coffee overdose.

Nicole nods. "No questions."

We continue walking. "Well, that killed about five fucking minutes." Nicole kicks a rusty can off the side of the road. "Christ. It's only nine twenty-two."

I sigh.

Nicole shrugs. "You think we'll get a ride sometime?"

"Yeah. Sometime."

"Well, stick out your thumb, because, Goddamn, it's cold out here."

We don't have to wait long. A lady with Coke-bottle glasses picks us up in an old station wagon.

CHAPTER NINETEEN

The lady drops us off a few miles down the highway, like suddenly she decides picking up two random hitchhikers isn't such a good idea.

It probably isn't.

We look around. She leaves us on the shoulder, then turns off the highway where there's a cluster of houses. We watch as her broken taillight sputters and blinks. Her car becomes a dot on the horizon.

I smell my clothes. "I reek. Mold, mothballs, potpourri, and BO."

"I'd kill for the perfume department at Macy's right now." Nicole sniffs and scowls. "What's the deal with BO, anyway?"

I open my mouth and Nicole holds up her hand. "Rhetorical, okay?"

I nod.

"You know, don't you?"

"Know what?"

"Why we have BO."

I shrug. "Kinda."

Nicole shakes her head. "Save the science talk for later. You're so random," she mutters.

I don't get it. I don't get her.

Nicole fidgets and gnaws on her nails. "Fuck, I could use a smoke."

I could use some Pepto. But it looks like we're both out of luck.

I listen to Nicole talk all afternoon until we get to a town called Battle Mountain, Nevada. Right off Highway 80. The name of the town doesn't sound familiar, so I pull out the map.

"Oh crap."

"Oh crap what?" Nicole asks.

"We should've changes routes. Back at Winnemucca. Gone to US Ninety-five."

"So?"

"So now we've gone way out of the way."

"So we take the scenic route. No biggie." Then she starts talking about some guy named Domenico Raccuglia. She's white noise—like a radio that you forget is on. At least I'm getting used to it.

I watch her. I doubt Nicole's mouth has ever run out of batteries. At a 7-Eleven on the outside of town Nicole steals a couple of hot chocolate packets. We fill Styrofoam cups we find in the garbage with tepid water from the gas station tap and stir the chocolate with our filthy fingers.

"Do you, um, ever feel bad about stealing?" I ask.

"Do you ever feel bad about eating?" Nicole asks between slurps. She licks the last of her chocolate from the cup.

I stare at my cup. It has a red lipstick stain. My stomach turns. I suppose it would sound ungrateful to tell her that styrene is seeping into our fat cells as we drink, opening us up to a slew of health problems including the big C.

But the chocolate tastes so good. I swallow it down, clumps of powder sticking to my teeth. Food first. I'll deal with the carcinogenic effects later.

Funny. Three days ago you wouldn't have caught me touching Styrofoam, much less drinking from it. Back in the elementary birthday party days, when I got invited—occasionally—I'd bring my own cup just in case the family wasn't eco-conscious.

We leave the bathroom and my stomach feels a little better. I tuck my hands into my coat sleeves and walk behind Nicole down the road. It's too dark to hitch, and we have to find a place to sleep for the night.

We find the bus station and hide behind an old Dumpster. I wonder how far out of the way we've gone. At least a hundred miles. I look at the map again. We'll go to Wells, then north on US 93. Probably better than backtracking to Winnemucca. Crap. Crap. Crap.

I lean my head against the freezing metal of the Dumpster. It seems like any sleeping arrangements on the street have to do with trash and transportation. I sigh and close my eyes, drifting to sleep.

"So what do you expect out of all this?" Nicole asks, jerking me awake.

"What do you mean?"

"I mean, you think this aunt will just open her arms wide and say, 'Come and be the daughter I never had'?" Nicole says.

That was hypothesis one—pre-Nicole. "Is that what you expect from your dad?" I say.

"Jealous?" she says. "At least I know where he is."

I am jealous, but I don't say anything. I wonder if her dad

will take us both in. Now that's a ridiculous hypothesis.

Nicole keeps talking. I come back to her voice when she's saying, "If she gave a rat's ass about you, you'd have a collection of American Greetings birthday cards with crisp five-dollar bills tucked inside. Well?" She raises an eyebrow and looks me up and down. She likes using snail mail as a proof of love. So she has some postcards. Big deal.

"Well what?"

"Have you even been listening?"

I don't answer. I don't have time before Nicole repeats, "What do you expect?"

"I guess I haven't thought about it." Big lie. That's all I think about.

"So we're going four hundred miles hitching, freezing our asses off for something you haven't thought about?"

"More like five fifty," I mutter.

"I didn't ask you to come along."

"You're so—" Nicole starts to say.

"So what?"

"So fucking green. You probably think that if you click your heels, you'll end up at home with somebody named Auntie Em. Jesus, Jeopardy, for being so smart, you're about as retarded as they come."

"And you? So you have a bag of postcards and a map. A

Mafia dad on the run." I scrape some muck off my jeans. "At least I'm doing something about—"

"About what?"

"About my life. I'm not waiting around for somebody to make my decisions." I pull my legs to my chest and pile on old supermarket ads for blankets. I cough—my throat itches.

"So you're my inspiration. A regular James 'Whitey' Bulger," she says. "I'm just not gonna make a movie out of you."

"Huh?" I ask.

Nicole rolls her eyes. "It's like I have to explain everything to you. Bulger. *The Departed*. Jack Nicholson."

I close my eyes and refrain from saying, "Now look who's random."

"Anyway, if you can find family, why can't I? Especially since mine is a lot easier to find. I don't have to chase a box of paycheck stubs and letters."

"So go to Chicago and live happily ever after with your dad."

Nicole shrugs. "I will."

At least her dad gets me off the hook. I've gone through a bazillion hypotheses in my mind, and they all end up with me alone. Without Nicole. And I'm okay with that. I look at Nicole. She's right. I only care about my plan. But what's wrong with that? Looking out for myself?

When did everything get so complicated?

Nicole is chewing on her fingernail. "Well, it's not like I have an address. How will I find him in Chicago? Should I just hang out at the Sears Tower waiting for him to drop by?"

"So look in a phone book." All I want to do is sleep.

"He's probably changed his name a thousand times by now. I can't look up 'Nicole's Dad.'"

I sit up, causing an avalanche of supermarket ads. "And this is my problem how?" I feel weighed down by her and then guilty for feeling that way.

"We're a team, right? Cosa Nostra?" Her arms are wrapped around her body now, like she's hugging herself. "We're in this together. Remember the rules." She almost sounds hurt.

I sigh. "Listen, *Capone*, I'm just trying to find a way to get to eighteen, okay? Finish high school and go to college. I just need to make it to eighteen. If I can do that at an aunt's house in Boise, Idaho, or Wherever, U.S.A., I will. You can do the same. Get on the internet. Find your dad. Whatever."

"So you can use me, then throw me away. Like trash."

"How have I used you?" I ask, settling back against the wall.

"You've been eating, haven't you? Oh, the self-righteous morally correct won't shoplift. No. But she'll reap the benefits of it."

"I could shoplift, too. It doesn't take a genius."

"It takes skill. I'm not a hack lifter. I take pride in my work." Nicole moves away from me. "Fuck, it's cold. What day is it?"

"Thursday, November twelfth?"

"I would have to pick the coldest fucking winter to run away. Christ." Nicole puts her hands in her pockets.

Technically it's still fall, but I don't say anything. My throat itches, and I say, "I need cough drops or something. Maybe NyQuil. Yeah. That would be good."

Nicole rolls her eyes. "Add it to our shopping list next to your lotion-scented triple-ply Charmin."

I swallow back a reply and close my eyes, wishing I could shoplift everything I needed; kind of wishing I was more like my dad. He wouldn't be sleeping behind Dumpsters. My lids burn against the pupils and I rub them until I fall asleep.

CHAPTER TWENTY

I run through the plan of the day in my head. I have to stay true to the purpose, follow the procedure. That's what I need to modify. I take out the MapQuest map I printed in Reno.

Purpose: Find a way to get to Aunt Sarah quicker

Hypothesis: If I can find Aunt Sarah's exact location, I can call collect and avoid another couple hundred miles living on the streets.

Materials: MapQuest map, Nevada library card, Mom's box, a bigger library—maybe one in Elko, a public pay phone

Procedure:

1) Get to a library

2) Reread Aunt Sarah's letters to my mom to see if I missed any specifics

3) Search Boise databases for Sarah Jones

4) Get her phone number

5) Call

6) Then what? I have to think about what I'll say. I'll figure it out, though.

Variables: Aunt Sarah: Does she still live in Boise? Will I find her number? Box: Will it have more clues as to where I can find Aunt Sarah?

Constants: Me, Nicole

I think through the experiment again. I don't know if Nicole should be classified as a constant or not. Other than that, though, everything's pretty foolproof—precise. Not much can go wrong with it. We just need to find the library.

I take out the letter with the flower.

"It's pretty," Nicole mumbles. I didn't realize she was awake.

"Yeah."

"I wonder what flower it is," she says.

I shrug. "We could look it up."

Yeah. Like I really need to spend my time looking at flowers. It seems anything can throw me off course. It's hard to keep things on track. It's hard to think about what I'm really supposed to be doing when my stomach aches. I'm getting pangs—the contractions last about thirty seconds, then subside.

I'm hungry.

"What's the theme?" Nicole asks, lighting up a cigarette. She found a half-smoked one on the street. At least she's recycling them now.

I swallow down some saliva and debate about whether I should suck on some snow. I scoop some from a drift near the road. It's black from exhaust. Better not. "Your pick today," I say. We're taking a break, lying on our packs behind some thick sagebrush bushes. I close my eyes and soak up what little warmth I can.

"The theme of the day, then, is . . ." Nicole pauses. "Hmmmm. The theme is—"

Nicole nudges me. "Hey. Are we going to talk about the theme or not?"

"What is it?" I sigh.

"You fell asleep."

"Oh. Sorry. So what's the theme?" I ask again. I pull

out a T-shirt and put it on top of my sweater. Another layer might help get rid of this cold.

"Ahh, forget it."

I shake my head and rub my eyes. "So what do you think your dad's like?" I finally ask.

"Way better than my crackhead mom, that's for sure."

"Oh," I say.

"Yeah. I think he was on some kind of undercover gig when he met her. I can't imagine him actually falling for her. Maybe it was a one-nighter and I could get a T-shirt that says RESULT OF ONE NIGHT OF BAD JUDGMENT AND A WORSE CONDOM."

I laugh and say, "The odds of getting pregnant in a one-time encounter are about three to five percent. Just taking in a few variables, of course. So you'd be a pretty uncommonly cool T-shirt."

"I'm like the lottery." She smiles. She looks pretty when she smiles.

I shake my head. "Nah. You're more likely to get hit by lightning than win the lottery. Either way, though, you're a rare specimen."

She laughs. "That doesn't make it sound so bad."

"It isn't," I say. "It's procreation. Perpetuation of the

species. Somebody's sperm has to fertilize somebody's egg. So why not create a you—a one-of-a-kind you with your very own genetic structure and all the doodads that go with it?"

Nicole smiles. Science, when explained right, makes a lot of people smile. When science works, it's magic.

"That's pretty nice," Nicole says.

"It's doubly nice your dad sends you postcards." I mean it. I wish I had something like that. Anything to show that somebody out there is . . . out there.

Nicole blushes. "It is. So, um, what's with the science stuff anyway? Your dad and mom into it or something?"

My eyes and nose sting. I think hunger has made me more emotional. I don't know where the science comes from. It's not like Dad did anything very scientific in his life. I always feel like Dad and I just coexisted—nothing in common except for half his DNA. Mom might have been a science person. I've never thought about that before, and it makes me sad. Another missing piece to the puzzle. I think I just like science because I do.

I don't have to be anything like Mom or Dad.

"We better get moving. While it's still light," Nicole says. "We can talk and walk."

I have a feeling Nicole can talk and do anything. The soles of my shoes slap the cracked road, kicking up pieces of loose gravel as we walk.

Nicole inhales and smashes her cigarette butt on the sole of her shoe. "Fuck. It's the last one. So," she repeats, "what's with the science stuff?"

I bite my tongue and look at the shredded cigarette paper and ashes. I force a smile. "I guess the enchantment, you know?" I say.

"I thought scientists didn't believe in hat tricks and all that mumbo jumbo," Nicole says.

"That's the thing. Science *is* magic." I smile.

"How so?" Nicole asks.

"Who else can take mold and save someone's life? Or take one cell and create a kidney?"

Nicole shrugs.

"A magician."

"I've never thought about it like that," Nicole says. "That's kinda cool."

"Kinda."

"Magic," Nicole whispers.

"Magic." I nod.

"Okay," I say. "Your turn. Why the mob?"

Nicole puffs on her hands. "The rules are clear, you know. Black and white. I kinda thought a scientist would get that."

"Try me," I say.

"They live by one law: loyalty. The whole idea is that if you're in, you're in. There's no real gray area. Parents are supposed to be like that."

"*Supposed* is the operative word."

"Exactly."

"Yeah." Plus it's pretty impossible to parent from the can. Maybe that's why he signed those papers.

Nicole's eyes light up. "Loyalty, though. Think Pablo Escobar. He ran a pretty tight business when he was in jail. Then they hunted him after he escaped and killed him on the roof of a house in Medellin, Colombia. He was shot in the chest, leg, and ear. The ear was the fatal shot, and some people think he did it himself. You know—killed himself to be free. He wasn't gonna let them take him down."

"And that's admirable?"

"Yeah. It's like saying 'Fuck you' to the system."

"By killing himself?"

"Yep. That takes balls. He went down free."

Death is freedom?

Maybe for some.

Nicole spits out the grass and says, "I hope I wasn't chewing on jackrabbit piss. Wanna hitch?" She looks up at the sky. "It's gonna be dark soon."

"Yeah. Let's try to get to the next town, anyway. Maybe there'll be a 7-Eleven where we can hang out until morning."

"I can get us some more Swiss Miss shit. And maybe a pack of cigarettes. Fuck, I need a smoke."

I rub my stomach. The human stomach can secrete up to three liters of gastric acid per day. I think mine has to be secreting double from the intense burning I feel. I can just imagine the acid working its way through my intestines and gastric walls. "That'd be nice, actually. The hot chocolate." I decide not to ask her to lift the Pepto-Bismol.

"What, you don't have any special requests? Besides toilet paper, cough drops, and Pepto, of course."

My stomach spasms again. "Nope."

We put on on our packs and walk to the highway. A trucker for some fruit company gives us a ride to Carlin, Nevada.

CHAPTER TWENTY-ONE

"You can't be here. You gotta go. This is my spot. Go. Go. Go. Gooooooooooooo!" He holds his hand out toward us, then jerks it back, retreating to a corner where he taps on the wall. He coughs four times and blows on his fingers.

The boy wears a thin coat. The soles of his shoes are fastened by old pieces of tattered string. The left side of his face is totally scarred from a burn—the leathery skin drapes in brown folds, pulling his left eye taut. It's a horrific contrast to the right side of his face. Through the filth, it's easy to tell how beautiful he was. And his eyes—a winter green. Like pine.

"Go!" He balls his fists. "Go. I don't know you.

Tallywhacker. Go go go go go. This is my spot." He coughs four more times and blows on his fingers again.

It's taken us three days to get to Elko because we spent two days in Carlin shoveling snow for food. And then walked the whole way to Elko. Nobody would pick us up. Twenty-two miles doesn't sound far. But it sure feels far when you're walking in the snow and haven't eaten much. My hands are covered in blisters. Once in Elko, we found an empty construction site near the airport. And now we're stuck in here with a freaked-out kid.

I'm tired.

Real tired.

Nicole moves toward the boy. I pull her back, but she shrugs me off and says, "Kid, we just want to sleep. We won't do anything to hurt you, so relax already."

I wonder who he has run from. If it has anything to do with his face, he definitely did the right thing.

I pull some jelly out of my pack. "Why don't you eat this?" I offer.

"I don't," he says, then freezes. I watch as tension builds up in his whole body. He trembles, then coughs and snatches it out of my hand. "Tallywhacker, asswipe," he mutters, blowing on his fingers. He returns to the corner.

"We're just going to sleep over here." Nicole motions to the other side of the room. She turns to me and mouths, "Nutcase." She starts to talk. Big surprise. Blah blah blah . . . "We'll only be here one night. No more, kid. So take it easy." The endless stream of words seems to calm him down.

Nicole and I back-walk and lie down, resting our heads on our packs. I turn on my side and face the boy. My eyelids feel like lead. I try to keep them open—to keep watch—but I can't do anything except curl up into a ball and fall asleep.

I shiver. No matter what I do, I can't get warm. I squeeze my eyes shut, trying to cut off the cold; trying to stay in a world of dreams. Sometimes sleep is the only place that makes sense anymore. I perceive the change in light outside. Dawn's lavender skies replace the inky night. I give in to the cold and morning, finally opening my eyes.

"It's colder than a well digger's ass in the Klondike," the boy says in a quiet voice. He's lying down, his face just inches from mine—his green eyes luminous.

I jump up. "God! What the—" I shout, moving back

until I'm against the wall. Nicole startles awake. "What? What happened?"

The boy sits up. He cocks his head to the side. "Tallywhacker, asswipe. It's cold." He tenses his jaw, coughs, and blows on his fingers, balling his hands up into fists when he stops blowing.

"Ass where?" Nicole asks, rubbing her eyes.

"It's colder than a well digger's ass in the Klondike," I whisper, then smile. The boy smiles.

"You're okay," he says, and taps his fingers on the ground. "Asswipe," he says. "It's cold."

"Dude, what's with the language?" Nicole asks.

He blushes and his whole body gets tense. Then it's as if there is an explosion of movement: coughing, head jerking, and blowing on fingers followed by a string of obscenities. He comes up with some pretty original word combos.

Nicole sits up. "Nice." And we both giggle.

The boy coughs. "Come on. I'll show you something." He motions for us to follow him and jerks his head to the side. He hop-skips through the room and out into a field. The sun has risen; rain drizzles down. Rays of sunshine break through clouds shining on drops of rain, creating a kaleidoscope of color.

The boy coughs and jerks his head. "The Devil's gettin' married."

I look across the empty field toward the mountains, then back at the boy. His eyes radiate light. He turns to us. He taps his chest. "I'm Klondike." Then he taps my shoulder four times and Nicole's as well.

Nicole motions to me. "She's Jeopardy. And I'm Capone." She owns that name. Chicago. Cosa Nostra. Weird Mafia facts. A dad on the run. She's a definite Capone kind of girl.

I pause. "Yeah. Jeopardy and Capone."

I don't know how long we stand in that field, looking at the "Devil gettin' married." I just know I stop feeling the cold.

CHAPTER TWENTY-TWO

We strap our packs on our backs. I look around for Klondike, but he has disappeared. I want to thank him for the morning and put two more jellies where he slept the night before. We walk until noon, when Nicole slips into a 7-Eleven to lift us something to eat. I think again about asking her to get me some Pepto-Bismol. Or even Tums. Anything to stop the burn. I don't know if it's from anxiety or hunger anymore.

I wonder when I'll stop feeling hungry. But I know that's a dumb question. Biology makes sure the body never stops feeling hunger. Maybe I'll get used to it.

"Do you feel like we're being followed?" Nicole asks.

I turn around. The black asphalt shimmers in the

afternoon sun. There's nobody. "No."

"Why are you so quiet?"

"I'm just thinking about food." And what else would I be with Nicole talking all the time. But, I admit, I kind of like it. She has some pretty funky stories.

Nicole gnaws on a piece of beef jerky. "Christ, this is spicy," she says. "Makes me Goddamn thirsty."

"Well, you stole"—I look at the name—"colon cleaner jerky. What do you expect?" I tried one bite, but the burning was too intense. Plus it's gotta be bad for my stomach. I wonder if she can steal tea bags. That's not too much to ask. Hot water and a tea bag. I clear my throat.

Nicole looks at her package and shrugs. "What's the theme of the day?" she asks.

"Your pick," I say.

"Okay," she says. "How about the most beautiful thing you've ever seen?"

"Uff."

"Well?" she asks. She swallows and sticks her tongue out. "This stuff burns going down." Nicole rubs her throat. "Can't even fuckin' eat it."

"Well, what did you expect? The wrapper has a guy farting fire."

Nicole studies the wrapper. "Pretty tacky."

"What? You now have scruples about colon cleaner jerky packaging?"

Nicole looks at me. "Ha. Ha." She leans against the speed-limit sign. We've been trying to get picked up for about an hour.

"Next time steal something less, um, leathery," I suggest.

"Have you ever heard the expression 'Beggars can't be choosers'? Well, the same goes for shoplifting."

"Okay. Sorry." I try one more bite of jerky. It tastes like the sole of a shoe that's been dipped in Tabasco. My throat's been bugging me enough as it is. Oh well. I tuck the jerky into my pocket for another day.

"Well? The most beautiful thing?"

"Give me a minute."

Nicole sighs.

"Okay," I say. "There are these things called diatoms—a type of phytoplankton. Anyway, I had a really amazing biology teacher when we lived in New Mexico. He took us to an exhibition of molecular photography. It was like looking at perfection. Nature is perfect—even in its tiniest, microscopic forms."

Nicole nods. "But nature made humans."

I think about that. "Really, how we work is perfection. How we grow and are born. It's just everything gets messed up afterward."

"Wonder why."

"I think free will."

"Free will?" Nicole asks.

"Well, instinct doesn't have malice, you know. It just *is*. Humans, though—" I pause.

"Are shit."

I shrug. "That's one way of putting it."

Nicole says. "Anyway, molecular photography. Never heard of it."

I stretch. "And you? What's the most beautiful thing you ever saw?"

"The Devil gettin' married," Nicole shades her eyes. "Do you see that?"

I look down the road. I don't know how we haven't noticed him. Klondike approaches us with his strange hop-skip.

"I knew we were being followed."

Klondike coughs, balls his fists, and jerks his head. "I want to come with you. Tallywhacker, asswipe." He taps my shoulder. "Okay?"

I shake my head at Nicole. Two is hard enough as is.

With three, nobody'll ever pick us up. And we'll be stuck walking the rest of the way to Boise. My feet are already feeling pretty raw.

This is not part of the procedure. I've already changed the constants to include Nicole, but not Klondike. In science, you can't just keep adding facts to fit the existing experiment. And I don't want a new experiment. I don't want to start over.

I look back toward the city that has faded in the distance. It's there. At least that's what the billboard for the Bob & Tom Show on Coyote FM 94.5 says. On the other side of the road there's a billboard about erectile dysfunction. We've walked over an hour, and I realize I forgot to look for the library in Elko.

I take little consolation in the fact that forgetting helps the brain conserve energy while improving short-term memory and recall of details like . . . like what? What could be more important than finding a phone number for Aunt Sarah? It's not like I misplaced my keys. I forgot a critical step in the procedure. It's like I blew off the entire procedure altogether.

It must be the hunger.

Klondike crosses his arms and says, "I'm coming."

Nicole stares down at her shoes. She doesn't say anything. I look Klondike in the eyes. "You're too young to come with us. Go back to Elko."

"I'm twelve."

I scowl.

"Eleven."

I raise my eyebrows.

"Ten. Old enough. Tallywhacker, asswipe. I'm old enough on my own, I'm old enough with you." His voice changes whenever he says "tallywhacker" and "asswipe" to a gruff sound; then he goes back to talking like normal.

"No, Klondike." I look to Nicole for support, but she still just stares at her feet. "Sorry. We can't take you."

"So I'll follow. I'm not with you, just on the same road as you. Tally—" He coughs and balls up his fists again. Klondike taps Nicole on the shoulder.

I get up and walk down the road. Too many changing variables. Nicole catches up to me, with Klondike following at a short distance.

"What do we do?" I ask.

"He's ten," she says.

"Why do you always want to look out for the younger kids?" I ask. And if something happened to one of them at

Kids Place, it always got fixed. I always figured Nicole was behind it. Especially with how they all hugged her when she got back from the hospital.

"You did. Billy. The new boy at Kids Place. You stopped the Triad from hazing him. Even I couldn't have stopped it. Not like *that*. How is that different from what I did?"

"Because I did it for me. Not for him." I hate to admit that. It sounds selfish, but it's true. He was just a positive result.

"Well for whatever reason, you stood up for somebody. And Klondike needs us. He shouldn't be on his own. God knows how he's survived this long,"

"How long is this long?" I ask. "Maybe people are looking for him."

"Did you get a look at his clothes? Hair?"

I nod.

"Long."

"Yeah. Okay. But he's not our responsibility."

Nicole squints in the sun. She lowers her voice. "He kinda is. I mean he's in this same mess. We're all in it together."

"So now *anybody* who lives on the streets is part of us—some kind of wacko version of the mob?" I shove my hands in my pockets. This is not procedure. It can't be, because then we'll never make it. I'll never make it. I've got to go back to my original, basic purpose.

Purpose: Find Aunt Sarah

Hypothesis: If I find Aunt Sarah, she will take me into her home and I won't have to be in foster care, and we will be a happy family.

But that hypothesis doesn't work. Because it doesn't include all the constants: me, Nicole, and now Klondike.

Hypothesis: If I show up at Aunt Sarah's door, old locket in hand proving I'm her niece, with two other runaways, she'll close the door on our faces and call the police.

We're two too many and too much baggage. I hate this hypothesis. It's way worse than my others, and then the procedure will have to include convincing her to open a kind of foster home for runaways from Nevada. I sigh.

"God, what's that smell?" Nicole asks.

Klondike skips up to us. "What did you want me to do, let it crowd up around my heart and kill me?"

I inhale and then pinch my nose. "Gross, Klondike." But I can't hold back a giggle.

Nicole and I exchange a glance. She hands him a piece of beef jerky. "Come on."

CHAPTER TWENTY-THREE

I've decided I'm being pretty negative about the plan—and absolutely unscientific. There's no proof to show that Nicole and Klon will want to stay with my aunt Sarah. Actually, Nicole wants to find her dad. And Klon? I'm not sure. Moreover, there's no proof to show Aunt Sarah will even want me to stay. My scientific procedure has, so far, been a big shot in the dark. So I think about it all afternoon. We finally get a ride in the back of some guy's sheep truck, minus sheep, to Jackpot, Nevada. And I come up with something that will work.

I think.

Purpose: Find Aunt Sarah and Nicole's father

Hypothesis: If I can find Aunt Sarah and explain the

situation to her, she might let me stay with her on a trial basis with Nicole until Nicole finds her father.

Materials: Nevada library card, the locket and box of letters, Nicole's postcards

Procedure:

1) Get to a library to research more about the Boise restaurant connection

2) If I can't find more about Boise, get to Boise

3) Find somebody who knows Aunt Sarah and get her number

4) Call collect

5) Say, "Surprise! It's your long-lost niece. I've got a locket to prove it."

6) If that all works, look for Nicole's dad once we're living with Aunt Sarah (procedure to come)

Variables: Klondike: Will he want to stay with us? Will he find a new place to live? Information on the net: Will I find a phone number for the restaurants? I can't very well call any restaurants collect and ask for Sarah Jones, so I need to be pretty certain. Aunt Sarah: Will she even care? That's a variable I hate to think about. But people are so unpredictable.

Constants: Me, Nicole

I can see the glaring problem. The new hypothesis doesn't include Klon. But I've decided he's too new to the trip to include in the method. Maybe he just needs a change of scenery. Maybe he'll find somebody else to travel with. No sense in getting all fussed over him. My details are pretty shaky when I think about the whole procedure, but I can't imagine *all* scientists having everything cut and dried from the beginning.

I sigh. I'm thinking the scientific community ought to come up with another method. Or maybe social scientists do something different altogether. I should look into that.

We make it to Jackpot, the last town in Nevada before Idaho. Klondike can't walk too fast. And he's always stopping on the side of the road to check out rusted cans, abandoned campsites, road kill. He's especially interested in road kill.

He's a little boy.

Klondike sleeps on a pile of cardboard boxes we found. His threadbare coat hangs midstomach, too small to button. His stomach is concave, an empty cavity beneath his covered rib cage.

✿　✿　✿

"What's the big deal? So instead of two, we're three," Nicole says. "And he needs us."

So when did Nicole go all UNICEF? Geez. "The more people, the more complicated," I finally say. "He looks younger than ten years old. And nobody wants to pick up kids unless they have some kind of weird porn ring in their basement or something. And I'm not particularly interested in showing up on a carton of milk."

"You're so clinical," Nicole says. "It's like you don't give a shit about anybody but yourself and your Goddamn locket."

"Why is looking out for myself so bad?" But that's what Dad did. And look where that got us. I clap my hands on my arms and rub up and down. Stupid weather. Too bad Dad didn't get caught in summer.

"You know what happens to people who don't look out for others? Watch each other's backs? They end up alone." Nicole straightens her back and huffs.

"Well, you're certainly the model of being surrounded by friends and loved ones," I say, and hold back from mentioning the clear absence of friends her age at Kids Place.

I stare at Klondike. He shivers and coughs. Nicole's

right. I take off my coat and put it over him. "He doesn't have any clothes that fit, and that cough sounds pretty nasty." I turn to Nicole. "You think you can get some cold medicine at the drugstore tomorrow?" I wouldn't mind some either.

Klondike coughs so hard, I worry his ribs will explode through his paper-thin skin. His eyelids flutter open; then he curls up into a ball, wrapping my coat tight around him. Nicole and I wait until the coughing subsides. All we can hear is the quiet wheeze of his breathing.

"A drugstore," Nicole mutters. "With all the meth heads it's not easy anymore—Sudafed freaks." She talks to herself and sighs.

"I'll help you," I say.

"Help me what?"

"Shoplift."

Nicole raises one eyebrow. "We're not doing some kind of chemistry lab here. It's shoplifting."

"So?"

"So I'm gonna have to teach you."

"Okay, fine. You teach me."

"In return for what?"

"I'll show you how to read." It's something I've been

thinking about. Another procedure, another hypothesis.

Nicole sucks in air. "I know how to read."

"Okay," I say. I pull a piece of newspaper from the pile I have on top of me. "Read it."

Nicole stares at the paper in my hand. She pushes it away. "Whatever. I don't have anything to prove. I'm not stupid," she mutters.

"Just because you can't read doesn't mean you're stupid. It just means you never learned." I shiver and cover myself with the newspapers. "You don't have anything to lose," I mutter.

"What's the theme?" Nicole asks.

"Can't we drop it today?"

"The rules were one theme per day." Nicole rubs her hands together and puffs on them.

Yeah. And my original method didn't include either Nicole or Klondike or living on the streets or the cold or the hunger. I hate that Nicole's rules are easier to follow.

"Okay," I say. "Something we wish we did before. Something we regret."

Nicole fidgets with her coat buttons. "I don't regret not being able to read. So get off your My Little Pony and stop looking down on me. You're such a fuckin' snob."

"I'm not a snob."

"Yeah, you are."

"I am not."

"You think you're better than me. So you can vomit science facts. Big deal. So your daddy's a 'white collar' criminal." Nicole shoved her hands up the coat sleeves. "He's no better than me shoplifting hot chocolate at the convenience store. He just wears a tie doing it."

I want to defend Dad. I wish I could tell her that's not the way it is. But it is. I've known it all along. And I like the nice house and clothes anyway.

I lean my head back against the cement wall.

"I tell you," Nicole says, "you gotta be pretty fuckin' smart to get through school not knowing how to read. Plus who needs it? Capone didn't get through school, and look where he ended up?"

"Um. Dead. I figure."

"Yeah," she sighs. "But he was untouchable. He never got killed in all those years. He died of a heart attack, at his home. The greatest mob leader of all time died of a heart attack. In his home. Brilliant."

"A bit anticlimactic," I say. I was hoping for something more mobster-like. Pablo-like.

She shakes her head. "That's the genius of it. Simplicity."

Her knowledge of how mobsters have died is slightly disturbing. "So what does this have to do with him not finishing high school?" I ask.

"He was making over one hundred million dollars a year at one point. In the nineteen thirties. Who needs high school?"

We sit in silence. I rub my arms and ask, "So how do you do it?"

"Do what?"

"Get through school without reading," I say.

"Memory," she says.

"Memory?" I ask. "Like how?"

She pauses, then says, "The Bodele Depression. Billions of grains of sands are moved by the wind all around the world, blown across the Atlantic on trade winds. It's a place where all travel begins."

I stare at her.

"Close your mouth. I told you I'm not stupid."

"No kidding," I mutter. I feel a pang of jealousy. If I had that memory, I wouldn't have to study so hard. "How do you do that?" I ask.

"What?" she asks.

"Remember. I only said that once. When I thought you weren't listening."

"I dunno. I just do."

"But I don't get it. *How?*"

"Okay. When I listen, I picture my brain opening up. My brain's one of those nineteen twenties bars. You know, filled with flappers and smoke and jazz music. The golden Mafia age, okay?"

"A bar? Your brain is a bar?" I ask.

"You wanna hear it or not?"

I nod.

"So anyway, each person in the bar holds information for me. So when somebody says something, I create a new person depending on the information. The Bodele Depression is a cleaning lady, sweeping up the dust, peanuts, and trash. She's a descendent of slaves but sings blues and jazz when everybody leaves the speakeasy at dawn. Maybe later on she'll become famous. I just need more facts to build her up."

I stare at her. In awe.

"But I have to be interested in the topic to make up the person."

"You were interested in the Bodele Depression?" I ask.

"Yeah. Hitchhiking sand." She smiles. "You oughta see the ones I cooked up in sex ed—especially when we went through the venereal diseases. Real characters."

"I'll pass," I say. "You know. Technically nothing is ever forgotten, physiologically speaking. It's just a matter of recall and retrieval from the wrinkles of the brain. It's like you're a master. Think of what you could do if you could read." My voice fades. Part of me likes having the upper hand there.

If Nicole learns how to read, she won't need me. My stomach burns more than my throat for a second. Isn't that what I want, though?

Nicole wipes her nose and leans against the cement building. I watch as she gnaws her fingernails down to the nub. In a weird way, I'm glad Nicole is here. It makes everything less lonely.

"So do you want to learn?" I finally say.

"To read?"

"Yeah. To read."

"What? So you can save me from myself? So you can feel good about stooping to my level? Maybe you can even put it on your college résumé in bold letters: TAUGHT RUNAWAY TO READ THE NEWSPAPERS SHE WRAPPED HERSELF IN DURING THE NIGHT. Yeah. That's way Nobel-worthy. For sure. At least I can read the headlines and stock reports before I freeze my ass off and die. Real useful."

"Look who's got a chip on her shoulder now," I say.

"So what's it to you whether I can read or not?"

"I just don't want to eat another piece of colon cleaner jerky. And I want to learn how to shoplift."

Nicole doesn't say anything for a while. "Okay. Deal." She pauses and pushes up her sleeves to scratch on a scab. "So what's the theme of the day?"

"Regrets."

"I don't like that theme."

"My choice," I say.

Nicole leans back against the building and closes her eyes. Her jaw tenses. "Do you have any sisters or brothers?" she asks.

I shake my head. "Not that I know of." I rattle the box. "Maybe something here will tell me otherwise." I laugh.

Nicole doesn't.

"I did," Nicole says. "And now I don't. That's my regret."

"How?" I ask.

Nicole looks away. "Crackhead mom in Yerington. Brought all sorts of freaks home. Stupid whore."

I don't say anything for a while. "I'm sorry," I finally say.

She says, "Kids are supposed to have normal, you know? Macaroni and cheese and lemonade stands and all that shit. Not what we had. Not what she had."

Normal. That would be nice. "Yeah." I pile another bunch of newspapers on top of me. At least I've never felt unsafe with Dad. He might be a con, but he never hurt me. Not really. Does it count that I was sometimes his decoy? So I fell down a few times on slippery floors at banks and office buildings. Four fractures and one serious break— all ending up in cozy settlements. Does that make him a monster?

I look at her arms and remember the cuts she has—two big ones on her wrists—lengthwise.

I wonder who found her. In time.

Will she find her dad after I get to Aunt Sarah? Will she be safe?

"And you, Jeopardy. Your big regret?" Nicole interrupts my thoughts.

I pick at a hangnail. "Five minutes of chasing Jimmy Sanchez around for a hair ribbon."

"Huh?"

"It was satin. Pink. I remember my mom had braided it into my hair that morning, and he yanked it out."

"A hair ribbon?" Nicole sneers.

"So I came home late after kindergarten. Five minutes too late. And they couldn't bring her back. Science," I say, "like magic, is all about timing."

"Oh." Nicole looks in my eyes and looks away.

We sit in the cold alleyway. There's a pizza restaurant around the corner. Garlic and tomato sauce almost cover the smell of cat crap and pee. Maybe someone will throw out a half-full box. I'll go look later. I shiver and lean against the wall, trying to find a way to get warm.

"It was cool of you to give Klondike your coat," Nicole mutters. "We can share mine."

I move to her side. "You got paper and a pencil?"

"Yeah."

"Are you tired?"

She shakes her head.

"Tonight we can start," I say.

"Start what?"

"Reading."

"And stealing?" she asks.

"Tomorrow."

"Deal."

"Deal." I guess this will be our normal.

Klondike lies next to us curled in a ball. His hair is matted and flops down over his face, covering the leathery skin. His chest rattles when he breathes.

We crouch together under the light of the neon pizza sign. And we begin, one letter at a time.

CHAPTER TWENTY-FOUR

"**G**et up!"

The heavy boot lands on my back. Dizzy with pain, I roll away and crouch in the corner. Nicole and Klondike scramble over to me.

"Who left the cage open so these animals could get out?" The skinhead kicks again, his boot crushing Klondike's side. I can hear the sickening crack of bone and pull Klondike toward me. He whimpers.

"Fuck, you're ugly. Nobody should let you out during the day," a second says. The three of them wear black army boots and painted-on blue jeans. They have chains for belts and their knuckles are chapped and scarred. They all have serpents tattooed on their necks. I stare at the tattoos, trying to distinguish what snakes they've chosen. It's like they're clones—three of the same being. I wonder which one is the original and which ones are copies. I stare at their tattoos and label them Cobra, Rattler, and Mamba.

"Jeopardy," Nicole elbows me. "Snap out of it."

Klondike tucks the scarred part of his face against my chest. "Tallywhacker, asswipe." He coughs, holding his hand out toward them.

I jerk it back. "Don't touch them," I say.

Klondike's body trembles and he taps my shoulder frantically. "Asswipe, asswipe, asswipe," he repeats.

"What did you say to me, you microwaved piece of shit?" Cobra asks.

"Asswipe. Tallywhacker," Klondike says, cradling his side. He coughs six times, then hiccups.

"Shut up, Klondike," Nicole says. "Jesus Christ, Klon. Just. Shut. Up."

Klon snaps his mouth shut and his whole body tenses up until he has another flurry of fits and tics. "I can't help it. Asswipe, tallywhacker. Goddammit." He clenches his fists tight then trembles all over. Every time he says something, his voice drops to that gravelly, creepy sound.

I try to cover Klondike's mouth, but he jerks away, repeating himself over and over again.

"You're human shit, littering up this place." Cobra steps forward.

I look down the alleyway. We're at least two hundred yards from the street. Cars trickle by.

Nicole flashes me a look. She has her lighter out. I grab onto my piles of newspaper and twist them together. "Hold on to me, Klondike," I say. "Don't let go."

He coughs, blowing on his hands.

The three move toward us, their fists closed. "Now," whispers Nicole. She lights up the pile of newspapers and each of us holds our torches in front of us. Klondike shrieks and cowers in the corner, blocking himself from the fire; Nicole turns to him and loses her footing. Rattler grabs her hair and throws her to the ground. He punches her in the mouth, blood spattering his shiny black boots.

"Looks like we've got ourselves a prize here, guys." Rattler starts to unzip his pants. "Breakfast with a filthy slut."

Cobra and Mamba laugh, their bald heads glistening with sweat.

Nicole's eyes turn dead then. I look from Rattler to

Nicole to Klondike kneeling behind me, whimpering about the fire. The snakes are focused on Nicole, holding her down. My stomach burns. Nicole dropped her lighter, and I edge toward it until it's within my reach. Nicole has turned away from us. Mamba is on his knees, pinning her down.

I take a deep breath, snatch the lighter, and ignite a handful of newspaper. I run at Rattler, putting the burning newspaper underneath his shirt. He stands abruptly and shrieks, fanning the flames. "Stupid bitch. Stupid, stupid bitch!"

Nicole knees Mamba in the groin and scurries away. He rolls around groaning.

The fire burns Rattler's shirt and spreads all over his back. The flames dance and work their way up toward his head. Everything smells like burning flesh. I gag.

He panics and starts to run, his screams deafening.

"Stop, drop, and roll, asshole. Stop, drop, and roll!" Cobra hollers, running after him. "Son of a bitch! Stop! Drop! Roll!" Cobra grabs Rattler and the two roll on the ground together, dowsing the flames.

"Get off me, you flame dick." Rattler tries to push Cobra off. "Jesus, are you trying to hump me or something, you sick queer?"

"Fuck, man, I'm just trying to put out the fire." Cobra looks hurt. He and Rattler are tangled together a few yards from us. Everything has a burned smell.

Mamba keeps saying, "My balls. My balls."

Klondike won't move past the fire—some papers and trash have begun to burn. "Not fire. I can't do, tallywhacker, asswipe. Not fire."

Nicole finally drags him away, somehow carrying him in her thin arms. "Grab that." Nicole points to a wallet that has fallen on the street. I grab for it, then just kick it into a puddle, leaving it behind.

"We'll find you, you Goddamn whores!" One of them calls after us. I look back to see the three of them standing together—Rattler in the middle, holding out a now-melted synthetic-fiber jacket. "You'll pay for this!" they scream.

We run up Main Street, slipping into a casino called Cactus Pete's.

"Find the bathroom," Nicole barks. I lose my sense of direction with the casino's mirrors and dizzying lights. Klondike moans and whimpers. "Hurry!" Nicole says.

She and Klondike follow me past the hotel reception and we slip into the women's bathroom. We cramp into the handicapped stall. Nicole blocks the door.

"Tallywhacker," Klondike croaks and hugs himself—his body an eruption of spasms. "I hate fire. I just can't, asswipe, tallywhacker. GODDAMMIT." Klondike taps his face and blows on his fingers.

"Shut up, Klondike," I snap. "Just shut up for a second. I can't think."

With that, Klondike's tics worsen. I lean my head against the bathroom door and swallow back the knot that blocks my throat. "I'm sorry, Klondike. I didn't mean—it's—never mind."

"Are you"—I turn to Nicole—"are you okay?"

Her lip trembles. "Yeah. I'm okay." She rubs her arms. "No big deal."

"I'm, crap, Nic—"

"Capone," she says.

"Capone." I try to steady my breathing. What am I supposed to say?

"I said I'm fine. Okay? Just drop it," Nicole squats on the floor and rests her head on her knees. "Where's the wallet, Jeops?" Nicole finally says.

"I, um. I didn't take it."

"What? It could've had cash. We could've used it."

"I couldn't."

"Why the fuck not?"

"I burned him, okay? He might be"—I lower my voice—"he might be scarred. Forever and ever. It's not like I needed to steal his wallet on top of everything."

Nicole clenches her jaw and says, "It's good you're considerate about a rapist's things. God knows we wouldn't want him to have a couple of visible scars so he can't hide the monster inside so easily." Nicole slumps to the floor.

"I didn't—" I stop talking. "Capone, it's not that. It's just . . ."

She turns to me. "It's just what?"

"I don't know. I'm trying to do things the right way here."

"What's the right way?" Nicole asks.

"I don't know," I say.

"Christ." Nicole chews on a hangnail until it bleeds, her hands chapped from the cold. "Nice time to get all high-road on us. He was a Goddamn prick."

"I'm hungry," Klondike mutters between croaks.

Suddenly I feel like we're just stuck in a box with no way out. My fingers still smell burned. I push open the door and rush to the sink—heaving colon cleaner jerky. It burns twice as bad coming back up and my stomach spasms. I rinse out my mouth, then slump in the corner. The bathroom door sways open and three ladies with mile-high bangs and camel-toe jeans come in blathering on about some cute cowboy. Two pass an aerosol can of spray back and forth, and we're stuck in a sickening fog. The third comes out of the stall and they leave the bathroom, clomping away in wedged heels.

They don't even see us.

"She is so yellow-listed," Nicole says.

"Huh?" I ask.

"She didn't wash her hands—totally antihygienic. I mean, gross." Nicole turns to me. "You know what kinds of germs there are on hands?" she says. "I mean you probably *know*."

Viruses, bacteria, parasites—the correlation between disease prevention and hand washing is irrefutable. I start to go through the numbers in my head, trying to remember what last I had read about it. Nicole looks at me and smiles.

Things are okay.

Then she turns to Klon. "Klon, you've got to keep a lid on it when we're around psychos who want to kill us."

"I can't." Klondike shivers, coughs, blows on his fingers,

and taps Nicole's shoulder. "I can't help it." He tries to cough again but grabs his side when he does. So he replaces the cough with a strange croaking sound that comes deep from the back of his throat. "That's why I have to live alone. That's why"—he puts his hand to his face—"I hate fire," he says, touching his scars and jerking his hand back. "Tallywhacker."

We wait for what seems like forever for Klondike to settle down. His breathing evens out.

"Do you think you're badly hurt?" I ask Klondike. "I mean your side."

Klondike nods his head, jerking it up and down. "I'm fine, though. Just the fire. Asswipes. The fire." His voice drifts off. Then he croaks.

"Think." I press the palms of my hands to my eyes. "Just think." God, I wish I had Pepto-Bismol. I look from Klondike to Nicole to the mirror. We're a mess. We look and smell like street kids. That guy probably has second-degree burns all over his back—at least. I hate getting spattered by grease when I grill cheese sandwiches.

It feels wrong that I'm worried about a guy who would've raped Nicole.

I go to Nicole and put my hand out, pulling her up.

"You okay? Really?"

She nods. "Just a little shaky. Thanks," she says, "for helping me out." Her lip is swollen where the guy punched her.

I do a superhero stance and salute her. "Well, ma'am, there you have it—just a run-of-the-mill morning in the life of Super Jeopardy. I'll kill 'em with boredom every time." I exhale. "If the fire didn't work, I was ready to start to recite the periodic table and balance equations. That would've done it."

Nicole laughs. "I owe you one."

I shrug. "I hope I never have to collect."

"Me, too," Nicole says. She turns to Klondike. "You okay?"

He coughs, then midcough changes it to a low, thundering croak. "There has to be evil so that good can prove its purity above it." Again he touches his burned face.

Nicole and I both look at Klondike. "Where do you get that stuff?" I ask.

"Pa's sermons. Pa says that . . ." He strains his neck and lets out a long, steady croak. "Evil is always possible. Goodness is a difficulty, and he that spareth his rod hateth

212

his son: but he that loveth him chasteneth him betimes. Always showing me the business end of a stick. Then"— again he touches his face—"it was the demons."

My head pounds. Klon talks in Bible-Appalachian-who-knows-what speak. Nicole's stuck in some black-and-white make-believe Mafia world. And they both look to me for answers. "Okay," I finally say, and turn to Nicole. "Nic—"

"Capone," she interrupts.

"Oh yeah. Capone, can you get one of those DO NOT ENTER, RESTROOM BEING CLEANED signs?"

"Sure, Jeops. Your lesson last night was stellar, but we're just getting through the vowel sounds." She rolls her eyes.

"Okay. Crap." I rub my eyes. "Just get one of those yellow triangles that you see cleaning people have."

Nicole nods. "Give me ten minutes."

"We'll wait here."

About five minutes later she comes back with five different signs—WET FLOOR, DO NOT ENTER, KEEP LEFT, WATCH YOUR STEP, RESTROOMS BEING CLEANED. I put the last one outside the door and try to jam the lock. "Well, you're thorough. And fast."

Nicole shrugs. "Ha. Ha."

"We probably have about ten minutes, okay? We need to clean up," I say. "Strip down."

Klondike points to the stall. "You wait there. When I wash, you wait there," he says. "I'm not gonna be without a stitch in front of a couple of girls." He points to the stalls.

"We don't have time." I motion to the door. "Somebody could come in at any second. So let's just get cleaned up."

None of us moves.

"I have one ball," Klondike finally says.

"Huh?" The light in Nicole's eyes comes back a little.

He blushes and scowls. "One ball, nut, gonad, tater, nugget, testicle. One."

Nicole and I burst into laughter.

"It's not funny. Tallywhacker. It's not," he says, lip quavering. Then he croaks four times and taps his groin.

"I'm sorry, but"—I hold my stomach—"it's just that . . ." Then I cry. I let the hot tears spill out. I blow my nose on the scratchy toilet paper. "Let's get cleaned up," I finally manage to say, and put my head under a stream of lukewarm water.

"First memory," Nicole says.

"What?"

"Theme of the day. First memory."

I scrub my hair with the liquid soap, pulling at the tangles, wishing for the bazillionth time I had straight hair. "Do you really think now's the time?"

"What's the diff whether it's now or later in the day?"

I clench my teeth when I pull my fingers through the knots. Chunks of hair come out. I think back to when I was little, trying to piece memories together. It seems like the memories I have of my mom are a jigsaw puzzle with pieces missing. I never get the complete picture and only remember random things about her.

"Playing sleep," I finally say. "My mom liked to play sleep. She'd wrap herself in blankets and say, 'Let's play sleep.' And to play, I had to be very, very still and close my eyes. Then she'd let me lie next to her. Sometimes she'd even hug me. That was nice. When she'd hug me."

"Weird."

"Yep," I say, and peel off my shirt. "Yours?"

Nicole pauses, then takes her shirt off, too. Her belly is covered with cigarette-tip–size scars. She points to one right above her belly button. "This one. One of Mom's boyfriends." She starts to soap up her stomach. "I think I wet the bed or something," she says.

"How old were you?" I ask.

"Three. I dunno."

"Wow," I say.

Nicole shrugs.

"Did it hurt?" I look at the countless circles all over her stomach. "I mean did it hurt the same every time?"

Nicole turns to me. "Every fuckin' time. You know what, though? Every time one of her fuckhead boyfriends got on me or something, after she sobered up, she'd tell me about my dad. How he's on the run, you know. He's big in the organization. And Yerington. Fucking Yerington is too small for somebody that big." She scrubs her body and says over the sound of water, "Those stories, the postcards—they're the only real things I've ever had, you know?"

My stomach flip-flops. "What about your sister?"

Nicole shoots me a sharp look. "She's gone now. What does it matter?"

"In Heaven?" Klon asks.

"I don't know about that Heaven and Hell and stuff," Nicole says. "Are there rules?" She looks at Klon like she's waiting for a definitive answer.

"All children go to Heaven when they die." Klondike strips off his shirt. The scar continues down his left shoulder all the way to his waist. When he takes off his pants, we see how it covers the entire left side of his body. He blows on his fingers and croaks. "But let judgment run down as waters, and righteousness as a mighty stream." Klondike jerks his head. "Heaven—no matter what—because children's souls are immortal."

"You think?" she asks. "And when, um, do the doors to the Pearly Gates close? Like, um, when we turn eighteen? Sixteen? Do God and Peter and Gabriel and all those other guys have a legal adult age?"

I can see her doing the math in her head. Klon stares at her for a while. "I don't get it."

"Never mind," Nicole says. "But you think she's really in Heaven? Is that possible?"

"I know," he says. "You'll see her again when it's time."

She turns away from us. "Maybe," she mutters.

We're quiet, listening to the whine of the bathroom pipes. I swallow. "And your memory, Klon?"

"Water. My baptism in the icy waters," he whispers. "Everything except for that and the fire is gone. Except the hate. How she looks at me with hate," he says. He taps his head and shrugs, making that low croaking sound again. "Fire and water. That's why I had to go. Ma's eyes and the demons."

217

The three of us stand in the bathroom—everything exposed. The only sound is the rhythmic drip of water from a leaky faucet.

"Hey. You okay?" I ask. Klondike's side has started to swell—a light bluish color is spreading around his ribs where one of the snakes kicked him.

He nods and tries to pull his too-small shirt over his head. I fish a semiclean one out of my backpack and throw it at him. "Wear this."

"Thanks," he says, shivering.

"Colder than a well digger's ass in the Klondike?" I ask. He grins.

I hand him my coat. "Keep it. We'll find another one."

"Find?" Nicole asks.

I shrug. "You know what I mean."

"Yeah. I know."

We finish cleaning and try to comb through each other's hair. No lice or nits yet, as far as I can tell.

"So what's the plan?" Nicole breaks the silence.

The plan? It's totally ad hoc. Every time I try to create a hypothesis and procedure, anomalies come up and I'm scrambling to make sense of everything. Maybe a good scientist would be able to come up with methods to work with the change in elements. Maybe I'm a really bad scientist.

Finally I say, "I think we need to get out of here. That kid, you know. He could be pretty hurt. I think, um, that I could probably get in big trouble for that."

Klondike taps my shoulder. "It's okay." He croaks four times.

"Yeah," I say, trying to ignore that sick feeling I have in my stomach.

CHAPTER
TWENTY-FIVE

We walk through the casino unnoticed. That's a good thing about a border town. People come and go and nobody pays any attention at all. We find the diner. I pull out all the cash we have left. "Five dollars and sixty-seven cents," I say. I'm trying to remember where we've spent the money: coffees mostly, I guess.

"We can dine and ditch," Nicole says.

"Yeah. But then a waitress gets stuck with the bill. That's not cool."

Nicole rolls her eyes.

"Just because people have been bad to us doesn't mean we have to do the same," I say.

"Oh. The scientist is into karma?"

I shake my head.

"Okay, Girl Scout. How do three people eat with five dollars and sixty-seven cents?" she asks.

I look around the casino floor for nickels, quarters, anything. The swirly red design makes me dizzy. Some old lady spends the last of her change and slips off the plastic stool. I watch her black silhouette against the morning light. All alone. She has no one else but a stupid nickel slot machine.

"The feeding of the five thousand. Luke nine, verses ten to seventeen," Klondike says, and then lowers his voice in that creepy Darth Vader way, "Asswipe."

People look up from their slot machines and then go back into their gambling daze.

"Nice, Klon," I mutter.

Nicole scowls. "What the hell is he talking about?"

"You know, when Jesus multiplies the bread and fish," I say.

Klondike clenches his fists. I look where he's looking.

His hand lifts up to touch the nickel slot and I slap it away. "We'll get in major trouble if you touch anything here." I turn to Nicole. "You know that story—when Jesus has one loaf of bread and five fish or something and five thousand people eat. But it's just a dumb story. Miracles don't really happen in real life," I say. Unless you pay for them, I think.

Klondike recites the Bible verses, tic free. He balls his fists. It's as if an electric current runs from his toes up to his head. We watch as he twitches, coughs, croaks, and taps both of us when he finishes. Every time he coughs, he grabs his side. His coughs are more wheezes now than croaks.

"Miracles," Klondike says after a fit of tics, "aren't really miracles at all. Tallywhacker, asswipe. They're just people doing what they should. At one time or another, we all get to have one. I can't wait. ASSWIPES!" he says in that freaky deep voice. Loud. Again people look our way.

"Geez, Klon," I say. Nicole drops her head.

He jerks his head and blows on his fingers. "I can't help the demons. I don't mean to." He clenches his jaw. "Sorry."

"It's okay," I say.

Nicole sighs. "No big deal. We all have our weird shit to deal with. Jeopardy here, she's a walking Discovery Channel, you know. She spurts out science facts about anything from the reproductive cycle of tsetse flies to belly-button lint."

I clear my throat.

"What?" Nicole asks. "You have no interesting facts about belly-button lint?"

I refrain from telling them that a professor in Sydney, Australia, conducted a thorough study of navel lint. He found that most lint migrated up from underwear as opposed to down from shirts. It has to do with the frictional pull of body hair dragging tiny fibers *up* to the belly button. I wonder who *that* character would be in Nicole's mobster bar. Maybe I should tell her. Just to find out.

Nicole laughs. "I know you do. That can be another theme of the day: Everything you know about belly buttons."

"Yeah." I turn to Klondike. "And Capone, here, is a walking Mafia-freak tape recorder. And a kleptomaniac on the side."

Nicole curtsies. "I must say I'm pretty good." She holds my locket in her hands. I touch my neck.

"When?"

"Ahh, that's the beauty. You'll never know." She smiles

and dangles the locket in front of me. "Your auntie Em." She smirks.

I snatch it from her. "Cute. Don't take this, okay?"

"Just trying to prove a point."

"Point proven." I put the locket on and tuck it in under my shirt.

The corners of Klondike's mouth curl up. "I'm hungry," he says, ending with just one cough. He looks more relaxed, like being weird is our normal. So that makes things okay.

"C'mon. Maybe we can get something to eat," Nicole says. We leave the diner area and stare at the grocery store across from the casino. "Lesson one, Jeopardy."

"Okay."

"You like magic. It's like being a magician."

I glare at her.

"Really. Just a different kind. Maybe you want to trick some cells in someone's body. I want to do a little trick of the eye. You have to misdirect the audience. They'll be looking at what you *want* them to look at while you lift what you really want, okay? Grocery stores are easy," Nicole continues. "They're big. Not a lot of security. And they have lots of small things, easy to pocket." Nicole nudges me. "What are you waiting for?"

I stare at the store and the people going in and out. It would be easy. No problem.

Half an hour later I come out.

"What'd you get?" Nicole asks.

I shake my head and hand her the latest grocery store ads. "Look. With some of the money we had left, I got us a bag of generic cereal and powdered milk. That should last us a while. We still have some change left over."

Nicole rolls her eyes.

"I'm sorry," I say. "I couldn't. I got scared . . ."

How can I explain to her that I just don't want to become my dad? It's one thing when I can pretend the food is from a legitimate source, but another when I can't.

I shrug. "Maybe you could hone your teaching skills a bit. Or maybe I should do some practice shoplifting beforehand."

"Practice shoplifting? Christ," Nicole mutters.

I should construct a procedure. A procedure for stealing. I ask Nicole to go through the steps again.

"There are too many scenarios," she says.

"Just humor me. Give me one."

She does, and then I construct the plan in my head.

225

"What are you doing?"

"I'm making the plan—procedure. To steal."

"Huh?" Nicole asks.

"Listen, you've got your bar. I've got my hypotheses. It helps. Just let me think."

Purpose: Steal food

Hypothesis: The average human body needs between 1,200 and 1,800 calories/day. If we don't get our calories over a period of a couple of months, our bodies will enter a state of starvation and irrevocable organ damage. And then we'll die. Therefore, I need to steal food so we can eat and not starve to death.

Materials: A big jacket, fast hands

Procedure:

1) Borrow Nicole's jacket

2) Go to the grocery store cereal aisle where there are all the fruit bars

3) Slip fruit bars in coat sleeves

4) Browse other aisles

5) Leave with fruit bars

6) Eat

7) Starvation avoided

Variables: Security devices: What kind of security does the store have? Cameras? Mirrors? People wandering the aisles? Identify and act accordingly. Me: How cool can I be? Will my face give me away?

Constants: None (unless hunger counts)

"Okay," I say. "I'm ready."

"So your hypothesis and procedure make it okay now?" Nicole asks.

"Kinda."

"Well, let's eat first. You can steal lunch." She laughs. It's like she knows I can't. "It's not like you can go back into the same store."

"Oh. You didn't say that. I could've, um, changed my plan."

"Common sense, Jeops. Open up the cereal."

We open the cereal and the powdered milk. I find an old coffee tin and pour in the powdered milk. Then I go to the grocery store bathroom for water. I pass by the cereal aisle and go through the procedure in my head. But I don't have the jacket. I didn't ask Nicole for it before coming in.

Improvise, I think. I've got to stop being such a

coward. I have to prove that I can do it. So I shove the bars in my shirt and tuck it in. Just as I'm to the door, a man taps me on the shoulder.

I untuck my shirt and the bars spill everywhere. I turn to get away, sloshing the milk all over me, running out to Nicole and Klon. "Run! Run!"

I try to run without spilling any more of the milk. When we get a few blocks away, my front is covered in gooky powdered milk substance. And half our cereal has fallen out because Klon ran with the bag open.

Klon, Nicole, and I look back at the trail.

"Hansel and Gretel," says Klon.

We nibble on the rest of the cereal, licking the crumbs from the palms of our hands. We take some side streets, backtracking, walking through Jackpot's neighborhoods. "What happened back there?"

"I dunno," I say. "I tried."

Nicole says, "Part of success is getting over the initial fear. That's good practice." She laughs. "But God, I'm hungry." We walk in silence for a while. Even Nicole can't find anything to say at the moment. "Where are we going?" Nicole finally asks.

"We need a map," I say. "A road map."

"Yeah. Like that's gonna be a real help with your sense of direction. What happened to the MapQuest paper, anyway?"

I pull it out, soaked with milk. I've been keeping it under my shirt—a safe place. Now all the roads and numbers look blotchy. I take off my shirt and pull a warm sweater on. It's like cold and lack of food have frozen my brain. I wad up the shirt and shove it into my backpack. "Stupid. Stupid," I grumble.

"Nice striptease, Jeops," Nicole says.

"I'm cold," I say. "And we need a new map."

"Well, I can steal one from a gas station," Nicole offers. "Or do you want to?"

"Ha. Ha." We walk for a while. The sun is up and it's not as cold as before. I rub my arms, glad to have at least a sweater on.

Then I see it. "That's what we need."

The three of us stand outside the doors. I almost want to go and hug them.

"Another library?" Nicole asks.

"Yep. Maps. Internet. MapQuest. Google Earth. Warmth. Everything." I turn to Klondike. "Do you think you can keep your croaks to a minimum?"

He shakes his head, and his body jerks in a series of movements. "Probably not."

I shrug. Nicole sighs. Klondike croaks and says, "Tallywhacker, asswipe."

"It doesn't matter," I say. "Ready to go in?"

"Another library," Nicole mutters and pauses at the door. "Goddamn, these places make me nervous."

CHAPTER TWENTY-SIX

"Are you kids here for the program?"

"Yeah," Nicole says. She looks around the empty library. "We're early."

The librarian smiles and peers over a pair of thick-rimmed black glasses. She has spiky purple hair and nose piercings. She turns to Klondike. "You're not from the high school. Shouldn't you be at Jackpot Elementary now?" she asks him.

"Tallywhacker," he croaks, and taps her on the shoulder.

She bites her lower lip and says, "Excuse me?"

"Nothing." I push Klondike behind me. "He's a cousin from out of town. He has my teacher's permission to be here. He just says stuff."

The librarian hesitates, her hand resting on the phone.

I put on what I like to think of as Dad's make-an-insurance-claim face—stoic with a touch of angst. It's like I can physically see Dad and copy his expression perfectly. And that makes me kind of uneasy.

She slips her hand off the phone and points toward a table. "Go ahead and help yourself to juice and muffins before the presentation begins. It'll be a busy morning."

I don't exhale until I'm way out of her range.

"Score. Food," Nicole whispers. "Who'd have thought?"

The three of us head to the food table. "The muffins look real good. Asswipe," Klondike says in that guttural voice.

"Jesus," Nicole groans. We turn back and see the librarian staring at us. She half smiles and goes back to working on her computer.

Nicole licks her fingers and grabs a second muffin. "I think we should come to the library more often."

I roll my eyes.

Klondike is on his third muffin before I even finish my first. "Let's not try to look *too* hungry," I say. "I'm going to find some maps." Maybe I'll look for a botany book, too. Maybe I'll look for the flower. Aunt Sarah's flower. I tuck the envelope with the flower in my jeans pocket. It's my favorite letter.

I scarf down the last bite of muffin and shove a second up my sweater sleeve. I look at the coat rack in the front hall of the library. There's a heavy black coat hanging by the door. Maybe, I think. Maybe. I just hope it's not the librarian's.

I find a highway map of the western states and trace Highway 93 to Twin Falls; then from Twin Falls, we can take Highway 84 to Boise.

It doesn't look too far away. Maybe we can get there today. Maybe today we can find Aunt Sarah.

I tuck the map under my arm and head to the photocopy machine.

A bus pulls up and a bunch of teenagers spills into the library, ruining the comfortable silence. They rush to eat the muffins and juice, stuffing the food in their faces. They probably aren't even hungry.

I look back and see Klondike's body tense up. I try to wave Nicole down, but she's filling up on another glass of juice. It dribbles down her chin a little. The acid in the juice has to be a killer on a cut lip. I look from Nicole to Klondike to where Klondike is looking.

"Oh God," I whisper. My feet feel like they're stuck in drying tar.

Klon is jerking his head and muttering something.

"No!" I push through the crowd of students, but it's too late.

Klondike coughs, spattering muffin everywhere. "Tallywhacker, asswipes," he croaks in his strange voice. "Stay away," he says. "Just stay away."

"That's her! She's the one who burned Martin! These are the street kids who attacked us." I can't believe those kids are in high school. I mean who gets up early in the morning to go out and beat up homeless kids before school? What happened to sleeping in as late as possible? It's like we're stuck in some kind of vortex. Everyone whirls around us.

Klondike's body comes alive in a burst of movement. Nicole drops her juice and starts to back toward the main entrance, her face pasty white.

The librarian moves toward us. "What's going on?"

"Those kids are the ones who burned Greer. Some homeless druggies who tried to kill us," Cobra says. His eyes are nothing but hate. I look down and see his heavy boots and cringe, rubbing my sore back. "They stole Martin's wallet, too."

My stomach clenches thinking about the stupid wallet I kicked into the puddle.

"What's wrong with him?" somebody says, pointing at Klondike.

"Jesus, look at his face."

"Is that what reeks? Is that the stench?"

"Oh my God. They're homeless. So gross. I mean, totally gross. Like gonorrhea gross," somebody says in a lilting singsong voice.

"Somebody has to do *something* about them. I mean they're, like, um—like gonna hurt us or something."

Everybody starts to talk at once. It's like you can see all their brains turn into one group-think mass. Their neurons pulse rationalized conformity.

The librarian and I lock eyes for a second before I pull Klondike out of the crowd and run toward the door. Nicole's waiting for us outside, the beautiful black coat in her arms. "What took you so fucking long?" Nicole asks, tossing me the coat.

I hesitate for just a second, then shrug it on. I need a coat.

We run.

A bunch of students runs after us, but halfheartedly. They're probably afraid they'll end up like Martin. Or like Klondike.

After a few blocks, Klondike grips his side and stops running. Nicole and I slow down and walk with him. I take off the coat and hand it to Nicole. "Why don't you take it? I'll wear mine and Klon can have yours."

"What? So you can be clean from any sort of association with stolen goods? What the fuck?"

"It's just . . . It's different stealing from a big corporation. But this is probably that librarian's . . ." My voice fades.

"What? You thought living on the streets would be like living in that posh little house of yours in Reno?"

"It's just. It's not what I imagined would be happening, you know? It's not supposed to be this way."

"Not everything in this fucking world is black and white, right and wrong, Jeopardy." Nicole shakes her head. "It's about loyalty, okay? Haven't you ever heard the code?"

"Code?"

"We"—she sweeps her arm around to point us out— "we are together. We as a group come first—before birth, before family, before God. None of us are going to be like that leech Sammy Gravano. *We* come first—as a group. And when you worry about a fucking coat or wallet or what's right and wrong, it's like we can't trust you."

"What?" I say. "We're *not* the mob. We're three runaways with no money chasing a box of my dead mom's things." I mutter, "We're. Not. The. Mob. And *somebody* better worry about what's right and wrong or—"

Nicole clenches her jaw. "There's no such thing as cosmic karma or whatever you're thinking. Remember Capone? He got away with it all. He died of a fucking heart attack. You just don't get it." Nicole huffs and repeats, "Before birth, before family. Before God. It's the code."

Klon squints and croaks. "Cappy," he says, "nothing comes before God. Asswipe," he squeaks. "Stop fighting."

I sigh. We're like a bad joke. A preacher, a capo, and a scientist are going on a road trip. . . .

Klondike croaks and mutters things under his breath, only coughing a couple of times. "Tallywhacker, asswipe."

"Let's drop it," I say. "I'll wear the coat."

"Fine." Nicole walks ahead. "Just remember we stick together. That doesn't just mean walking down Highway Eighty or wherever the fuck we are. It means more than that."

"Okay. I get it."

Klondike jerks his head to the side and does his hop-skip, keeping up with Nicole's and my pace. He croaks and says, "Sorry about your mama."

"Thanks," I say.

"Me, too," Nicole says.

"It doesn't matter," I say. Probably a bit snippy.

Nicole shrugs. "I'm just saying I'm sorry. Can't you even take an apology? Jesus."

"Don't get your knickers in a bunch, Cappy," Klon says. "Everything's okay now. We're together."

I ruffle his hair, then shudder thinking about the state *my* knickers are in. Gross. Klondike stops to look at a dead bird in the road. He pulls on one of the feathers and tucks it into his pocket.

"Cappy," Nicole says. "I like that."

"Better than Capone," Klon says. "More girly."

I'm starting to get used to the kid.

I turn back to see the black silhouette of the librarian against the sun, her purple hair a splash of color against the desert backdrop.

TWENTY-SEVEN

"**N**ice work, Jeopardy. Your first act of thievery." Nicole beams with pride, as if she were responsible for my accidentally stealing a map. "Where are we?"

"Here. Jackpot, Nevada."

"Where are we going?"

"His name is Martin Greer."

"Who?"

"The kid I hurt."

"So?" Nicole bites her lower lip.

"It's just. His name is Martin Greer. It was better when he didn't have a name, you know."

Nicole shrugs. "So what are we gonna do?" she asks again.

I pause. "I think I'm going to turn myself in."

Klondike and Nicole gawk. "Turn yourself in for what?" Nicole asks.

"That kid. Martin. He could be really hurt. And I need to go and explain what happened."

> **Hypothesis:** If I go to the police, they'll take me into custody. If they take me into custody, I'll have a chance to tell them my story. If I tell them the story, maybe they'll give me lunch and a bunk to sleep on. And they'll have to call a relative. They'll have to call Aunt Sarah because relatives in federal prison don't count. They'll search for her because I'm too expensive for the state to maintain. And I'll have a family. And I can sleep. Inside. And be warm. Just until they find her. I'm just so tired.

And my throat hurts.

"Did you just walk off the stupid bus or something?" Nicole kicks at some gravel. "Have you taken a look at us? And they'll believe the nice local boy was going to rape me? This isn't *Law and Order*. This is real, Jeopardy. And you'll be in the system forever."

Sometimes I worry finding Aunt Sarah is more science fiction than science. And all of this is for nothing. "Why are you such a skeptic?" I ask. "The system can't fail everyone."

Nicole glares at me. "Yeah, you really trusted it. You were in it, what, a month? Two months? And you decided to split." She turns to Klondike. "How long were you in?"

Klondike taps my shoulder. "Everything burned because of me and the demons. And Pa—tallywhacker, asswipe—" Klondike turns his head toward the sun and lets out a long, low croak. "The wicked flee when no man persueth. So I ran. And keep running. Because of the demons inside of me."

We're in the parking lot of the last restaurant on the edge of town. There are several trucks parked side by side in the front of the restaurant. People scarf down hot turkey sandwiches, spaghetti, chicken pot pie—diner food at its finest. And Klondike thinks he's possessed.

I sigh. "You don't have demons, Klon," I say.

Klon shakes his head. "I bring bad luck. I bring the Devil wherever I go." He looks away from us. "I'll go alone now. Asswipe. For the wages of sin is death. I am a sinner.

Tallywhacker. I have demons."

I look at Klon standing before us in his rags and want to tell him everything's going to be okay.

> **Hypothesis:** If Klondike knows he's not possessed but probably has Tourette's, he'll feel better. Won't he? Or maybe he'll realize he lived with horrible, ignorant people who treated him terribly and made him feel bad about who he is.

Does everybody need to know the truth about things? I've always thought so, but now I wonder. Will it help me to know the truth about Mom?

What is her truth? What is anybody's?

I hate these vague questions with no answers. No hypothesis. No procedure. Just variables that are out of my control.

I'm trying to order things in my mind when Nicole says, "Klon, people treated you like shit. You aren't the sinner. They are. You didn't deserve that burn, so something amazing will happen to you one day—one of your miracles. That's what Jeopardy's karma is all about."

How come she seems to make things so clear? Breathe,

I think. Just work out a new procedure to find Aunt Sarah. I need to stick to the purpose: Find Aunt Sarah. That's the purpose. That won't change.

"Are we gonna hitch?" Nicole asks.

"I don't think it's a good idea," I lean in and whisper. "We kind of stand out, you know." I say in a louder voice, "Klon. You're coming with us. We stick together. That's the code, right?"

Nicole nods. Proud. Her stupid Mafia code, but it makes more sense than anything I seem to come up with: before family, before God. Our moms and dads aren't getting any parent-of-the-year awards. They're even too screwed up for Dr. Phil. It's like we've thrown every genetic quirk into a vial and *ka-boom*—major dysfunctional offspring.

Klondike shivers. I cup his hand in mine. "You aren't evil, Klon. You're the best person I've ever known. We're going to find my aunt Sarah and Cappy's dad. And we're all going to be okay." That sounds about as cheesy as they come. Geez.

But Klondike seems happy about it.

"A man's heart deviseth his way: but the Lord directeth his steps." He wipes a tear from his eye and taps my shoulder. "So what are we gonna do?" he asks.

I wish I could call Dad. He'd know what to do. Well, he used to. Until he gave me away to the State of Nevada.

An image of Martin Greer lying in a hospital bed flashes into my mind. I erase it. If I hadn't stopped him, Nicole would be really hurt. And probably Klon and me, too. The rules have changed. I need to change with them.

We watch big trucks pull into the parking lot, gravel popping off mud flaps with profiles of naked ladies on them. I wipe my nose and still smell the burn of flesh.

Klondike sits on his heels and croaks.

"I'm not sure what we should do," I finally say. "I'm—"

"Scared?" Nicole asks.

"Yeah." I rub my hands together.

"Welcome to my life," she says. She sits next to Klondike. "You know, though, this is turning into a very cool road trip."

"This is *not* a road trip," I say.

"Not exactly, but kind of."

"Not at all," I say. "Road trips are supposed to be fun."

Nicole smirks. "I bet this is the most fun you've ever had. I mean, really. When have you ever just lived like this—taking one moment at a time?"

Every single day with my dad, I think. And I hate it. Why is everybody's definition of fun spontaneity? Why isn't it okay to want predictable? Normal? Normal would be fun.

"So? What's your big plan, Jeopardy?" Nicole asks.

That's the problem. Every plan I put into place falls apart. Nothing is under control—especially Nicole and Klon. They're the two most erratic variables in this whole mess. I just need to keep the purpose the same. The hypothesis and procedure can change. There are many roads to get to the same destination.

God. I'm starting to sound like Dad during his motivational speaker days—*Eight Steps to a Better You.* All for a nominal fee, of course. (Cash only, please.) Focus, I think. Just focus.

Hypothesis: If we can get to Boise, we can find the restaurant on Main Street. If we can find the restaurant, somebody there might know Aunt Sarah. If I have more information about Aunt Sarah, maybe we can get off the streets.

Everything starts to unfold in my mind, make sense.

Procedure:

1) Hide in somebody's truck to get out of Jackpot
2) Get to Boise
3) Find Main Street
4) Find the restaurant where Aunt Sarah worked
5) Find more clues about Aunt Sarah or find Aunt Sarah. (Who's to say she isn't still there?)

The method will work. It has to.

"So?" Nicole throws a rock, skipping it across the pavement. She's irritating—that all-knowing attitude.

"We need to get out of Jackpot. That's my big plan of the day," I say. The gravel has started to dig its way into my butt, and I shift positions trying to find some comfort on the craggy rocks.

"Well, remember the rules. One: No names. Two: We don't fall asleep, and three: We stick together, okay?" Nicole stands up and brushes dust off her pants. "That's why a code is good. It makes things clear."

I sigh. For someone who never seems to follow any rules, she sure sticks steadfast to the ones she makes. I survey the trucks, looking for Idaho plates. There's one with a tarp tied down over something lumpy. The license plate holder says TWIN FALLS—BOISE—JEEP CHEVROLET. "That's our ride," I say. "We need to get under that tarp."

"How do you know?" Nicole asks.

"It's an Idaho plate. The license plate holder says Twin Falls. If they bought their truck in Twin Falls, maybe they live there, too. So I imagine they're heading back to Idaho as soon as they scarf down their hash browns and watery coffee." I turn to Klondike. "You okay with this?"

Klondike nods and taps his fingers to his head, coughing weakly. Then he goes back to croaking, cradling his side. Nicole crosses her arms in front of her. "And if I'm not?"

"You have a better plan?"

"No," she says.

I point to the truck. "Then get under the tarp."

Nicole bites her lower lip. "Let's go for a ride."

TWENTY-EIGHT

We huddle in the truck. And wait.

And wait.

Nothing happens. Nobody jumps in and revs it up.

What seems like hours pass. I pull out the envelope and let the dried flower slip into my hands. I understand what Nicole means about having something real. Aunt Sarah sent something to Mom—more than words, more than paychecks—something that meant something to her. That's real.

"Nice, Jeopardy. What do we do now?" Nicole asks, interrupting my thoughts. "I think my ass has frozen to the grooves in this fucking truck bed."

I put the flower back into the envelope and peer out from under the tarp to see if I can catch a glimpse of anything. The sun is high above us. It's got to be noon or early afternoon. At least the sun warms up the heavy tarp. It's warmer inside than out. "We can't risk getting out here where other people might see us. What do you want to do?"

"Nice wasted day." Nicole rubs her arms.

Klondike croaks and cradles his side.

"Are you okay, Klon?" I ask. "Your side's hurting a lot."

He drums the truck bed with his fingers. "I'm fine. Just tired."

"Sorry about the truck idea, guys," I say.

"Well, we're here now," Nicole says. "At least nobody's messing with us."

That's true.

Klondike taps me and puts his arm around my shoulder.

"Let's take a nap," Nicole suggests. "I got first shift if you two want to sleep."

"That's okay. I got first shift. I owe you guys," I say. "If nothing happens in half an hour, let's get out and find another ride, okay?"

"Perfect." Nicole yawns. "A half hour of uninterrupted sleep. A half hour of safe." She sighs.

Nicole and Klondike lie down. She turns to me before

sleeping. "Just half an hour."

"Yep. Just half an hour."

"Don't sleep. Rule two."

"I won't."

But I do.

And I don't wake up until I hear the door slam and the tread of heavy boots outside the truck. Somebody opens the bed of the truck—the heavy tailgate thunking down. I pinch Nicole awake and put my fingers to my pursed lips when she looks at me. She motions to Klondike, but I shake my head. The last thing we need is a croak.

"Goddamn tarp keeps coming loose," a woman grumbles, tightening the ropes from the outside. Instead of getting in the truck and driving away, she walks away, her footsteps growing faint.

I push on the tarp, but it doesn't budge. I feel the closeness of it; the musty air; the stench of gasoline, the sensation of being shut in, trapped. I push harder.

Hypothesis: If we don't get out of the truck, we'll die of hypothermia or starvation or carbon monoxide poisoning or all of the above.

Well, you really only can have one cause of death, but the others would just make things all the more uncomfortable.

I kick on the tarp. "We can't get out."

Nicole pushes. "Help me out here." The two of us throw all our weight into the tarp.

I stumble on Klondike and he sits up straight. "Tater," he says, and croaks.

Again we lean against the tarp trying to loosen the ropes, but nothing moves. I can feel my throat close up, stopping oxygen from getting to my lungs. "I can't breathe," I say.

Nicole pulls me back. "Just relax, okay? We wanted a ride. We'll get one."

"We've gotta get out of here." I claw at the canvas until sweat beads on my forehead and drips down my back. Everything starts to smell like body odor, feet, and exhaust fumes. I pound even harder, my chafed knuckles bleeding against the tarp's taut surface.

Nicole clutches my shoulders. "Relax. We're fine. Nothing's wrong."

Klondike twitches and taps my shoulder. I push him off. "Don't touch me. Not now. We've gotta get out of here." My throat closes, and I can't breathe. I wake up with Nicole shaking my shoulders.

"You totally passed out," she says. "Are you okay?"

She actually sounds concerned.

"We're stuck," I whisper. "You know how long it takes to die from hypothermia? The moment our bodies lose heat faster than we can maintain it, everything goes downhill. We shiver. The cold kind of freezes our brains and we can't reason. We won't even *know* we're going to die. Then we'll lose control of our small motor skills, slip into comas, go into organ failure, and die."

"Well, none of us are shivering. The only one here who has made bad decisions is you making us climb into this stupid truck. So I think we're fine," Nicole says. "Don't get all unzipped on us now. It's not like we're going down like Giovanni and Pietro Ligammari."

I lay my head on the cool metal of the truck bed and squeeze my eyes shut, preparing for one of Nicole's twisted mob anecdotes.

"They found them, father and son, hanging from the basement rafters, face-to-face. At first they said it was suicide, but not likely." Nicole whistles. "Now that's fucking brutal."

"Why do you even *care* about how those people

died?" I ask, then say, "I don't think Klon should hear those things."

Nicole sighs. "Ah. He's heard worse. You know, there's an Italian mob boss who's in jail now who some people think should be made a saint. His name is Bernardo Provenzano. They're big on the religion thing, the mob. Big-time Catholics. The Italians, I mean. And the Chinese, the Triad, are into Guan Yu, the Taoist God of brotherhood. The Reds, the Russians, I'm not so sure about. Are they commies or something?

"Anyway, all these mobs are into religion. Like that Bernardo Provenzano. He could say all this Bible shit," she whispers, "kind of like Klondike does. You know, I've been kind of wondering what he meant when he said miracles were just people doing what they should do in the first place."

I squeeze my eyes shut even tighter, trying to get the vision of two Mafia guys with bulging eyes hanging from a basement ceiling out of my head. I curl up tighter. "I haven't thought about it," I say.

"You don't listen good, Jeopardy."

"How do you know all this stuff about the mob anyway?"

"True Crime Channel. In one foster home I had a TV

in my room and watched it twenty-four/seven. It was pretty great until they decided to move to Africa or someplace to start up an orphanage there. Real hippies, give-back-to-the-world shit. They shipped off to Africa and I was shipped back to Kids Place. Not cool. Sure kids in Africa need help, but so did I."

"So all these Mafia facts have their own personalities in your nineteen-twenties bar?" I ask.

"Yep. But that's not too hard. They're people. You just have to put the actual person there. It's the Darwin's friendship theory shit that needs extra work."

I sigh and start to recite the periodic table to myself.

Nicole keeps talking. And talking. Her words filling up the tarp. With all her hot air we should take off any second and float away. She goes on and on, her words running together like one endless sticky strand of glue. She taps me on the shoulder. "Or what?"

"Or what, what?" I ask.

"It's not like we've got anywhere to go. Or is Auntie Em expecting you for dinner?"

"Be quiet," I say, and try to pretend we're outside. Free. "Please. Just. Be. Quiet."

"It's nice here," Klondike says. "Cozy and warm." Then

he croaks, rubbing his side, blowing on his fingers.

Nicole huffs, "Nice fucking road trip."

"This is not a road trip," I mumble. I want to ring her neck but don't have the energy. Plus, if I open my eyes, I might lose it again. "Everything sucks right now," I mutter.

"This is not a road trip," Nicole mimics. "Of course not according to your scientific definition of a road trip. What is it? Roadeth Trippeth: The act of going in a car to a specific destination with a cooler of Coke. Whoopeee. Fun. Get over the pity party, Jeopardy. Christ." She gnaws on a nail.

Klondike croaks again and says, "The sun don't shine up one dog's ass all the time." He turns to Nicole. "Stop stirring the turd. I'm tired." He lies back down.

"Okay," I say. "Let's forget about it."

We sit in silence in the truck for a while until I ask, "Why did you want to leave Kids Place with me anyway?"

"We already used up our theme of the day."

"It's been a long day." I can feel it's already evening. A long, wasted day.

"Same twenty-four hours."

"It's not a theme, Cappy. It's just a question," I say.

She lies down and closes her eyes. "No questions."

"Whatever," I sigh, and I lie back down. I curl up in a ball and hold my stomach. I picture the acids working their way through my gastrointestinal tract, eroding part of my small intestine. The hole will be small at first; then it'll grow. Perhaps later I'll develop an ulcer in the lining of my stomach. It might bleed and I'll get iron-deficiency anemia. Then, over time, it will turn into cancer. And I'll die a lingering, excruciating death.

"Charles Carneglia," she says, just as I'm drifting off to sleep.

"Huh?" I say.

"Charles Carneglia—the go-to guy for the mob when they wanted to dissolve hits in acid. You listened to my stories at Kids Place. It's like I'd been talking for nine years, but you *heard* me." She pauses. "With you, I'm real."

I swallow back the knot that forms in my throat. I'm either getting really sentimental or sick. My throat just hurts all the time. "It's hard *not* to hear you with how much you talk," I mutter.

"Yeah," whispers Nicole. "I didn't talk the one time it counted, and I've been talking stupid shit ever since."

After a bit I say, "They count."

"What count?" she asks.

"Your stories."

We're quiet. Klon croaks. I rub my arms and find a comfortable spot. "You know, even if I feel bad about that Martin kid, it doesn't mean I wouldn't do it again, okay? Just conflicting emotions, I guess."

Klondike quietly taps on the truck bed, croaking softly. Nicole finally says, "Let's do short-a words until I fall asleep. When I do, you get first shift, Jeopardy."

"That's fair."

"Don't fall asleep," she says.

"I won't," I say.

"Bat—b a t, cat—c a t, fat—f a t . . . ," she begins. She's a fast learner and continues with "an," "am," "ad" words until her voice gets heavy with sleep and she drifts off. Her last word, "dad."

I try to stay awake. Really. But I end up breaking rule number two . . . again. I don't even feel the rumble of the truck on the highway. I am so, so tired. We jump awake when the flashlight shines on us. I hold my hands to my eyes to block the glaring light.

"Get the hell out of my truck," she says.

CHAPTER TWENTY-NINE

"Well, don't just sit there staring at me like some dumb deer on the road. Get out of my truck."

We stumble out of her truck, stiff from so many hours curled under the tarp. Our breath comes out in silvery puffs. We stand in the driveway of a country home—soft yellow light filters through the windows.

"You fell asleep," Nicole says through her teeth. "Again."

I rub my eyes. It's so hard to stay awake. "Well, we got a ride, didn't we?" I say under my breath. It's not like staying awake would've changed anything.

"So? You runaways?" The lady stands with hands on hips. She wears a heavy flannel jacket and wranglers—

worn cowboy boots peeking out from under the jeans.

"No!" I say—too loud. I step forward. "We're, um, on a road trip." I glance at Nicole. "And we're trying to go cross-country on our own for our senior project." Yeah. That sounds good. "So we, um, hitch rides and—"

"And hide out in the back of people's trucks," the lady finishes. "You're a bad liar, kid. Real bad."

"Asswipe," Klondike croaks, then says a slew of obscenities. He taps the lady's shoulder and croaks. "Sorry," he says. "We just needed a ride."

I blush. Nicole tugs on Klondike's elbow, which only makes his tics worse. It's hard to remember that it's better to ignore him.

"We're sorry," I say. "He can't help the stuff he does and says. We're just looking for my aunt. Sarah Jones. She lives in Boise. Really. That's the truth."

The lady gnaws on her lower lip. "I must've picked you three up in Jackpot. And the last thing I need is to get busted for toting around runaways—no matter what you're doing." She looks the three of us up and down. "So either I call the cops or you head along your own way. Your business is none of mine."

We nod. That's a good thing about people—a total lack

of interest in anything not directly related to them. Think about it. AIDS, hunger, global warming, genocide—this happens daily. And we don't care. Apathy is the disease of the developed world. The more bad stuff happens, the less people care. And that works for us.

"Well," she says. "Get going. I don't want to see hide nor hair of any of you by the time I'm done unloading the truck."

We turn to go when Klondike doubles over in a coughing fit, holding tight onto his side. I rub his back and Nicole tries to keep him still. The coughing must be killing his ribs and bruised side.

When the coughing stops, Klondike sits. "I just need to rest. Just a minute," he says before letting out a soft, low croak. He leans his head on Nicole's bony knees.

The lady eyes us over the bulky boxes she heaves to the edge of the truck. I go to her. "Um, can we have a couple of minutes? To rest?"

The lady nods.

"And just something hot for him. It can be hot water."

"This isn't a twenty-four-hour truck stop, honey, and I don't need trouble," the lady says with lips pursed. But her eyes aren't cold.

"Please," I say. I look back at Klon, eyes closed, resting against Nicole. Nicole motions for me to join her. Move on. But Klon needs something warm.

The lady nods. "You are a sorry-looking bunch. When's the last time you had anything decent to eat?"

I can't remember.

She gnaws on a toothpick. "I need help with these boxes. You pull a muscle or throw out your back, I will deny you were ever here, okay? I can't afford a nasty lawsuit by some snots like you."

I cringe. Dad's done that. His idol for a time was the McDonald's hot-coffee lady, though he did concede that the finger those people found in Wendy's chili was going a bit far. There are limits. Even for Dad. Or at least there used to be. My stomach tightens. I hate missing him. He doesn't deserve it.

Nicole pulls Klon up. Everyone stares at me. The lady says, "You the head of this gang?"

"I guess," I say.

"Well, are you three going to help or not?" she asks.

"We just need something hot for him, ma'am," I say. "If we help, will you get him something?"

"I'm Jan, not ma'am. If you're going to haul my boxes,

you'd better know my name."

I begin to introduce us when she holds up her hand. "And I sure as hell don't want to know your names."

"Go sit over there, Klon," I say, and motion to a place next to the garage. "We'll take care of the boxes." Nicole and I unload the truck and set the boxes in the garage. Then we sit next to Klon, waiting for Jan to bring him a hot drink.

She comes out with a cup of steaming liquid and hands it to Klon. He looks at Nicole and me.

"Go ahead," I urge. "You need it."

Klon sips at the liquid and cups his cold hands around the mug. His twitches subside for just a moment. I exhale. It's like I haven't taken a breath since we left Jackpot.

"Do you even know where you are?" Jan finally asks.

"No," Nicole says. "But it won't be long until we figure that out."

Jan shakes her head. "Lord help me. Come inside." She takes the empty mug from Klon and turns toward the door.

We stare at her.

"I'm not going to ask again." She turns and walks up the porch, leaving the front door open.

Nicole glares at me. "You've definitely gotta have some

kind of sleeping disorder. Jesus, Jeops, we could be on the moon for all we know."

"I can assure you we're *not* on the moon," I say.

Nicole rolls her eyes. "C'mon." We trip up the crooked steps of the old ranch house. Smoke spills from underneath a door in the entryway.

"What the hell are you doing up? Do you have any idea what time it is?" Jan barks at a closed door. "And put out that Goddamned cigar. You're gonna set the house on fire!"

A door opens. It's a coat closet. A tiny woman half the size of Jan peeks her head out. Her wiry gray hair is pulled back taut in a barrette. A thick cigar dangles from her lips and she has a monstrous can of Lysol clutched in one hand. She nods at us and shuts the door again.

"No wonder she likes us," Nicole whispers. "They're just as nutty as Klon."

I look over at Klon. I can tell he's relaxed. His croaks got quieter as soon as he saw the lady in the closet.

Jan walks ahead of us. "Follow me," she says, pushing through the cluttered hallway. "Watch out for Ganesh."

We walk by an elephant statue covered with candle wax. It teeters on the edge of a wooden table with three legs, the fourth made of old magazines. The living room isn't much more organized. Every inch of wood-paneled wall space is covered with trinkets from all over the world. Nicole picks up a dusty yellow box and opens the lid. Twelve tiny dolls fall into the palm of her hand. I try not to groan, sure she's going to steal them when Jan turns back. "Guatemalan worry dolls."

"What?" says Nicole.

"Asswipes," Klondike croaks and taps on the yellow box.

"Worry dolls. You tell them your problems before going to bed, and they help take care of them while you sleep."

"Tallywhacker," he says, and holds his side.

Nicole smiles. "That's nice." She looks at the room, her eyes scanning all the exotic contents.

"Looks like you kids have a lot of worries of your own."

I clear my throat, not looking up.

Tap tap tap tap. Klondike plays on my shoulder. I try to shrug him off but he taps harder.

"Some," says Nicole. She stares at the dolls in her hand. "Where did you say they were from?" she asks. "The dolls?"

"Guatemala. Central America."

Nicole holds the dolls in her hand. She clasps it shut. It would be so easy for her to steal them, but I watch as she

264

lets them fall back into the tiny box and puts it back on the shelf. I sigh, relieved, trying to ignore Klondike's loudening croaks. The good thing is that Jan doesn't seem to care about what Klondike does and says.

"Wait here," she says. When she leaves the room, Nicole turns to me. "You thought I'd take them, didn't you?"

I shrug.

"I don't steal what I don't need. That's not cool."

"Okay. Sorry. It's just—"

"I'm not your dad," Nicole says.

I feel the blood rush to my cheeks.

Jan comes into the room with a pile of blankets, three mugs of hot chocolate, and a box of graham crackers. "Like I said, this is no luxury hotel. You'll have a good breakfast and baths in the morning. Good night."

The next morning Jan wakes us up before the sun has risen. We rub sleep from our eyes. I pull the blankets tight around me. She hands us three threadbare towels. "You can stay the day and one more night. I need help unpacking those boxes. You'll get your three meals. But tomorrow you're out at sunrise." She sniffs. "From the smell of things, you all need to shower and wash those clothes. You know how to wash clothes, don't you?"

We nod.

"Breakfast will be ready at seven thirty."

I look around for a clock, rubbing the sleep from my eyes.

Jan shakes her head. "An hour and a half. So there's the bathroom, here are the towels, and here's some laundry soap. Hot water's expensive. So keep the showers under five. The dryer beeps when the clothes are done." She points to a door. "There's the kitchen. Don't be late." She hollers down the hall. "Did you hear that, Nancy? And put out that Goddamned cigar!"

Nancy peeks from the closet and sprays her Lysol can in Jan's direction. I wonder if she sleeps there. I stare at the rotary phone and worry if she'll call the police.

Jan says, "Your business is none of my own." She looks us over head to toe. "I can see you're not bad kids. But you're not taking the right road, that's for damned sure."

The three of us stare down at our toes. Klondike whispers, "Tallywhacker, asswipe," then taps my arm.

"One more night." Then she turns on her heel and goes into the kitchen while we get washed up.

The hot water trickles out of a rusty showerhead and I jump away to turn up the cold.

I don't want the shower to end. I scrub my hair and use her conditioner, my curls coming unknotted. Nicole pounds on the door, "Five minutes! Switch!"

I stand and look at the filthy water that swirls around my feet and splashes up my ankles. Just one more minute, I think. Just one.

Nicole pounds again and I step into the steamy bathroom, the mirror fogged up. My skin is itchy and red.

Nicole gets into the shower. "Klon's sleeping again."

"Yeah?"

"Yeah. What's with that?" Nicole asks.

"You know. On average a person will spend a third of his life asleep."

"That explains why you can't seem to keep your eyes open. Ever." Nicole shouts above the spatter of water. "Christ, what a lot of wasted time."

"Nah. It'd only be a major evolutionary glitch if sleep didn't serve some purpose—memory, learning, rest, who knows? All animals sleep. Scientists study it all the time. Humans need at least seven hours a night to be fully rested. And Jan probably woke the roosters up."

After a while the water turns off and Nicole steps into the bathroom, wrapping her body in the towel. "Well?"

I'm sitting on the woven rug on the bathroom floor. "Well what?"

"Aren't you gonna go get Klon? It's his turn."

Our clothes are in the dryer, so I tiptoe around the house in a damp towel, leaving little puddles wherever I go. Klon is sound asleep, a towel wrapped around his shoulders, curled up against one of Jan's bookshelves. I shake him awake and steer him to the shower. When he's done, the three of us sit in the steamy bathroom, listening for the beep of the dryer.

When we're cleaned and dressed, it feels like heaven— our clothes soft and warm against our skin.

Jan bangs some pots in the kitchen and whistles a tuneless song. She dumps piles of steaming porridge on our plates.

We spend the day organizing boxes of trinkets so Jan can take pictures to sell on eBay. Klon sleeps most of the day.

At dinner we sit around the table. I lean in and jerk my head back. It smells like burning socks.

"Potato, kale, soysage casserole," Jan says. "Our favorite."

The lady from the hallway leans her bony elbows on the table and stoops over her plate, plunging her spoon into the casserole. She finishes everything on her plate and creeps off down the hall.

I crane my neck to see where she's going.

"Back to the closet," says Jan between mouthfuls.

"Of course," says Nicole.

Klondike smiles.

They say hunger is the best sauce. Not tonight. The pasty casserole sticks in my throat and I drink several glasses of water to keep it down. Still, bite by bite, I eat until my plate is clean. Klon and Nicole are on second and third helpings. Jan offers, and I accept more, refilling my water glass. Food is food. No matter how bad it tastes.

Klon's head nods and he jerks it up, his eyes wide. It's early, but Jan ushers us to the den where we slept last night. "You three need to sleep. Good night."

"You gonna look at your letters again?" Nicole asks.

"Maybe," I say.

She nods. "I look at my postcards lots."

"I understand." I pull out the letters and we both look at the faded flower. "I like this one the most. It feels more—"

"Real." Nicole finishes my sentence. "What's the letter say?"

I read:

Dear Michelle,

Reading Mom's name aloud is weird to me and I pause. Michelle. Michelle Brandt. Then Michelle Aguirre. Then Michelle Brandt Aguirre—loving daughter, wife, and mother. Dead. I clear my throat and read on.

> *I didn't know the world could be so big outside of the farm.*
>
> *The tourist season is crazy with people coming in from all around the world. Before the snow has melted, the hikers arrive. And they come from Europe, South America, Asia—even Africa. The tents fill with aromas from around the world: curry, olive oil, sardines, and greasy sausages. Every group I take has a different menu.*
>
> *I've been on three tours with Michael Jones now. Michael Jones. He couldn't sound more American if he tried. At first, I found his presence to be irritating. He's quiet. Too quiet. He's not charming—at all. Not like your Michael. But over the*

past several months, guiding groups into the mountains, I'm starting to think there's something there in that huge frame. (He's over 6'5"—a giant!) The other day, after coming back from a two-week backpacking trip with a Japanese group (I never want to eat seaweed and wasabi again), he gave me this flower. He said, "This is a piece of our home." Our home. What does he mean by that?

But it made me feel like I found my place—something you and I have both always searched for. And I couldn't think of anyone better to send it to.

I thought you could use it more than me.

This is my home now. I'm never going back. It could be yours, too. Yours, Michael's, and Amaya's. Come home.

Love,
Sarah

I fold up the letter and put it back in the envelope. "Wow," says Nicole.

I nod.

"What's the next letter say? Did she get it on with the giant?"

"That's the last one. The last one dated before—" Before Mom died. What else would Aunt Sarah have had to say? "The only other things that come after this letter are the paycheck stubs."

"Intense," Nicole sighs. "You think she's in Boise?" Nicole asks.

I shrug. "I hope so. You think your dad's in Chicago?"

"Probably." Nicole holds the flower in her hand. "It's all about this flower. This is the key," she says.

"Maybe."

Then Nicole and I start short-e words. She knows more than she thinks. She just gets her vowels mixed up. We study until my eyes stop opening after I blink. Klon has been fast asleep for at least an hour.

We lie down in the den, bundled up, warm and full.

"Not all people are shit," Nicole says.

"No. I guess not," I agree, and fall into a dreamless sleep.

CHAPTER THIRTY

Purpose: Find Aunt Sarah

Hypothesis: If I can find Aunt Sarah, we'll be okay. I don't know why, but I just know things will be okay when I find her.

Materials: Mom's box, the locket

Procedure:

1) Get to Boise

2) Find the restaurant where Aunt Sarah worked (works)

3) Find someone who knows Aunt Sarah (if she's not at the restaurant anymore)

4) Get in touch with Aunt Sarah

5) Start a new life

Variables: The restaurant: Will it still be there? Will somebody remember her? Will she be there? Aunt Sarah: Will she take us all in? Will she know what to do? Am I ready to have somebody else make these decisions?

Constants: Me, Nicole, Klon

"I'm not gonna say, 'Call me if you need help.'"

We stand on her porch, and she hands each of us a sack lunch.

"I don't want to see or hear from any of you ever again, okay?"

We nod.

"The nearest town is four miles south of here."

The three of us look around. I look toward the mountains and sun and turn around on the porch.

"Lordy, Lordy," she says. "That way." She points to the left. "You have problems, tell 'em to the dolls." She hands Nicole the box of worry dolls.

Nicole cups the box in her palm. She looks up at the lady. "Than—" she starts to say.

"Bye." The screen door hangs crooked on the hinges and doesn't quite shut. Jan yanks it and it bangs on the frame, the inside door slamming shut.

"Thanks," Nicole whispers.

We stand on the porch for a second. I see the curtains in the living room part to the side. Two beady eyes stare out at us behind a veil of cigar smoke.

"Let's go," I say. But I feel better about things. Funny what a good sleep and food will do. It's like this can really happen. We will find Aunt Sarah, and everything will be okay.

We walk the four miles into a town called McCall. I pull out the map. "Ugh," I groan.

"What?" Nicole looks over my shoulder.

"We're here," I point out McCall. "North. And we need to go south. One hundred miles out of the way ."

"Oh." Nicole shrugs. "The scenic route again."

"Looks like it."

We sit down on a bench on the main street, resting our feet on the backpacks. "I guess we can hitch to Boise," I say.

"Okay. Which way is Boise?"

I look at the map. "This way." I point down the street. I turn the map around. "I think."

"You suck with maps," Nicole says, then looks up and says, "St. Sti. Stib. Stib. Stib. Ah, fuck it." Every sign she sees, she tries to sound out. Because of it, she's more tic-y than Klondike. She'll be talking, midsentence stop and try to make out a word, then continue just where she left off. Klon takes advantage of those times to look for road kill. He says he's never seen a dead raccoon and would really like to.

"Stibnite," I say.

"Oh." Then she looks at the map. "So where are we? You lost on that thing?"

I sigh. "Kinda."

Nicole takes the map from me. "Jeopardy, what kind of practical things do you know? Not SAT knowledge. Just stuff that we need to know to get by."

I think for a while. All my practical knowledge has to do with getting packed and leaving when Dad got caught. But we've never been on the streets. Not like this. I shrug and say, "I can read."

"Bite me," Nicole says.

"You asked. And it's practical." I lean my head back against the bench and close my eyes. So far our reading-for-stealing skill swap hasn't gone well. The short vowels haven't been a problem, but Nicole thinks every vowel should have just one sound. So she gets irritated with long vowel sounds and especially with "y" being considered a vowel at all. And we haven't even begun to look at diphthongs.

As for shoplifting, after my grocery store debacle, I haven't had the guts to do anything except take free fliers from the store counters. Shoplifting isn't as easy as it looks. Nerves of steel. And mine are more like rubber bands.

Before, four miles wouldn't have fazed me, but lately I've been short of breath and so, so tired. Klondike holds his side when he walks. His breathing has become really shallow. Maybe we should wrap his ribs in something. I'm about to ask him about it when he says, "It's prettier than a speckled pup in a red wagon."

We look around. The trees on the mountains that border the lake are dusted with snow; the lake, a crystal blue, looks like melted ice. Nicole opens up the box of worry dolls. Tucked inside, under the tiny dolls, are two five-dollar bills.

"Look!" She shows us. "Maybe our detour was worth it," she says.

We walk south.

"Next lesson, Jeopardy." Nicole stands outside a convenience store. "Stealing with two is easier than one. Like if I go in with you and act all suspicious, then it's easier for you to steal something. It's called being a decoy. Oh, and another one. A good one. But not with your decoy. Slip something in someone else's pockets. Wait till they walk out first and set the alarm. Then walk out right behind them. It works like a charm."

"But we don't need anything," I protest.

"You think these sack lunches will last forever?" Nicole asks. "Plus I could use a cough drop or something. My throat's killing me. We'll do it together. I'll be the decoy."

I take in a deep breath, so deep it feels like the cold from the air forms icicles on my rib cage.

Klon squeezes my hand. "You can do it." He coughs.

I *need* to do it. I swallow. My throat feels scratchy, too.

"Okay." We go inside the store and mill around. Nicole hangs out in a corner, with her back turned and hunched over. Way suspicious. An old man sits behind the counter reading his newspaper, ignoring us because he's more interested in some coup in Africa. I grab a bag of cough drops and exhale. It'll be easy. All I have to do is put them in my coat.

Then I look back at the counter. The man clears his throat; the newspaper rustles as he turns the page, and I drop the cough drops. When I lean over to pick them up, my head hits a shelf and Band-Aids, plastic bottles, and cold-pill boxes fly everywhere.

I pile everything back onto the shelf. The man peers

over the paper, nods, then goes back to reading.

My hands are shaking so hard, all I can do is shove them into my pockets and head to the door. "Thanks," I say, and leave.

Nicole follows. "Get anything?" Nicole asks. "You sure made a racket."

I shake my head.

"Christ," she mutters. "And my throat hurts."

Klondike looks tired. He leans against a wooden post and cradles his side in his hand. I should've at least gotten him some aspirin. But I just can't seem to go through with it.

Outside of town a man in an old Ford pickup stops for us. He shouts through the window, "Jump in back—I'll take you until we get outside of Boise. This ain't legal no more, so keep your heads down."

"Thanks!" We jump into the truck and huddle together. Any other day I might've loved the feel of the crisp wind on my face. But today everything aches from my ears to my throat—even my skin. Klondike shivers, and I wrap my arm around him. He coughs. But not his usual cough. A sick cough.

"You okay?" I ask.

He's asleep, though, before he can answer.

CHAPTER THIRTY-ONE

"This is kinda fun." Nicole adds another stick to the fire. The man dropped us off at a campground on the outskirts of Boise. We were pretty lucky that he took us all the way from McCall to Boise. That's like a hundred miles. In Nevada, that took Nic and me about three days to cover. We never got real long rides.

The only thing that sucked was crouching down in the back of a metal truck bed for two hours, trying to keep from freezing in the wind. We huddled to cover Klon and tried to protect his chest. I can't believe I didn't steal those cough drops.

The campground is closed for winter, so nobody's here. There's even a bathroom we got into by jimmying open a window and wiggling through. A real bathroom. Okay. No water or flushing. No toilet paper. But at least it's a toilet.

"I've never been camping before," Nicole says.

"A million-star hotel," says Klondike, staring up at the sky.

We all look up. Klondike points. "There's the Big"—he jerks his head and croaks—"Dipper. And Orion."

"You know about lots of stuff, Klon. Where'd you learn?"

"My pa." He croaks four times. "Before he died. He loved me more than any of them, and when he died in the fire, Ma said it was okay. But I could tell from her eyes it wasn't. She wanted to exorcise the demons—asswipe, tallywhacker. Fuckit."

We're quiet. We wait until he settles down and continues his story.

"We were filling the oil lamps for evenin' services. I had Pa's pipe in my pocket and I had to light it. I can't help the demons. Fuckit."

We watch as the embers glow and fire dances, casting shadows. A spark flitters into the black night, and we follow it with our eyes.

"Pa shouted, and the oil spilled and I dropped the

281

lighter and he fell on me—hotter than the hubs of Hades. Then he died. I've got the demons. And the scars because of the evil inside."

"Klon." I put my hand on his arm. "You don't have demons. It was an accident because of—"

Klon shakes his head. "Had to light it. The demons were talking to me. Tallywhacker, asswipe. So Ma couldn't look at me anymore and sent me to the home. Just for a while, she said. But I knew. She hated me. No one looked at me anymore. So I left. It's the demons' fault Pa died. My fault. I'm a demon inside and out." He croaks and shakes his head back and forth so hard it makes me dizzy. "Asswipes."

"You don't have demons. Really." I take a deep breath. Maybe my earlier hypothesis was wrong. Maybe knowing the truth will be good for him. "I think you have something called Tourette's syndrome," I say.

Both Nicole and Klon look at me. Nicole finally speaks. "There's a *name* for what's wrong with Klon? Way cool."

Klon croaks. Then he says, "Tallywhacker. The name is demons."

I shake my head. "Tourette's. It's a neurological disorder. It's like there's a glitch between your nerves and your brain. You can't help it. There's no cure. Even though lots of people

282

don't know about it, a bunch of people actually suffer from it. I mean, your mama might not have understood it and thought you had, um, demons. But you don't."

"No shit," Nicole says. "Now *that's* practical knowledge."

"Gee. Thanks," I say.

Klon doesn't talk for a long time. Tears blur his eyes and slip down his cheeks. "No demons," he whispers. He looks at me. "Are you sure?"

I nod. "Pretty much. It's something that's part of you when you're born. You can't help it. It's just who you are. Kind of like me having curly hair or Cappy having brown eyes. It's just who we are, you know? It's called a genetic makeup. Lots of people talk about nature versus nurture. But honestly, people are born the way they're going to be."

"So all those assholes at my mom's house. All of them were born to be *that* way?" Nicole asks. "And I'm born to be *this* way?"

Klon says, "Cappy, there's nothing wrong with you."

Nicole ruffles his hair. "You're a good kid, you know?" Nicole looks back at me. "What about me? Is everything set? Like, you know, *everything*?"

I pause. I'm not sure what she means by *everything*. "It's not like nature can decide *everything*. We're born with what we've got, right? It's our job to do the best with the good parts and work with the bad parts, I guess. Or else everybody could blame everything they've done wrong on a DNA strand."

"So what's wrong with your DNA strand, Jeops?" Nicole asks.

I'm the offspring of a con dad and depressed mom. Either I'll end up with a brain that gets so fogged by gray, I'll take prescription pills and live a dry-toast life, or I'll spend my life cheating, stealing, lying, and never having a real relationship with anybody—not even my own kids. But to have kids I'll have to have sex someday, and the likelihood of that is even more remote than me finding a long-lost aunt and her taking in a niece she doesn't even know to live with her.

Nicole and Klon watch me. I sigh and say, "Plenty."

We're all quiet for a while. Klon looks at me through the smoke in the campfire. "You sure? Tourette's?" He repeats the word several times and croaks. "Tourette's."

I nod.

"Ma would like to know that," he says.

"I think she would," I say. "Do you, um, know where she is?"

Klon doesn't answer. "You're my miracle today." He comes over to me and taps my arm, making a soft croak.

I don't know if the ache in my throat is because I'm feeling sick or because of Klon. I swallow and blink back my tears. I'm definitely getting way too sentimental.

Klon points up at a falling star.

"Meteor shower," I say. "You know that scientists estimate up to ten thousand tons of material falls to the earth each day. But there's only one documented case of a woman getting bruised from a falling meteorite." My voice steadies.

"Somebody actually got hit by a falling star?" Nicole asks. "That's fucking cool. Wicked conversation starter. 'Hey, why do you have a big bandage on your head?' 'Got hit by a star last night.' 'Man, I *hate* when that happens.'"

I laugh and wonder if insurance would cover that kind of thing. Maybe in the small print it says "Head injuries caused by meteor showers not covered." Dad'd get it covered. Honestly, though, I don't think it would feel too great to get hit by a mass of space rock.

"But if stars keep falling like that, will they disappear—

asswipe?" Klon furrows his brow and looks worried.

"That'll never happen, Klon."

"How do you know?" he asks, and croaks.

"Because . . ." I pause. I don't know how to answer that scientifically, so I say, "Because stars are magic, and magic never disappears."

"Will Tourette's?" Klondike asks after a series of tics and tapping.

I shake my head. "I don't think so. But you'd have to see a doctor to be sure."

Klondike croaks then looks up again. "Another one! Fuckit. Look up!"

"Make a wish," Nicole says, and I look up just in time to see the light fizzle.

We're all quiet for a while. I wonder what they wish for. Nicole and I scoot close to the fire, but Klondike stays pretty far away. "You need to keep warm," I say.

"Not by fire," he says. He's wearing every extra T-shirt and sweater we had packed in our packs, plus my jacket. "No fire," he whispers. But there's a calm about him that I haven't seen before. He looks almost happy.

We open up the sack lunches Jan packed for us, having saved them for as long as I could. She made us some wraps filled with an indescribable meatlike substance that makes bologna look gourmet.

"I think it's got to be soy based," I finally say. "They're probably vegans or something."

"What's a vegan?" Nicole asks.

"Somebody who doesn't eat any kind of animal product—not even cheese or eggs or honey or anything."

"That's dumb," Nicole says.

"Why?" I ask.

"Because only people who've never been hungry would be so picky about food," says Klondike. He's already scarfed down his share. He rubs his side and croaks, blowing on his fingers.

I hand Klon my last bite. "I'm not real hungry, Klon. Have this."

"Thanks," he says. "Theme of—asswipes—the day. Fuckit. Goddammit I can't help it. Tourette's. Tourette's. Tourette's," he whispers.

"Don't sweat it, Klon. We don't," Nicole says.

Klondike jerks his head and blows on his fingers.

"So what's the theme of the day?" I ask.

"Judgment Day," Nicole suggests.

"Judgment Day?" I ask. "What do you mean?"

"What will God say to you when you get to Heaven? *If* you get to Heaven?"

I shrug. "I don't believe in God. So nothing, I guess."

Klon grabs my arm. "You have to believe. You must."

"Why?" I ask.

"Look up." The sky looks like it's bursting with light from the stars. "That's why," he says.

An explanation of the Big Bang feels pretty empty right now.

We're quiet. "What about you?" I say to Nicole.

"What about me what?"

"What will God say to you?"

"Depends if I get there in time, right, Klon?" She laughs. Hollow. But it's not funny.

Klon and I stare at her through the smoke of the fire.

"C'mon, guys. Just kidding." She throws a twig on the fire, its bark peeling back burning black. "God won't want me anyway. He'd say something like, 'Why didn't you call? Why didn't you call?'" She pauses. "I wonder if he sounds like James Earl Jones." She laughs again.

"Call who?" I ask.

"Nine-one-one," she says. "What other number do you learn in kindergarten? Forget it. It's nothing."

I feel something tightening around my chest—a dull ache sets in. Klon reaches for Nicole's hand. Nicole shrugs him off and says, "Lighten up, guys. It was supposed to be a joke. God talking, meeting us up in the clouds. You're both stuck with me; Christmases, birthdays, whatever. Speaking of," she says. "let's change this topic. Klon, what was your favorite birthday present?"

He doesn't speak for a long time, then says, "I never got one."

"Huh? That's insane! All kids get presents." Nicole looks real embarrassed. "Oh. Are you a Jehovah?"

He jerks his head to the side and croaks. "Nope. We just don't celebrate what the Bible doesn't celebrate."

"But when is your birthday?" Nicole asks.

Klon shrugs.

"No idea?" I ask. Nicole and I exchange a glance.

"Nope," he says. "Maybe today. Maybe yesterday. Maybe tomorrow. I don't know." He inches a little closer to the campfire.

"You cold?" I ask. Even though Klondike has my coat, he shivers all the time. He needs more clothes. Somehow we have to get him some good sweaters or something.

"Nope," he says, and croaks, scooting back.

"Hey, Klon? How come you decided to come with us?"
It's something I've wondered about.

He twitches and says, "The Devil got married." He taps
his fingers on his temple, then runs them through his hair.
"A million-star hotel." He looks up at the sky. "The world's
too pretty not to share," he says, followed by an avalanche
of obscenities.

"See, I don't think demons like to share," Nicole says.
"You've definitely gotta have that Tourette's thing. No
demonic possession here."

Klon beams. I can't believe people would tell a kid
he's possessed by demons. That has to be not only the
least scientific, most ignorant approach to life but also
the meanest thing you can do. All these years Klon's been
running away from nothing.

"Who'd you share it with before?" I ask. "Before we
came?"

"Different people here and there. Fuckit. Joe. I liked
Joe. He was nice. Older than footprints. But the rain
was comin' down like a cow pissin' on a flat rock. He fell
down and never got back up. Fuckit. Then—tallywhacker,
asswipe—they came for him and took him away. I waited
until he was gone. He looked lonely. . . ." Klon lets out a

290

huge croak and a flurry of tics. He taps my arm. "I never want to be dead alone. You'll wait with me?"

Nicole turns on her side and looks at him. "We'd never leave you, Klon."

A wet leaf in the fire hisses, its crimson edges curling inward until it burns. "What's with you two?" I finally say. "It's like you're both on some freaky mortality thing. We're fine. We're young. Nobody needs to meet God in Heaven or wait with anybody who's dead." I try to control the tremor in my voice.

"It's just street talk, Jeops. It's always there, you know."

"What?"

"Death," Nicole whispers, like saying it aloud will call it over. "It's always there. You just don't feel it as much sitting in front of a flat-screen TV watching your Discovery Channel reruns. It doesn't mean anything, okay? It's just talk."

We're quiet for a while. The only thing we can hear is the crackle of the fire and Klondike's raspy breathing. I find three sticks and hand one to each Nicole and Klondike. "Let's pretend we're roasting marshmallows. My dad and I used to roast marshmallows out on the barbecue."

Klondike grins. "I like that. Pretending." He scoots a

little closer to the fire, caught up in the game. "I had them once. Marshmallows. Like Heaven. Asswipes."

Nicole smiles at me. We spend the rest of the evening eating pretend s'mores with roasted marshmallows. Klondike's the best at pretending his stick catches fire and he has to stomp out the invisible flames. Then he acts like his marshmallow is gooey, and he pulls on it and lets the sweet sugar fill his mouth. He shivers and croaks. But at least he's closer to the fire.

I fuel the fire before we go to sleep. We listen to the sizzle of the leaves and twigs. Red embers burn, throwing off heat with their flames. I stare up at the sky through the hazy smoke of the campfire. So many stars to wish on.

Maybe I'll call Dad. I can just call him and hear his voice. Ask him what I should do about everything. Will he know?

Will he care?

"The s'mores and shit. That's pretty high class," Nicole says, breaking the silence. "Your dad doesn't sound like such a bad guy,"

He isn't. I know that. It's just that he gave up on me— on us. And I don't know if I can forgive that.

Nicole stares at me through the popping campfire.

"Yeah. He's pretty okay. Most of the time."

"Does he know you're looking for Auntie Em?" Nicole asks.

"I think so. He's the one who told me about her." I pull on the locket.

"That was cool. So he didn't totally fuck it up."

I listen to Klondike's wheezy breathing and Nicole's stillness. We're almost there. Almost to Boise. And in a way, I don't want to get there and find her, because I don't know what will happen. I can't even come up with a reasonable hypothesis for what might happen to me, Nicole, and Klon. My head pounds and I can feel a slow ache creep up my body.

I stare up at the sky—billions of stars light-years away. I've never wished on stars before. It's something totally unscientific. But tonight I make a wish instead of a hypothesis or procedure. Maybe somebody up there really does listen.

Maybe.

CHAPTER THIRTY-TWO

"I still don't know why we can't stay here. Asswipes." Klon has moped all morning. It took Nicole and me about an hour to convince him to leave the bathroom.

After two nights sleeping under the stars with a cozy campfire, the third night it was as if the sky opened up and dropped down thick curtains of icy rain. At first the freezing drops pelted us one at a time. We jerked awake and ran to take cover in the bathroom while the storm thundered on the corrugated fiberglass roof. We couldn't talk above the clamor of the pounding rain, so we huddled in the center of the bathroom watching as rainwater seeped through the window until the storm cleared. Klon coughed for hours.

In a way, I want to drag it out, too. "You're stalling,"

Nicole said to me the second night before falling asleep.

I am. We're at the edge of the unknown and maybe at the end of the road. We might no longer be "we" after this. Nicole knows that, too.

"We're out of food," I finally say.

"So we'll pick berries," Klondike pleads.

"Klon, if we walk about two minutes out of the campsite, we can see the golden arches. It's not like this is the place for foraging for berries. Plus berry season was a few months ago. It's almost winter, Klon. We need to find someplace warm."

"Almost?" Nicole asks rubbing her hands on her blue jeans.

"Technically, it's not winter until December."

"Technically my ass. It's raining ice. It's fucking winter." Nicole shakes her head. "It's been winter ever since we left."

"And what if we don't find a better place?" Klon asks. He croaks and squeezes his eyes shut really tight. A new tic. "Asswipes."

"I'm hungry, Klon. C'mon," Nicole says. "We'll find a way better place than this dump. It's time to move on."

Klon hesitates. "Where?" he finally asks.

Nicole looks at me.

"The airport," I say. "Let's go."

We have to look presentable. We have to look okay. That might make the difference between foster care and family.

Purpose: Find Aunt Sarah

Hypothesis: If we show up at the restaurant where Aunt Sarah works all cleaned up and looking good, she'll see me, recognize me because I look just like her deceased sister, and invite us to sit down for hot chocolate and cookies.

(I can't make myself go further than that with the hypothesis. I need to stop there.)

Materials: Mom's box—the locket's especially important; the paycheck stub; new clothes

Procedure:

1) Go to the airport

2) Steal a suitcase

3) Find a bathroom in a restaurant, hotel, library, whatever. And clean up.

4) Find Main Street (just ask around)

5) Find the XXX Grill restaurant

6) Find somebody who knows Aunt Sarah—or Aunt
Sarah herself

Variables: The restaurant: Will it still be there? What if
it's got a new manager who doesn't know Sarah Jones?
Aunt Sarah: What if she doesn't care? What if Nicole
was right about that? What if she cares about me but
not about Nicole and Klon?

Constants: Me, Nicole, Klondike

Even though I'm terrified, I feel a slight buzz of
accomplishment. I made it to Boise. This is where she might
be. I look at Nicole and Klon. Klon is squished between us
in the back of a 1980's Chrysler Imperial. Nicole stares out
the window.

"Why the airport?" Nicole turns to me and asks. "What
happened to Main Street?" It's the first thing any of us has
said since we got a ride. The lady is nice. She doesn't speak
much English, but she seems like she wants the company
even though we don't talk.

She takes an exit and leaves us at a gas station. She
points. "Airport," she says.

"Thanks!" we say. I notice she watches us through her
rearview mirror.

We walk to the airport, past people lugging heavy suitcases on wobbly wheels. The place is packed. Perfect timing. "Again. Why the airport?" Nicole asks.

"We need clothes—for Klon."

Nicole shrugs. "I've never been inside an airport before." She looks around at the expensive gift shops. "But I don't think this is the best place for shoplifting."

Klondike is fixated on a woman who wears tight leopard pants and a nice pair of silicone-enhanced boobs. "Tits. Tits. Big nice tits." He jerks his head. "Tallywhacker. Tits." He turns to me, looking helpless. "I can't help it. Tits. Goddammit," he says.

I yank on his arm. The woman's boyfriend looks like he has steroid-enhanced muscles. "Klon, c'mon."

"Tits," he says in his gravelly voice, then croaks.

"Follow me," I say.

We weave our way through the horde of passengers. It looks like fun. Going somewhere. Having a suitcase. Having a plan.

We follow the signs to baggage claim. Conveyor belts carry suitcases around—suitcases that miraculously pop out of a shoot from the top. People push, shove, and heave suitcases off the slow-moving belts. Airport workers pull some bags off to make room for more, piling them in the center between different flights.

I turn to Nicole and smirk.

"I don't get it," she says.

"A hefty percentage of these bags won't get claimed because people miss flights, bags are sent to the wrong destination, etc. The airlines have insurance for this kind of thing."

"Sounds familiar."

"Huh?"

"Grocery stores." Nicole shakes her head. "Don't you remember anything we talk about?"

"Sorry, instant replay," I mutter. There's something slightly irritating about the fact Nicole remembers every stupid conversation. Ever.

"So?" Nicole asks.

"So we pick a bag. Just one. And we wave and pretend we're bringing it to our mom and dad. Okay?"

Somebody pushes past Nicole and bumps into Klondike. "Fucker," Klondike whispers. "Tits and ass. Asswipe."

I roll my eyes.

"Tits."

"Go stand outside, Klon. Wait for us over there." I point

to one of the exits. "We'll be there in a couple of minutes." I watch as people avert their eyes when Klon walks by them. Some people even gasp.

"Assholes," Nicole says. "As if they're walking specimens of pure beauty."

"Yeah," I agree. "Let's get a suitcase. Hopefully," I say, "it'll have a toothbrush."

Nicole curls up her lip. "Ewwww. You'd use somebody else's toothbrush? That's so foul," she says.

I stare at her. "Cappy, we've been drinking from cups we fish out of the trash. I don't see much of a difference there."

She shakes her head. "You've gotta draw the line somewhere."

Yeah, I wonder, thinking about Nicole's arms. Did she make sure she used only clean razors to cut herself? I shudder.

"What are you staring at?" Nicole asks. "What?" she asks again.

I rub my eyes. "Okay. Dibs on the toothbrush. You pick whatever else you want. And we all need clean clothes."

Nicole moves toward one of the conveyor belts.

"Over there," I say, and pull her to me.

"What's the diff?" she asks.

"We can't risk taking off the conveyer belt. We've gotta take one of the bags workers have piled in the center. Those people are either slow in getting off the plane or late or something."

"Oh. Clever, Jeopardy. So you've got a bit of thievery in you."

"We're not stealing. We're cleaning up after the inefficiency of airlines to get people's bags where they need to go."

Nicole rolls her eyes. "Did your dad always sugarcoat things like that? Stealing is stealing, Jeopardy. And sometimes it's okay, you know. It's not like you have to have a justification for everything. Haven't you ever seen *Les Misérables*?"

"What? Now you're a Broadway show expert?"

"Just saying," Nicole says.

I shrug. It feels better, though, to have a reason for things.

We walk over to the bags the workers have piled in the center. "Pick a black one," I say.

"They're all black," Nicole says.

"Yeah. Okay. Let's get one and go."

"Wow. It's like when you're a kid and go to a birthday

party and wonder what the surprise will be."

I laugh. I like the feeling of excitement building up, and I wonder if this is how Dad feels when he pulls off a scam.

"We should get Klon to pick it. He'd like that," Nicole says.

"Next time. That one looks good. Big." I point out a black duffel. There are four other duffels piled on the floor, so it's an easy target and one we can pass off as being a mistake in case we get caught.

"Cool, Jeopardy. I didn't think you had it in you."

"Neither did I." I need this, I remind myself, to up my chances at Aunt Sarah's restaurant.

Nicole clicks her heels three times. "There's no place like home," and picks up the heavy bag. We each grab a handle. I wave, "Got it, Dad!" The two of us walk to the doorway where Klondike waits.

We walk away from baggage claim as fast and calmly as we can.

"Fuck, this is heavy," Nicole says.

"I think we got a good one," I say, that tingly feeling still in my stomach.

We duck into the parking garage, dragging the bag behind a big SUV. MY CHILD IS A SUPER STUDENT AT

MAPLE GROVE ELEMENTARY SCHOOL is pasted on the shiny bumper.

"What's it say?" Nicole asks, trying to sound out some of the words. "Fucking sometimes 'y.' It can't decide whether it should be a vowel or a consonant. A total 'Johnny Boy' D'Amato—the closet gay mob boss. He got whacked, you know? You can't hide who you are."

"You're comparing the letter 'y' to a dead gay mob boss?"

"Yeah, so?" Nicole spends more time miffed at the English language than trying to learn it. But I can tell she's getting better. "My," she says, and continues to read. She gets all the words except maple, grove, and elementary. It's painfully slow, but I have to be patient. Like she doesn't get pissed every time I come out of a store empty-handed.

"Yep," I say, and repeat the whole bumper sticker.

"Dude, that kid probably gets the shit beat out of him every day." Nicole laughs.

Klondike shrugs, then jerks his head, tapping the bumper. "I think it's—fuckit—kinda nice. Tits. Asswipe. He has parents that love him."

I stare at the bumper sticker. "It's nice. But Cap's probably right. That kid's a punching bag."

"Plus you never know about the love part. I once had a foster home where the guy was some kind of big-shot doctor. He used to lock up all the food cabinets and the refrigerator, so his wife couldn't eat. He let me have dinner, but she could only eat celery. I lost like fifteen pounds in two weeks. They found out he'd been giving me some kind of funky weight-loss shit in my food and I had to go back to Kids Place. I was kinda bummed because at least he didn't try to get on me or hit me or anything. But a weird fucker." Nicole stares at the bumper sticker. "You never know what people's homes are like."

I nod.

Klondike coughs his raspy cough. "Open it. Let's see what's inside."

We open the bag and sift through a bunch of Styrofoam popcorn. The three of us peer inside. "No," I say, and pull off the plastic.

"Oh man," Nicole says.

"I can't believe it."

"Figures. No wonder it was so Goddamned heavy." Nicole sighs.

"Yeah. I didn't know people would be allowed to travel with something like this."

Nicole shrugs. "Maybe it died when he was on vacation and he didn't want to bring home Fido's ashes to the kids."

"Weird." I shake my head.

"Very."

Klondike pats the fur as if the dog were alive. "He's soft. What's his name?" he asks, and looks under the dog's leg. "Gonads. Two. Testicle. Balls. Nuts. Two." He coughs and can't catch his breath. Nicole and I rub his back until his coughing fit ends.

I look at the tag. "Lucifer."

"Really?" Nicole looks at the tag and studies the letters, trying to sound it out. "Somebody actually named their dog after the Devil?"

I shrug. "That's what it says."

Klondike jerks his hand back, then croaks.

"Pretty freaky that they froze him in a growl," Nicole says. "He'll end up spending his entire afterlife pissed off. You know, there's this guy called 'Joe the Boss.' They said he was the man who could dodge bullets. Once there was a hit on him, and the shooters missed—point-blank. The cops found Joe the Boss sitting in his bedroom with two holes in his straw hat."

"And?"

"Well. Nine years later they killed him when he was playing cards at his favorite Italian restaurant. Shot him to death. No more bullet dodging. Rumor has it he had the ace of spades in his hand. Pretty freaky, huh?"

"Freaky why?" I say.

"Ace of spades. The death card." Nicole shakes her head and pulls out her plastic bag of postcards and letters. She pulls out the card. "I always carry one around. It's kind of—"

"Morbid?" I say.

"No," she says. "A little freaky but mostly poetic. Death is freedom. Remember Pablo."

"So?" I finally say.

"So what?"

"So what does this have to do with a stuffed dog named Lucifer?"

Nicole shrugs. "They're both dead. And freaky."

I roll my eyes.

"We can try again," Nicole suggests. "We'll maybe get a brown suitcase this time. No more duffel bags."

"Too risky. There are security cameras everywhere." My heart sinks. I look at Klondike shivering. I pull off my last sweater—leaving me with a T-shirt underneath the black coat. "Here, Klon, put this on." It's not like we'll be on the streets much longer. Maybe we can find Aunt Sarah today.

He shakes his head. "I'm fine. Tits."

"Just put it on. We'll find something else along the way. Let's go find a place to sleep."

My body aches, and when Klon pats my back, it feels like he's pounding me with a hammer. I struggle to swallow down my saliva and look at the late-afternoon sun. I can't imagine finding Main Street today; I can't imagine doing anything but sleep. I just wanted new clothes, something clean. I sigh.

"Ahh, that's all right," Nicole says. "It was fun to go to the airport." Nicole nudges me. "C'mon. Let's find a place to crash."

Klondike nods. "My first time, too. I wish we could live in that—asswipes—campground. And roast marshmallows."

I ruffle his hair. It's greasy and clumpy. "Me, too." And I really mean it. "Maybe next time we come to an airport, we'll all get on a plane."

Nicole snorts. "Last I heard, they don't take hitchhikers on planes."

CHAPTER THIRTY-THREE

"Yes, I'll hold." I wait in the phone booth. We've found a boarded-up building near the airport where we can spend the night. Downtown is too far to walk before dark, and we can't risk getting caught on the streets at night.

I lied and said I was going to look for something in the area to help keep us warm. Nicole'll kill me if she knows I'm spending money to make a long-distance phone call.

"I'm sorry; could you tell me your name?" a woman with a nasal voice asks.

"Um, Beulah." My throat is on fire. Maybe I have allergies. "Hold, please." An instrumental version of "Dancing Queen" floods the phone line. Definitely not the kind of music I expect.

"Hello?" His voice sounds tired. Raw.

Silence.

"Hello? Is anyone there?" He shouts to somebody, "Nobody's on the line. Did you cut the call?"

Another voice comes on the line. "Hello? Hello? Yeah, I don't hear a thing, either."

"Hello?" He comes back on the line. "Are you there?"

I listen as the seconds tick away and open my mouth. But nothing comes out.

"Maya?" he says. "Is that you?"

And the line goes dead.

My head pounds. I find my way back to the warehouse. The street reeks of human waste. Small groups huddle around fires in the alleyway outside the warehouse— shadows dancing across gaunt faces. Nobody looks anybody in the eye. I weave my way in and out of small groups of teens. It's weird. I wonder how many people are homeless in Boise.

When we found the warehouse in the day, nobody was around. Where do kids like us stay during the day?

I guess they're not really like us. I mean we have a place to go. A destination.

I find Nicole and Klondike huddled outside the

entrance to the warehouse.

"Why don't we stay inside?" I ask.

"There's a body in there," Nicole says.

"A body?"

"A dead one," Klondike says. "And it's darker than God's pockets. Goddammit, it's dark. Asswipes." He lets out a long croak. A couple of kids scoot away from us. That's a plus. It's not like we want anybody too close.

Maybe we should've kept Lucifer. Natural nutcase repellent.

"Yeah. He's sitting up. Cross-legged. Frozen." Nicole describes everything about the corpse and says, "It's like Don Vito Genovese dying in prison of a heart attack. Total downer."

"Don't see the connection, Cappy." I brace myself for another of Nicole's totally unrelated mob stories.

"No glory, Jeops. Some kid dying in a warehouse all alone is just like a washed-up Mafia guy with high cholesterol. Pathetic. When it's time to go, you gotta make a statement."

"Capone didn't," I argue.

"Capone's nonstatement *was* his statement. Others, though, need more style. Go out with a bang, with purpose."

Like Mom, I think. I remember following her around the house in my socks so she wouldn't hear the pitter-patter of my feet on the cold floor. I knew where she hid her bottles and pills. I'd count them each day to make sure she wasn't taking too many. Dad pretended that everything was fine in the fairy-tale world he'd constructed.

I feel a pang of sadness. I watch Nicole, study her. I haven't had the chance to count her pills since we've been on the road. I just hope they're all still there. Déjà-vu.

"What?" Nicole says.

I swallow, the pain in my throat pretty much a constant—just getting worse, depending on the time. "I don't think it's pathetic. I think it's sad," I say. "Death isn't honor or glory or freedom. It's not romantic. Death is nothing. The absence of presence. A gap that you can't fill. The end," I say.

Klondike's eyes open wide. "And the promise of the afterlife? Eternal light? God?"

"Nice, Jeops," Nicole says. "Why don't you just tell him there's no Santa Claus while you're at it?"

I cradle my head in the palms of my hands.

Klon sniffles. "Are his eyes open?" he asks.

Nicole nods.

"You've gotta close 'em, Cappy."

"I'm not gonna close 'em. I'm not gonna touch him."
Nicole makes a face.

Klon trembles, croaks, then begins to tap my leg. His
eyes squint open and shut, open and shut—like one of
those pond frogs with bug eyes. I'm not liking his new tic.
It's kind of disturbing.

Klon coughs and grabs his side. "Then he's taking
someone else with him. That's how it happens. You have
to close his eyes or someone else will die. Asswipes,
tallywhacker."

"That's ridiculous," Nicole says, and rubs her arms.

"He sits like Buddha," Klondike says. "Buddha froze in
the warehouse." He taps us. "It's darker than God's pockets,
and he's alone. He has his eyes open, and he's alone. He
wants company."

I notice that a lot of the alleyway has cleared out. Few
groups remain. Death is a natural repellent, too. We don't
need Lucifer as long as we have the Buddha corpse.

"Maybe he's meditating or something," I finally say.
"He might not be dead."

"In his own shit?" Nicole asks. The more she talks, the
more horrified Klon looks. "That place smells like a sewer

in there. I think he's decomposing."

I shiver. "In this cold? He must've died several days ago then, if he's already decomposing. Way past the rigor mortis stage."

"Well, I wouldn't know the exact time of death, Jeopardy. I didn't bring my crime scene investigation equipment." Nicole shakes her head. "At least we're all biodegradable, huh? I mean he could stay there forever and just become part of the abandoned warehouse. We all could stay right here and biodegrade—only leaving a trace of brittle bones for some archaeologist to find two hundred years from now. But that would mean no glory."

I think for a bit. "Probably not Klon's breast implant lady. You know it can take up to five hundred years for plastic to decompose in a landfill. We've found a bazillion ways to ruin the world while we're alive, and we continue to do it postmortem."

Nicole looks down at her chest. "So I'm ecologically conscientious by not getting implants. Good to know I'm doing my part." She points to the warehouse. "Anyway, they call him Limp."

"Limp?" I say.

"Yeah. The guys who were sitting over there don't know

if he was Limp because he walks funny or"—Nicole points at her crotch—"limp. If you know what I mean."

"You asked people that?"

"It's a legitimate question, Jeopardy." Nicole nods.

"Why would you even want to know?" I ask.

"You know what's weird?" she says. "He can't be much older than us, you know. Just really gross smelling and looking."

I look down the alley. Most of the fires have died out. It looks as if everyone is gone. When I look hard, I can see people's feet or a stocking cap sticking out of cardboard boxes. There's only one streetlight working just a few feet from us, its dim light casting a soft glow. It's like this street is reserved for people like us: homeless. I clasp the locket. What do I expect from this aunt who might not even exist anymore? A miracle? A home? Family? Whatever that means.

Hypothesis: If I find Aunt Sarah . . .

I can't complete it. Maybe I'm just too tired to think.

Procedure:
   1) Find Main Street

2) Find Aunt Sarah's restaurant

3) Ask somebody for Aunt Sarah

4) Find Aunt Sarah

I'll leave the conjectures, variables, and all that other stuff for later.

Good. I have a procedure. Just for tomorrow. That's all I need, though. One plan a day.

I want to grab my backpack and sit on it. It's nice to have cleanish jeans, and it's not likely we'll get to a Laundromat anytime soon. I look behind Nicole and near Klon. "Where's our stuff?" I ask.

"I hid it," Nicole says.

"Where?"

"In the warehouse."

"With the dead body?"

"Well, he's not gonna take it." Nicole rolls her eyes.

"Yeah, but—"

Nicole leans in. "We can't be around here with nice REI backpacks. We'll get mobbed."

I nod.

"So I left them in the warehouse."

"Those packs are all we've got."

"Precisely," Nicole says. "And if we want to keep them, I had to hide them. Look around you. We're not on some high school trip where everybody compares ring tones and iPods. We've gotta be smart. We're looking too clean as it is."

I sigh. "Maybe we can take the ten dollars and—"

"We had a nice sleep the last couple of nights. We're going to find your mysterious auntie Em tomorrow. So suck it up for now."

"Yeah. Fine."

"It looks like we've got a long night ahead of us." Nicole looks around.

"Do we have any boxes?" I ask.

"Does it look like it?" she asks. "A box is a prime piece of real estate around here."

"So who gets first shift?" I ask.

"How about none of us sleep tonight. This place creeps me out."

I look over at Klondike. He's already fallen asleep, leaning against a green plastic trash bin. His breath comes out raspy; his chest rattles.

"He looks worse than before," I say. My throat is burning again. Maybe we all have tonsillitis.

"Yeah." Nicole sits down. "Let's sit back-to-back."

"Okay." I look up. No stars are out—none that I can see through the muck in the sky. "How are we supposed to stay awake?" I'm so tired all the time. Before, I needed a nice bed to be able to sleep. Not anymore.

"Okay. Let's go back to those vowels." Nicole pulls out a stubby pencil and ratty notebook. Her postcards spill out of the plastic bag.

Gotta give her credit for one thing: She's persistent. She really wants to learn how to read. Maybe I don't want to learn how to shoplift enough. I sigh and hand her the postcards that scattered on the ground. "You didn't keep your postcards hidden in the warehouse."

She pulls out a squished box. "I took your box, too. Just in case, you know, we couldn't get back in. We can read your letters later."

"Thanks."

"Okay," she says.

"Okay, long a." I write four-letter words on the paper.

THIRTY-FOUR

Nicole and I read all night by the light of the only sputtering streetlamp in the alleyway. We read until my eyes are blurry, and we both fall asleep. Back-to-back we lean onto each other until a garbage truck rumbles up the alleyway—the urban equivalent of a rooster.

I shake Nicole awake and go to Klon. His face burns with fever. He wakes with a start and shivers. "Klon, are you okay?" I can barely speak because of the fire in my throat. It's like my tonsils grow bigger every day. I wish I had gotten them removed as a kid. It's not like they do anything. I think that any structure of the human body that can be removed and not make a difference in the overall function of the body is obsolete. Like the coccyx and appendix—other totally useless parts of the human body that do nothing but cause pain. Stupid tonsils. I swallow hard and wish I had been the first to evolve into a non-tonsil human being. I tug on Klon's coat. "Klon, we need to get someplace warm."

He stretches and stands just before the garbage men clomp down the alley.

Nicole stands, and the three of us watch as other kids scramble out of their boxes and begin their day. What day is it? I wonder. I sometimes feel like all of time has been lost since we left Reno. I know it's November.

My tongue feels swollen; white clumps come dislodged from my throat, and I spit them out, wincing from the pain.

New hypothesis: If I don't treat my infected tonsils, the condition will get worse. If the tonsillitis gets worse, it can turn into quinsy. If I develop quinsy, then I will have to be hospitalized or could suffer a slow, painful death.

Then I won't have to worry about finding Aunt Sarah. I rub my throat.

"It's just a sore throat. Why are you so freaked out

about it?" Nicole asks. "You'd think you had some kind of fatal disease or something."

Obviously, she hasn't heard of quinsy. "Let's go," I say. I hope I don't produce much spit today, because swallowing is a killer.

"Where to?" Nicole says. "The world is ours."

Klon smiles. "Yeah. We can go *anywhere*."

If that's true, how come I feel so trapped?

"Main Street," I finally say.

"Main Street," Nicole echoes. She looks nervous.

"Okay!" says Klon, and croaks. As long as there's road kill, he'll be happy.

"So?" I say.

"So what?"

"Are you gonna get our backpacks?"

"Why don't you?"

"I'm not the one who hid them beside a dead body. And I don't particularly want to go see it."

"Fine." Nicole slips into the old building and comes out with our packs. I'd swear the sickly sweet smell of death has stuck to them. I gag.

"Oh, please," Nicole says. "Enough with the drama, okay?"

320

We ask around. We're not as far from Main Street as I thought. "Do you think," I ask, "it would be better to leave our stuff here? Hidden? Ummm, to not look so, well—"

"Well what?"

"Well, homeless, I guess. She might be there, you know, at the restaurant, and showing up with backpacks and helpless puppy expressions could freak her out."

"What happened to 'who gives a fuck about appearances'?"

"This is different," I say. Plus our backpacks smell like death. Really.

Nicole mumbles something and says, "Okay. We hide them next to Limp. Just today."

"Just today."

"Yeah, okay."

We weave through the streets of Boise. I cradle the box in my arm. It's a really pretty city. It'd be a nice place to live. Then I stop the thought. Hope equals disappointment.

We get lost about half a dozen times until we find Main Street. It wasn't as close as everybody said. I pull out one of the check stubs. "Okay. We're here. Now we just need to find the restaurant."

We stand and watch traffic whiz by. Klon, Nicole, and I look one way, then another. "Which way do we go?" Nicole asks.

I turn right. "Let's go up this way and come back down the other way. We'll stop in all restaurants that have 'Grill' in the name. There should be nine, according to MapQuest."

"Good plan," says Klondike. "Let's go." We almost bowl him over, though, because he's crouched down to stare at a pigeon in the gutter.

Nicole squints. "Look over there. That says—" She sounds out the letters. "Grill, something?"

I look up. "You know," I say, "I bet you need glasses."

"Do not."

"Tell me the letters."

Nicole squints. "Okay. I maybe need glasses."

"You can't see anything," I say.

"Sure I can," Nicole argues.

Klon laughs. "How many fingers do I got up, Cappy?" His voice is hoarse and his croaks have become soft moans. He holds his side.

"Ha. Ha." Nicole says.

"No wonder you never get your vowels right." I sigh.

Hypothesis: If I steal a pair of glasses at the drugstore for Nicole, she'll be able to actually see the letters to read them.

First, though, I have to steal.

"So what does it say?" Nicole asks.

"Not Grill. Let's go."

And we walk. And walk. Entering every single Grill restaurant on Main Street which happens to be, in my unscientific opinion, the longest, most awful street on the face of the planet. It's late afternoon when we get to the last restaurant before we reach our starting point again.

"C'mon, Jeops. This is the one. It has to be," Nicole says. She smiles. "Really. Don't look so down."

I force myself to swallow. We walk into the waiting lobby. Couples huddle together, dressed up, waiting to be called to their tables. Most of them have some kind of expensive-looking drink in their hands. Coffee-table books of the United States are displayed on a low, granite-topped table. Some people leaf through books while precariously balancing drinks. I cringe.

"Pretty swank," Nicole says. "This has got to be the place."

She and Klon sit in the corner. Several couples move away. I knew we should've washed up first. "Go on." Nicole pulls out a photo book for her and Klon to look through.

I take a deep breath and make my way toward the hostess. "Excuse me, could I please speak to a manager?"

She looks at me above rimless glasses, pulls them off, setting them on her solid-wood podium, and not-discreetly-at-all covers her nose. "May I ask who you are?"

You're a stupid restaurant hostess. Get over yourself. That's what I'd say in some get-gonads-and-speak-your-mind procedure. I'm going to do that. Make a procedure to follow to stand up to people—to tell people exactly what I think. That's what Nicole and Klon do. I look back at them. They're engrossed in a desert photo book.

I stand up tall. "My name is Maya. Maya Aguirre. Um, I think my aunt works here. So can you please get the manager? It's an emergency."

She hesitates, then turns on her heel and works her way through the crowded restaurant to talk to some guy in a suit. They dance around busy waiters, the manager schmoozing the customers. It feels like it takes them years to come back.

Before he says anything, I pull out the check stub

that has half disintegrated in my sweaty hand. "Um, is this check stub from this restaurant?" I show them. "I'm looking for a Sarah Jones." I hold my breath, trying to peek behind them. Maybe she's a chef. Maybe she's a bartender. Maybe.

The manager wrinkles his nose but takes the stub in his hands. He shakes his head. "I remember the place, though—the sign. It was a hot university hangout."

My heart jumps. "Where is it?"

He hands it back to me. "Sorry, kid. It burned down ten years ago or so."

I nod. "Um, thanks." I stare down at the stub. Sarah Jones. In the U.S.A. How easy will it be to find somebody with that name? I have a sinking feeling in my stomach like I've failed all of us. All of this was some stupid wild-goose chase.

The manager has his snooty vibe back. People in the waiting room are feeling uncomfortable. They want to have a nice evening, get away from it all. And we're just a reminder of the reality they want to escape. He clears his throat, "I'm going to have to ask you to leave now."

The hostess sighs and flutters her purple lashes at the people waiting. She gives them an apologetic smile.

Homelessness makes people squirmy.

Behind them I watch waiters take half-eaten plates of food into the kitchen.

"Just one more thing," I say. I'm about to ask where the old restaurant was when Klondike lets out a huge croak. He's torn out a picture from the perfect photo book and it bends in his filthy hands.

"Hey!" The manager pushes me aside and moves toward Klon and Nicole. "You're going to have to pay for that, kid. That's an expensive book."

I push over a glass from the table and it shatters on the floor, taking his attention away from Nicole and Klon. Before I follow Nicole and Klon out the door, I slip the snotty hostess's glasses into my pocket.

We rush out into the middle of traffic, veering around cars to cross the street, then take a side street far away from Main. We run until it feels like my lungs are going to explode. Klondike barely keeps up, clutching his side. He trembles in the wind, gripping the picture in his hand.

We collapse on a curb and sit huddled together. I turn my back to them, wiping tears off my cheeks. I wonder if it's scientifically possible for a heart to collapse from disappointment, because the pain in my chest is crushing.

It's probably just another cold symptom, I think.

Nicole puts her hand on my shoulder. "It's no big deal, Jeops. We'll find her. We have a whole box of clues to follow. Think about that flower," she says.

I sniff and wipe my nose across my coat sleeve. I nod and turn to face them, trying to pretend that everything's okay. "A whole box," I echo. "Can I at least see it?" My teeth chatter, and I hold out my hand for Klon to pass me the ripped page.

He shows me the picture of a desert scene. Sun shines through droplets of rain. "The Devil's getting married," Klondike says between wheezing breaths. He croaks. "Fuckit. It's for us, our beginning. Genesis."

I look from Klondike to Nicole and shake my head. What a great time to get sentimental. I sigh. "Thanks, Klon. That's really nice."

Nicole says, "We've gotta get back to our stuff at the warehouse. It's already dark."

CHAPTER
THIRTY-FIVE

We hug our coats around our bodies and walk back toward the warehouse—hope of a life in Boise all gone. The box's corners dig into my stomach and I hug it tighter, feeling angrier. More disappointed.

The cold bites at our noses and ears, and after we finally get oriented, it takes us an hour to find our way back.

"I don't want to sleep here again," Klondike says. "It's been too long. We stayed with him last night, but no more. Buddha. Asswipes." He lags behind. "It's bad luck they don't find him. Death brings death."

I grab his hand and pull him up with us, impatient and tired. "We stick together. We'll be okay. One more night."

We're standing at the end of the alleyway. I see the warehouse is still boarded up. I wonder what the protocol is for something like this? Shouldn't *someone* report it? "Death is near," Klon says.

"No shit, Klon. Death is in the warehouse." Nicole sighs. "You guys know about Machine Gun Jack McGurn?"

"No." Klon shivers.

"And we don't want to." Klon looks terrified and I try to calm him down. "We have no choice," I say. "Just one more night. I promise." We walk to the alley. Some kids gather around a fire they built in a trash bin. Others have already found their places inside ratty cardboard boxes.

The temperature drops. "We'll huddle together tonight. We'll be okay," I say. "We'll be okay," I repeat under my breath. We have to be. Aunt Sarah's not here.

And the pain comes back to my chest.

Nicole peeks inside the building and comes out smelling like death. "Jesus, that place is ripe. I can't see too good, but I think the packs are still next to Limp. When do you think they'll find him?"

Klon moves away from Nicole.

"Jesus, Klon. It's not contagious or anything. Anyway, that Jack McGurn really got the raw deal in the end. You know he was one of the shooters of the Saint Valentine's Day massacre—a top assassin in his day. But he was killed in a bowling alley of all places. Talk about a bum deal. A bowling alley. Who wants to die in bowling shoes? Rented, smelly, athlete's foot bowling shoes? How shitty is that? Anyway, when the feds found his body, they found a note next to the corpse: 'You've lost your job; you've lost your dough, your jewels, and handsome houses. But things could be worse, you know. You haven't lost your trousers.'"

The Mafia world is surreal. They even take the time to write bathroom-wall poetry after a big hit. Weird. My mind spins. Where will I find Sarah Jones from a bunch of letters and a dried flower? How is it possible?

"Hey. Snap out of it, Jeops." Nicole tugs on my arm. "Earth to Jeopardy. Are you even here?"

"Oh. Yeah."

Nicole shakes her head. "Anyway, I'm never going to die wearing a pair of bowling shoes. That's why I don't bowl. What an embarrassment."

"But bowling's kinda fun."

"I'm not taking my chances," Nicole says. "I'm gonna die in style."

"And how's that?" I ask. I just don't get it. The whole die in style thing.

"I'll die when *I* choose to go. You know? That's what I can control in this fucking shithole. My death."

Nicole looks angry. Something's off. Her eyes have that dead black look again. I shake off the feeling and figure it's just that we're all feeling pretty sick.

Klon's eyes have a glassy look to them, and it's like he slips in and out of consciousness. He finally says, "It's bad luck—so many days. All alone. That boy." He sighs. "And his eyes are open. He must be so tired."

"You can't be tired dead," Nicole says. "That's the whole point of the eternal rest, right?"

The wind whips up, and cold gnaws into every part of our bodies.

I shrug and shiver. It's weird to think that Limp maybe has a family somewhere. Maybe somebody's looking for him. Maybe not. I look at Klondike and wonder the same.

"Just one more night like this," I say. "Tomorrow we'll find someplace warmer. Tomorrow we'll get away from here. Maybe get to a library. Get more clues about where to go next."

Klon sighs.

"Really. It's like an adventure, and we're detectives trying to find Aunt Sarah. It's fun," I say. The words sound lame. "How are you feeling?"

"Like I was eaten by a wolf and shit out over a cliff." Klon croaks and squeezes his eyes shut, nodding his head back and forth.

Nicole and I both laugh. "Come lean on me," I say. I wish I had Klon's cool expressions. We should write them down.

"Okay," says Klondike. He falls asleep on my shoulder, his breath a raspy whistle.

Nicole sits on the other side of Klon. "I'm feeling pretty crappy, too. All this cold."

"Me, too," I say. "He's getting worse. I wonder if his ribs are okay."

"Ribs heal themselves, don't they?" Nicole asks.

"Yeah. It just takes time."

"He'll be fine."

"I hope so," I say. My eyelids feel like lead and my head bobs forward. I'm too tired to worry about Klon right now.

"Are you okay?" Nicole asks.

"What do you mean?" I say.

"Are you, um, okay that we didn't find Auntie Em?"

Nicole says. Her voice sounds strained.

I nod. "Sure." I try to sound convincing. At least the pain in my chest has eased up. "We'll be fine. We'll just find her somewhere else. And she'll take us in." It's the first time I say that—"us." And I realize it's what I want.

"Right," Nicole says.

"Really," I say.

"Well, if not, we've always got my dad." She half laughs.

"Plan B," I say before I catch myself.

"Plan B," she mumbles.

"Oh yeah!" I say. "Ta-da!" I hand her the glasses. The one accomplishment of the day. It wasn't a total loss.

She slips them on her nose and squints. "Hey. That's kinda cool. Everything looks like I'm staring into a fish bowl."

"Most likely they're the wrong prescription, but maybe they'll help. You should try them in the light. Tomorrow."

She puts the glasses in her coat pocket. "Thank you," she says. "Really."

"You're welcome. Though technically you can't consider that shoplifting," I say.

"Nah. That's just outright stealing." Nicole laughs.

"Maybe we're going wrong with you and should focus on pickpocketing instead of shoplifting."

"Ha. Ha."

"Really, though. Thanks." Nicole smiles. "So what's the theme of the day?" she asks. "We should stay awake." We listen to the wind and the rustle of papers in the alleyway. "This place creeps me out."

"Night creeps me out."

"Yeah."

Talking would help keep me awake, even if it means my throat hurting more. "Theme of the longest day on the planet," I say. "What's the first thing you're gonna read when you get good at reading?"

Nicole pats her chest. "My postcards. The glasses should help."

"I hope so. Do you, um, want me to read one to you? Just because." Nicole, except for that first day, has never even let me hold them. "Just to pass the time, anyway." For some reason I want a connection to somebody real. And postcards from a real dad seem like the best thing we've got. "I can read a couple of these stupid letters out loud, too. We can share family secrets or something lame like that. Just to kill time."

She nods. "Okay. Maybe if you read letters, we'll find more clues."

I shrug. "Maybe. Unless you want to practice reading."

"Nah. I don't really feel like concentrating so much tonight. My head's killing me. Read a few postcards." She hands me Chicago and two others behind it.

"Okay," I say. "Here goes. 'You'd love it here. The city has the biggest skyscrapers I've ever seen. And great pizza. I hope to see you soon.'"

"And the postmark?"

"Why the postmark?"

"Maybe it'll be a clue. You know, for Plan B. Besides, it's kind of cool to think that these pieces of paper began somewhere and ended up in Reno. And are now in Boise. All for"—she looks at the stamp—"twenty-eight cents. Way cheap travel."

"Not as cheap as hitchhiking sand from Chad."

Nicole smiles.

I read the postmark. Yerington. My stomach hurts, and that familiar burning churns up my esophagus. "Chicago," I say. I flip over the other two postcards she handed me. All of them have Yerington on the postmark. Was it her mom? It must've been. I guess she wasn't all bad. I read the postcards aloud. They all say basically the same thing.

"Pretty generic," she says.

"Yeah. But that's the point of a postcard. You don't write anything really important on one."

"How many have you sent?"

I think about it. "None. Not that I remember."

"If you take the time to buy someone a postcard and send it, you should write something better than 'You'd love it here. Great pizza.'"

"Okay. Will do."

"Okay," she says, "now read one of Auntie Em's letters. The flower one. I like it the best."

"You haven't heard the others."

Nicole shrugs. "I don't need to."

So I read the one with the dried flower. The alley is so dark, it's hard to make out the tiny handwriting on the crisp paper even though I've practically got it memorized by now.

"Now that's a real letter. Sure beats the hell outa 'great pizza,' 'great food,' 'Hollywood walk of fame.'"

I shake my head. "Nah. Your dad is just more to the point," I lie.

Nicole smiles and takes back the postcards. "You know," she says, "I'm not really sure what I'll say to him when I finally find him. You know what you'll say to your aunt?"

I shake my head. "Not a clue." And at this point, I'm not even sure if I'll ever find her. My one solid clue was a dead end.

We're quiet for a while. Somebody in the alley is snoring. Somebody else moans in his sleep. Night is a sad time. It makes us more invisible than we already are. It makes everything more real. I think about all those stupid survivor man shows on Discovery. Who needs to know how to survive in a swamp or desert when the real world is hard enough? I'd like to see those guys set loose in downtown Boise. Survive this, asshole, I think. It feels good. I mouth the word: asshole. Yeah. It feels real good to say that.

I finally say, "That's a good choice. Reading the postcards. Tomorrow you can try. With the glasses and better light." Even if she can read the words on the card, I doubt she'll be able to read the postmarks. At least I hope not.

"Yep," she says. "Tomorrow. And you? Now that you're

a professional shoplifter, what would you like to steal? For real."

I think for a while. "Maybe a phone card."

"Who do you have to call?"

I pause. "Maybe my dad. Just to hear his voice or something dumb like that."

Klon shifts positions and opens his eyes. "I'd call Ma. I'd tell her it's not the demons," he says. "Tourette's."

"I'll call her with my phone card, then," I say. "We can call her first."

Klon half smiles, then drifts off to sleep.

"Let's practice vowels." Nicole takes out the notebook. "Write bigger, okay?"

"You could've told me that before."

She shrugs. "Never let on to your weaknesses. Mob rule."

"Are there any others, besides the whole code thing?" I ask.

"Never lie," she says.

Figures there'd be some "thou shalt not lie" mob rule. I think of the stupid Yerington postmarks and pray those glasses won't work for her. We've got to find Aunt Sarah before Nicole figures it out.

"Hey, are you listening or not?" Nicole says.

"Yeah. Sorry. Just daydreaming a bit." I wonder if I can find a way to break those glasses tonight, just in case the prescription is close. Just in case she can read those tiny letters. "But isn't the mob, um, kind of over?" I finally ask.

Nicole laughs. She sounds sad. "Well, they're still around. But it's not the same."

I look around the alley and see black forms trying to keep warm. Home seems a million miles away. An impossible dream. I pull out a pencil stub and start to write in her notebook.

We practice letters, words, phonics. Nicole scribbles in her notebook writing sentences. It's almost dawn. We haven't slept all night, and the fire in my throat has spread all over my body again. Even my hair hurts.

"Do you think we can sleep a few minutes—just a few?" The night sky has turned lavender. We have another hour before sunrise.

"Good idea. I'm so tired," Nicole says. We lean against each other.

When I close my eyes, my lids burn against the pupils.

"Hearing your dad's voice isn't dumb, you know. He's

family," Nicole says just as I'm about asleep. "That counts for something," she says.

Klondike half opens his eyes. "You and Cappy—you're a good family." He smiles, croaks, and drifts back to sleep.

Tears itch my eyes.

CHAPTER THIRTY-SIX

"Clear out!" The voice booms in the alleyway.

Startled, I try to jump up but can't move. It feels like my entire body has turned into a Popsicle. My teeth chatter.

"This isn't a hotel. You need to clear out before we haul all of you off to the shelter!" The man speaks into a megaphone. The alley comes to life with people shuffling out of their boxes.

Klondike yawns and leans on me. "I'm too tired. Tits. Asswipe."

Nicole stands. "I feel like shit."

Three police officers walk up and down the alley, hitting wooden batons on their gloved palms. A woman officer comes up to us. She taps me on the shoulder. "You're new around here," she says.

I nod.

She looks at the three of us. "Your friend doesn't look so good there." She motions to Klondike. "He sick?"

Klondike's body tenses up. He twitches and lets out a massive croak.

The officer stares at the three of us for a while. "He looks awfully young. I think we should—" she's saying when the guy with the megaphone shouts, "It's in here. Jesus Christ, Lord Almighty."

She hands me a flyer for the Path of Light Home for Women and Children. "It's a shelter near the university. Much better than the streets, kid. Bring your friends." Then she follows the policemen into the warehouse.

"Looks like—" I can see the light of the officers' flashlight beams in the building. "Oh, man. It's Limp," somebody shouts, his voice muffled by the boarded-up windows.

"How many days?"

"From the smell of it, a while," he says.

With the cops distracted by Limp's dead body, the alleyway clears out. "What about our stuff?" I ask Nicole. She hid our backpacks next to Limp yesterday.

342

"You got your box?"

I nod.

"I got my map and stuff."

"Okay."

"Fuck the other stuff."

"We can't."

"Well, we can't very well walk in there and say, 'Oh. Excuse me. Could you pass me my backpack?'" Nicole helps Klondike up. "What's so important, anyway? All you ever do is collect trash in that stupid pack. We're already wearing all the clothes we have."

I swallow. It's like giving up on the last piece of something that makes us different from other kids on the streets. Without our packs we're just homeless teens—not teens on a trip somewhere.

"Christ, Jeopardy. What's so important that you left in there?"

"What about the dolls? The worry dolls and money?" We have a reason to get the packs.

Nicole pulls them out of her pocket. "I'm not a moron. I wouldn't leave money in there." Nicole stares at me stone-faced. She's about to say something—I imagine related to some mobster who got killed wearing an REI pack—when the same police officer pokes her head out of the building.

"You three, why don't you stick around for a couple of minutes, okay?" She points to Klondike. "How old are you, kid?"

Klondike grips my jacket. "No," he says. "No. I can't go back," he says, then coughs. Then he clears his throat again, and a massive clump of green phlegm comes up.

"Klon, it's cool. You're with us." Nicole squeezes his shoulder. "Nice loogie." She laughs. "Let's go." She leans into me. "We've gotta get away from the cops."

"Klon," I say, "are you feeling okay? Maybe we could go by the shelter. Just for a day or so. Or a clinic. There's got to be a free clinic around here. Just so you can get something to feel better."

He shakes his head and croaks. "I won't go. Please no. Fuckit. Not with them. Tallywhacker, asswipe, tallywhacker. People don't like deformed kids. People hate me when they see me. I want to be with you and Cappy. Please. Please. Tallywhacker." He taps my shoulder and squeezes his eyes shut, his body shuddering with the wave of tics.

I look at Nicole.

She pulls me aside. "You know what happens if we take him to a hospital? They call social services. Social services shows up and assigns him a caseworker who has about two hundred other kids filed away in a ratty briefcase. This caseworker finds a home willing to take the social reject—a scarred kid—saying she'll be checking up to make sure everything's okay. Well, her weekly visits turn into every two weeks, then monthly, then every other month because she has a hundred and ninety-nine other kids in shitty homes she has to visit. And before long, his file that was once shiny and new and on the top of this caseworker's to-do list is shuffled to the bottom of that ratty briefcase, and he's forgotten. And his foster parents are happy because they get that fat monthly government check and treat him like shit because of a scar and some tics." Nicole exhales and sighs.

I don't know where she gets the energy or the air for those kinds of speeches. I shake my head. "He's so sick," I say.

"We'll get him something. Okay? We'll go to a drugstore and get something. We can do it."

But I can't. I haven't been able to. And if Klon's health depends on me reading symptom labels and then shoplifting the right medication . . . I feel my stomach tighten and the familiar burn shooting acids everywhere. The ache is a constant now. And I think I'm used to it—being hungry, tired, cold, sick. But every part of me wants this all to end. I look at the brochure the police officer gave me and tuck it into my jeans pocket. I don't know how much longer it'll take to find Aunt Sarah. And I don't know if we'll live long enough to do it, the way things are going.

Klon's face is gaunt and pale. Dark circles ring his winter-green eyes. He tugs on my jacket constantly with one hand and covers his coughs with the other. "I'm fine," he says. "Just a cough. Fuckit. Cough."

I squeeze his hand, and the three of us leave the alley before the police come back out. Plus I really don't want to see Limp's body. We walk behind three others who have spent the night in the alley. One of them drops a scarf. Nicole picks it up and says, "You dropped this."

The three of them turn around, and one snatches it out of Nicole's hand.

"Geez," Nicole says. "Just trying to help." She has that tough Kids Place attitude. Cappy's gone. Nicole's back.

"Don't," one girl says, and tucks it into her coat.

346

"Don't be rude, ladies. Let's introduce ourselves. This is Mario and she's Baghdad." Mario is the one who dropped the scarf. "And I"—he bows—"am Charity, Boise's queen of the night."

Charity is as dark as charcoal. He has long curly hair and wears red stiletto-heeled boots. Mario looks like she's Klondike's age. She fidgets and twirls matted greasy hair around her thumb. The right side of Baghdad's face looks like a patchwork quilt of skin sewn together. Her eye is fused shut.

Nicole introduces us. "This is Klondike, Jeopardy, and I'm Capone."

Charity bats his fake lashes. "As in Al? Trying for the mobster thing?"

Put it that way, it does sound kind of lame. But I've gotten used to Nicole being Cappy.

"Give it out for free, Charity?" Nicole snaps.

I elbow Nicole.

"Don't worry, honey." Charity keeps up with us at a fast clip, his heels tapping on the asphalt. He primps his hair. "My merchandise ain't free. Quality, baby. One-hundred-percent royal lovin' has its price."

"Don't those shoes, um, hurt?" I ask. I look down at my

torn-up sneakers and don't feel so bad anymore.

"My trick left me high and dry last night, so I had no way to get home and change," Charity says.

"You have a home?"

"Baby, the streets are my home." Charity flashes a crooked smile. Three front teeth are chipped. "But I have a place where I keep my stuff," he whispers. "I can show you." He winks.

"I'm okay," I say. I stare at his shoes.

Klondike croaks and says, "Asswipe."

Nicole pinches his arm. "He doesn't mean it. He's, um, twitchy."

Charity's eyes narrow. When Klondike croaks again and taps Charity on the arm, Charity relaxes. "There was a kid like you around here for a while—he had some funky thing going on. Remember Cuss?" he says to Mario and Baghdad.

Mario nods. "Yeah."

Baghdad shrugs.

"Anyway, he went over about as well as a queer in Texas. You don't look like a bad kid. Just watch out who you call names around these parts. Right, Baghdad?"

Baghdad shoves her hands in her jeans pockets. Her clothes dangle on her like she's a wire hanger.

Charity smirks. "She hasn't talked since I met her. One

348

of these days I know she's just gonna come down with a nasty case of verbal diarrhea and tell us all what's up. Right, honey?"

Baghdad looks down the road.

Klondike shrugs. "I can't—fuckit—help it. It just comes out, you know. I don't mean it—asswipes, tallywhacker." Klondike blows on his fingers and blinks. "Sorry."

I stare at Charity head to toe—especially at the bright red boots. They are raincoat plastic and come up midthigh. He wears stockings, really tight shorts, and a red fishnet shirt under a jean jacket. He has to have been freezing last night.

"Darling, have you ever met a queen before?" Charity asks.

I shake my head. "Actually, no."

"Well, baby, I don't bite. Unless you pay me to." He grins that chipped-tooth grin. "But it's not polite to stare, okay?"

"Oh. Sorry."

We get to one of Boise's main streets. Traffic streams from both ways. Tires spray black water, splashing through the melted snow. "We're going to Rhodes if you want to come," Charity says.

"Rhodes?" I ask.

"The place to be if you need to hook up with something, someone. Or just be."

"We're fine," Nicole says.

Mario mutters, "I can't believe Limp didn't go to the Garden. That's where he should've gone."

Baghdad looks like she has a tear in her eye. She nods.

"Oh, that's total mumbo jumbo," Charity says. "All that voodoo just creeps me out. Limp is just fine where he died."

Mario shoves her hands deep into her pockets and says, "He should've gone to the Garden."

"What's the Garden?" I ask.

Mario looks at me. "That's where we go to die."

"Who's we?" I ask.

"We," she says. "*Us.*"

I shake my head.

"The urban outdoorsmen and -women. Bums. Homeless. Hobos, whatever you want to call us, okay, Jeopardy?" Charity raises his eyebrow. "And they call you Jeopardy because . . ."

"Anyway, that's where we die. That's the safe place to

do it." Mario is twirling her hair faster now.

"Rubbish," Charity says. He flips his hair. "It's like when people tell you a body new to sex rejects sperm, because darlings, we all know that no body would reject this package of power. Complete rubbish."

Mario glares. "Could you cut that weird talk? And it's not bullshit. It's true. The Garden is safe. It's a guarantee."

"For what?" Nicole asks.

"Heaven," Mario says. "No matter what you've done."

Baghdad nods.

Charity sighs. "Or maybe no matter who." Charity and the others walk on. Charity turns back. "You sure you three aren't comin'? Rhodes is where *everyone* goes when the alley's been raided."

"Maybe later. Thanks," Nicole says.

Charity looks at us. "Your friend here's looking a little green." He motions to Klondike. "Sometimes the Mennonite Fellowship on Twelfth Street gives out soup."

"What's that?" Nicole asks.

"You know. Banjos, tambourines, 'Praise the Lord' shit. It's soup." Charity smiles his sloppy red lipstick smile.

"Which way?" I ask. Soup sounds too good to be true.

"About twenty blocks past Rhodes. We can walk together." We follow them for a couple of hours. Then Charity points. "Go that way. Twelfth Street. You can't miss it."

Soup. All I want is soup. I feel like I could walk ten hours to get it.

CHAPTER THIRTY-SEVEN

"We better try to get out of Boise today, okay?" Nicole says. We're sitting on a park bench staring at a lake. I'm sure if it weren't for the fact that I feel like Klon's road kill semirevived, I'd actually think it was pretty. "So where to, Jeops?"

I don't know where to go to find Sarah Jones in the U.S.

"C'mon, Jeops. Think about the letters. There's gotta be something."

I pull out the box and go through the letters one by one, looking for any return address label. I empty the box and run my fingers along the sides and bottom. Under the lip, stuck to the side, I feel something, and pull up the lip. Stuck to it is a return address label. Everything's faded, though. "Hand me your glasses."

She gives them to me, and I look through them, trying to make out the letters—anything. A tear drips down my nose onto the box. Nicole pulls it away. "C'mon, Jeops. We'll feel better after we eat. Don't smudge our only next clue."

My stomach growls. After another forty minutes of walking, we finally find the church. And they're out of soup. The guy says there's another soup kitchen—across town.

"Where?" I ask.

"You know. Near the Basque museum. It's a nice museum, too," he says.

Nicole glares at him. "You've been inhaling too much incense. A museum?"

"A little culture," he says, and mumbles something else under his breath.

I refrain from mentioning we've got all the culture we need on our bodies. Ugh.

I take out the tourist map we got at some office while wandering around. I think that maybe pre–running away I should've probably come up with a learn-to-read-maps procedure. I find the Basque museum. It looks far.

"Where are we?" Nicole asks, looking at the map.

I shrug. "Around here. I'm pretty sure. But I think we should try to get to a library before leaving Boise. Maybe we'll get more clues." I look around. The neighborhoods have started to blend together.

"And muffins," says Klondike.

"So which way do we go to find a library?" Nicole asks.

"I think this way," I say. And we walk. We have nothing else to do. We can't just sit and freeze on the streets. Water from puddles sloshes up the holes in my shoes. At first I tried to dodge the puddles. But we're in Boise—the puddle capital of the United States or something. I look at the tourist map. It says, "City of Trees."

I look around. There are definitely more puddles.

We sit in a forgotten park surrounded by run-down brick houses. A big change from the manicured lawns and pretty homes we just walked by. Tufts of crabgrass poke through loose gravel. A rusty swing set teeters in the wind. I stare at the map. "I don't know if I've been looking at it right."

I hand the map to Nicole. "Well don't ask me," she says. "I sure as hell can't read it." She squints, crumples it up, and throws it in the snow.

I pick it up and wipe off the damp dirt. "What'd you do that for?" I ask.

"What good's a map if you can't read it?" she asks.

"I don't know," I say. "I just thought—"

Klondike has leaned back and fallen asleep in the gravel.

"He doesn't look too good," I say. I pat my pocket with information about the shelter. Just one night, I think. Maybe we can go for one night.

"Maybe," Nicole says. "Maybe we should hole up a day or two. Let him rest."

"Yeah." I nod. "We can go to that Path of Light Home."

"No way. We'll find Rhodes, get some meds. We'll be just fine without a bunch of Jesus freaks giving us a place to sleep."

"Well we spent the afternoon looking for soup from Jesus freaks. What's the difference?" I ask.

"Soup is soup. Shelter is obligation and getting reported to social services, and going back to where we started. You want that?"

Yes. I think. Suddenly Don and Cherry don't seem so awful. I can't imagine foster care being worse than this. Ever. Maybe I can look for Aunt Sarah from Don and Cherry's house. A phone. Internet . . . probably should've thought of that before all this.

"Klon." Nicole jerks him awake. "Wake up. Come lie

down here." She leads him to one of those cement tubes. I didn't think they were allowed in parks anymore—safety regulations and all. I clean out the spiderwebs and leaves from the bottom of the cement tunnel and help Klon scoot in.

Nicole pulls off her last sweatshirt and hands it to him. We both keep our coats. We need them. "Put that on," I say, "under your coat."

"Let's find Rhodes—where the others hang out. We'll be safer with others," Nicole says.

I haven't come up with a hypothesis. I feel like a hack scientist. We're just reacting now. There's no method to what we're doing. It's all basic. Instinct. And it's not working.

"We're in Boise, Cappy. How bad can it get?" I ask. It wasn't like Boise was on the U.S. top dangerous city lists.

"We could be in—where is Dorothy from?"

"Kansas."

"Exactly. Anywhere is bad at night. People are bad," Nicole says. "Or did you miss out on that 'don't talk to strangers' lecture in grade school? It's safer in numbers. Trust me. Plus the kids at Rhodes will have information we need."

"Like what?" I ask. I hardly think any of them are

357

pediatric pulmonary specialists. "And what about Klon? We can't just leave him." I look over, and he has already fallen back to sleep. I touch his head and his face is burning.

"He's too tired to come with us. He'll be better off here, sleeping. We'll get some medicine, okay? And we'll find Rhodes and the others. When we do, we'll come back for him. Then we'll use the worry doll money to go back to Rhodes in a bus." She holds the worry dolls in her hand.

"What makes you think we can even find Rhodes? It took us almost an hour to find a church that already ran out of soup."

"We've already walked by Rhodes. We just have to go where Charity, Baghdad, and Mario went—when we split up."

"And you remember where that was?" I ask. It feels like it was years ago. I wonder if runaway time is warped—just endless minutes.

"Pretty much. As long as we stay to these same streets, I think we'll be okay."

"Okay," I say. We shake Klon back awake. "We're going to find somewhere to stay, Klon. And get you some medicine." I hand him the box. "Don't croak if anyone comes by here, okay?"

Klondike nods, twitches, and lets out a massive croak. "Promise you'll come back?"

"We promise. We stick together," Nicole says.

He clutches my jacket between his fingers. "You promise you'll come back?" he asks again.

"We'll be back." I pry his fingers loose. "We'll find food and medicine." I hold my hand to his forehead. Every time he coughs, a little bit of blood comes up with phlegm. "Don't move. We'll come back for you."

"I won't—asswipes. Don't be long." He blows on his fingers and curls up in the cement tube. I wish we had more to keep him warm, but there was nothing else.

"Klon?"

He looks up at me.

"If people come around—" I look around.

Nicole points. "There. There are some trees over there. If you have to move or go pee or something, you do it there. But don't go far."

"Come back," Klon says. "I don't want to be alone."

"We'll be back before you wake up," I say. "I promise."

Klon nods and closes his eyes. Asleep already.

"Ready?" I turn to Nicole.

"You know where we are?" Nicole peers over my shoulder.

I look at the map of Boise again. "Yeah. Here."

"You don't sound so sure."

"I'm almost sure."

"Okay. Let's find Rhodes and get something for Klon."

CHAPTER THIRTY-EIGHT

"**P**ay attention to the area. So we know how to get back easy." I tuck the map into my inside coat pocket.

"I am."

"Look for markers, you know? And I'll look at the street names."

"Okay."

"God, I wish I was a homing pigeon."

Nicole stares at me. "Of all the things you could be in the world right now and you want to be a fucking pigeon. I can't wait to hear this one, Jeops."

I just need something to make sense right now. Everything's spiraled out of control, but homing pigeons—they make sense. So I talk. "You know, they've been used to send messages from the time of Genghis Kahn. They're the most reliable messengers in the world—pre–World Wide Web, of course. Scientists think that they either use the earth's magnetic field for orientation or spatial distribution and atmospheric odors. How cool is that? It would be like us being able to find our way back to Klon just by sniffing."

Nicole inhales. She turns and looks. "Yep. It smells like cheap hot dogs."

I look at the Hollywood Market. "Good marker. Remember that. The Hollywood Market. Irene Street."

Nicole smiles. "I'll just remember the smell." She coughs and says, "We'll find our way back. Don't worry. Let's get to a pharmacy before we hit Rhodes."

We walk through Boise's side streets and residential areas. Things start to get more commercial, and we finally find a drugstore. Nicole says, "Can you do this?"

I nod. "Let's come up with the procedure," I say.

"Are you for real?" she asks.

"Just humor me," I say, then go through the procedure out loud, step by step.

Purpose: Steal medicine for Klondike

Hypothesis: If we can steal the right medicine for Klondike, he'll get well.

Materials: Nicole's fast hands, our bulky coats, me as decoy

Procedure:

1) I'll go into the drugstore first.

2) Nicole will follow when another group of people come in, so it looks like she's with them.

3) I'll walk around the store, without stopping, until I get to the cold medicine.

4) I'll pause in front of the cold medicine Nicole needs to steal for thirty seconds.

5) I'll go to the candy aisle, near the front of the store and look suspicious, keeping all workers' eyes on me.

6) Nicole will steal the medicine.

7) Nicole will leave the store.

"But how will you get past the sensors?" I ask. "The alarms will go off."

"I've got it covered, Jeops. I'll take care of it."

"But how? For the procedure?"

"Why don't we do a more detailed write-up later? It's getting cold. I'll get by."

"Okay," I say, and continue.

8) I will leave the store a few minutes after Nicole.

Variables: Time: This has to be fast, efficient. No do-overs today. Me: I can't chicken out. I can't get all weirded out. I need to be strong. Nicole: How fast will she be able to steal? Security cameras: Are there lots? Will they have us on tape? Will they look for us?

"Are we going to be doing this procedure-thing all afternoon?" Nicole yawns.

"Okay. Okay. Last step." There are way too many variables to even begin to fathom.

Constant: Klon's sickness

"Ready?" Nicole asks.

I nod. My hands feel sweaty and face feels flushed. I walk around the store picking things up then putting them on the shelves. It's not hard for me to look suspicious. I don't even have to try.

One worker asks me if I need help, then starts to price things everywhere I go. I hear the bells on the door jingle and some voices but keep my head down. I walk around the aisles then stop right in front of the cold medicine. I pause for thirty seconds, counting one-Mississippi, two-Mississippi . . . until I feel like my head will burst. Then I work my way toward the door near the candy, not wanting to be in the back of the store when Nicole leaves. I just want to get out of here.

Nicole leafs through some magazines, passes through the cold medicine aisle, pausing just for a minute, then heads for the door. Just as she's about to leave, another lady comes rushing in and slams into Nicole. Nicole falls back, and a bag of cough drops and a box of pills spill from her jacket.

The man behind the counter rushes toward her, "You little snot-nosed wretched good-for-nothing shit! I'm going to call the police."

Nicole jumps to her feet. "Run!" she shouts.

I run, but the man behind the counter grabs onto my shoulders. I wiggle out of the coat and follow Nicole. We zigzag in and out of traffic, running into some Basque restaurant mecca. After twenty minutes, we stop, gasping for breath.

"Fuck," Nicole says. She searches through her pockets and pulls out dental floss. "This is all I got."

"Dental floss? I'm to the sander stage to get this shit off my teeth." I shrug. "It's okay. It's something." I sit down on the curb, rubbing my arms. I can almost feel the sweat freezing to my back. I cradle my head between my knees to try to stop the pounding.

"You okay?" she asks.

"Yeah." I lift my head up slowly, my teeth chattering. "Just feeling a little funky. Sorry I wasn't much help."

Nicole shrugs. "You looked guilty the second you walked in the store. That helped a lot. If it wasn't for that cow who ran into me, we'd have been okay." Nicole sits next to me. "That sucks about your coat. Goddamn. We left with less than we came in with." Nicole looks around. "Where are we?"

"Oh no," I say.

"What?"

"The map. It's in my coat."

Nicole stands up. "Shit. Who needs a map? It's not like you know how to read it anyway. We'll find our way back."

I nod. "What about Rhodes?"

"What time do you think it is?"

I shrug. "Two thirty? Three o'clock, maybe." The sun is still high in the sky—a yellow glow behind gray clouds.

"We'll find out where Rhodes is and get back to Klon."

"You think you can find it?" I ask. "You know I can't."

"No big deal," she says.

"No big deal," I mutter. But I have a sick feeling in my stomach.

We begin walking toward what we think is the way back to Klondike, just to get oriented. "Theme of the day," I say, biting on my lip, trying to keep my mind from my knotted stomach and shivers.

"Shouldn't we wait for Klon?" Nicole asks.

I shrug. "We can redo it and pretend we haven't done it. I just feel pretty crappy right now and could use the distraction."

"Whatcha got?"

"Sore throat. Fever," I say. "Same as we all have, I guess. Now everything sounds like I'm underwater, though." I jiggle my ears.

"Yeah." Nicole puffs on her fingers. "Let's share the coat, okay? I'll wear it for twenty minutes, then you do. Back and forth."

"Okay. Thanks."

"Okay. Theme of the day: your pick," Nicole says.

"I think it's your turn." I'm just counting the minutes until it's my turn to wear the coat.

"Well, I can't think of one, so just pick one."

"Okay. Um. Favorite person," I say.

Nicole blows her nose commando style. Gross but efficient. She looks at me. "You want me to teach you that, too?"

I looked at the snot drying on my arm. I flick off the dried flakes and they pull on my hairs. One of the perks of a runaway isn't Kleenex. "Yeah. I wouldn't mind."

She laughs. "You're okay, you know."

"Just okay?"

"Okay's a lot better than I think of most people."

"Fair enough." I clear my throat, pinch one side of my nose and blow. Snot covers my cheeks and drips down my chin.

"Nice, Jeopardy." Nicole giggles. "You might want to try to do it downwind next time."

"I'll consider that lesson number one."

Nicole says, "*That* you can practice. You've gotten better about the shoplifting stuff."

I nod. "Your reading's better."

"It is," Nicole agrees. "So I'll read street signs, okay? Reading lesson of the day."

"Okay," I say, hoping it's my turn to wear the coat. "So. Who's your favorite person?"

Nicole pauses. She looks at me and takes off the coat and hands it to me. "Holy fuck it's cold. No wonder your lips are blue. Shit."

"Thank you." I sigh when it's on. "Here." I unzip it and hold it open. "Maybe we can just put it over our shoulders."

"People will think we're total lesbos, you know."

I shrug. "I'm just cold." I haven't cared about what anybody thinks about me for so long now. It's just survival, I guess. You can't be too worried about public opinion on an empty stomach.

Nicole laughs. "Okay. Favorite person." She and I walk close together. "I have a couple."

"Really? Who?"

"I really dig Klon, you know? He's a quirky little shit."

"Me, too," I say, and laugh. "I especially like his croaks." I wait for her to say more. "And? Who's the other?"

"Hey, you're not fishing for a BFf necklace, are you?" Nicole laughs.

"Nah. Way cliché."

"This is okay, you know? You, me, Klon. It's a good road trip."

"It's definitely more memorable than having a cooler

of Cokes and snacks."

"Definitely," Nicole says. "And you?" she asks. "Who're your favorite people?"

I rub my throat and think. It's not dad. Klon's one for sure. I look at Nicole and sigh. It's a weird world when your favorite person ends up being the most irritating human being on the face of the planet.

Nicole smirks. "You don't hafta say what's already obvious. I'm your BFf!" She laughs and says it in a mocking tone.

I shrug. "It was inevitable. You've grown on me. Like fungus."

Nicole smiles. "Any particular kind?"

I shake my head.

"You'll find your aunt, you know. That'll be cool," Nicole says. "Real cool."

I nod. I haven't even thought about Aunt Sarah all day. Weird. Like my entire purpose has gone away and I'm just living day by day.

Ad hoc.

I finally say. "You know, we should get Klon a present. Have a birthday party for him. Today. When we get back. A big surprise. That'll make him feel better."

Nicole pulls on the coat, leaving my left side exposed. I tug back. "Keep it in the middle."

"Fuck, it's cold."

I hand the coat to her. "Let's switch back and forth. It's too hard to walk this way. Plus you reek."

"Yeah, and you smell like Bath and Body."

I look around. "What about the party?"

"I like it. We'll give him his first present."

"Maybe we can get him a cupcake or something."

"No. Marshmallows," Nicole says.

"Oh yeah!" I say. "Maybe we can roast them for real."

"Cool. Should I just steal them?"

"Doesn't mean the same, you know? Buying it with our money"—I motion to her pocket—"means a lot more."

"Good point," Nicole says, "but we can't spend more than two dollars. That'll leave us eight for bus rides and shit."

It's fun to think about Klon's birthday party—his first birthday present. A good distraction. We talk about all the ways to try to make it as special as possible. We find an AM/PM and go up and down the aisles, trying to decide. Finally, we pick a package of marshmallows and piece of Bazooka gum. It feels good to buy something.

We walk. It's like time passes, but we're in this weird warp where we don't even notice until the sun lowers. Nicole passes me the coat. "Look," I say.

"So?" says Nicole.

"Look inside."

Nicole looks in the window. "Oh shit."

"Same drugstore we tried to rob. We've gone in a complete circle," I say. "We're lost." I turn around and look down the street. God, I suck at directions. "Let's get out of here before he sees us." We hurry down the street.

"How long have we been walking?" Nicole asks.

I look up at the sky—the same gray sky we've been walking under all day long. "Two hours? More? I'm not sure." That warped-time thing again.

"Shit. We've gotta get to Klon."

"I know." I felt tears prick my eyes thinking of him huddled in some cement tube. Waiting for us.

Nothing has gone as planned. This isn't supposed to be so hard. I hate those people who say it's not the destination, it's the journey.

Screw the journey. The journey sucks.

A couple of police officers cruise the street. "Let's go ask them. We need to get back."

Nicole grabs my arm. "Are you stupid? We just robbed the drugstore down the street. We're obviously homeless. We can't just go up to a couple of Barney Fifes and say, 'Excuse us, could you happen to point us to where the twitchy kid is hiding so they won't take him away? He's real sick.' Jesus, Jeopardy, don't you get it? Don't you get who we are now?"

"I don't care anymore. We can't just walk around knowing Klon is alone. I'll go. I'll ask. You don't have to."

"What about Emerald City? What about Auntie Em? What about home? Do you think you'll find that in the system? Or Klon? It's like you have no idea."

"No idea about what?" I ask, walking toward the police.

Nicole grabs my arm. "You have no idea what they do to you. None."

I shake her hand off my arm and walk toward the police car.

Nicole turns around and pulls up her coat. "Look."

I turn back. "Pull your shirt down. Geez, Nicole, stop it. What are you doing?"

"Look," she says. Her back has the mark of a fire poker. "That was my mom's third boyfriend. He was her PO—the one who was supposed to keep us safe. So when he beat my sister to death, who was I supposed to call? Nine-one-one? The police were already there." Her lip trembles. "And social services are the ones who choose our foster homes—to keep us safe from our mom and her pervy asshole boyfriends." She shakes her head. "Never again."

"What about the nice people? The ones you stole from? What about the ones who are good to kids? The ones who went to Africa to help out? They're out there," I say.

"It's not your decision to turn Klon in. It's his. If you want to go, that's your deal. But Klon doesn't want that. When he does, then it's his choice, okay?" Nicole rubs her arms. I pass her the coat back. "I'll find Klon on my own. Death is better than going back there, okay?" Nicole says.

"How can you know that, though? How can you know dying is better? We can't know that," I say. "I'm sorry. I'm sorry for what happened to you, but Klon deserves to have a chance."

"Then we have to ask him," Nicole says.

"How can we do that when we can't even find him?" I'm close to tears. Everything is wrong. I can't reason with her, but she makes sense. In her own way.

"We'll find him," she says.

"And if we don't."

"Wait until dark."

"And then?" I ask.

"If we don't find him before it's totally dark, we go to the cops. Okay?"

"Promise?" I say holding out my hand.

"I'm not going to fuckin' pinky promise you. My word is my word. Okay?"

"Okay," I say.

The cops turn and look at us. One talks into a hand radio.

Nicole and I set off, walking as fast as we can. "Remember the Hollywood Market?"

"Yeah. The hot dogs."

"We can find that. It was on Irene Street."

We look up at the street sign. Brumback Street. "Um, do you remember a cross street?" I ask.

She shakes her head.

"Okay. We can't be far," I say. "All of this looks kind of familiar."

And we walk.

The sun slips below the horizon, leaving a purple sky to blanket us in cold. Every part of my body aches. I can't even swallow because of the burning pain in my throat.

We walk. Night creeps toward us. Nothing looks familiar. We ask for directions but nobody stops to help us. People just wrap their coats around them and clutch their purses to their chests. We walk in and out of shadows, trying to keep to the streetlights.

We find Twelfth Street and walk up the street, passing Ridenbaugh, Lemp, getting stuck on Heron as it runs into a park.

"The street ends here," Nicole says. "And this park doesn't look familiar. I don't get where we're going wrong."

I stare at the street signs. "Oh God." That knot returns to my stomach and tightens inside me. Panic washes over me, and I turn to Nicole. "We can't find him."

CHAPTER THIRTY-NINE

We follow the park until Thirteenth Street, then follow its edge. "Heron, Hazel, Bella—it's gotta be close," I say.

"Fuck," Nicole mutters. "Fuck. Fuck. Fuck. Fuck." She pulls out the worry dolls. "Help us find Klondike. Please. Help us," she whispers, and hands me one. "Your turn."

I count my breaths, in and out, in and out, feeling my lungs work and throat burn. My head feels light. "I have to stop. Just a second." I sit on a curb, slump over, and breathe some more.

We find Irene Street, but nothing looks familiar, so we walk to Harrison Boulevard and find a convenience store. We go in to ask for directions and the guy hollers, "You keep my business away. Out. Now. I don't wanna see nothing of you and your stupid friend."

"We're just looking for a park," I say.

"We're in Boise. The whole fuckin' town is a park. Out! Now!"

We leave the store. Somebody left a half-drunk cup of coffee on the corner. We share, slurping down the liquid, cupping the Styrofoam in our hands. Its aromatic vapors disappear, and we're left with brown sludge at the bottom of the cup.

Nicole nudges me. "Ask the worry dolls for something."

I hold one in my hand. "Please," I whisper. "Help."

"That it?" Nicole slurps her coffee. "I think they need you to be a little more specific than that."

I'm so tired. It's like in those dreams when you're running away but you can't move. All I can think of is getting to Klon, but my whole body feels like it's shutting down. I rub my eyes.

And it's supposed to be his birthday. But I don't even know the date.

Some birthday.

Flakes of snow spit down on us from the gray sky. I don't feel the cold anymore at all.

"We have to go." I try to stand. "Just one more minute," I say. I don't even realize I'm trembling until I look at my hands, blue nail beds, shaking to hold the worry dolls still. "Breathe," I say. "In and out. In and out." It feels like someone has wrapped his hand around my throat and constricted, making me work for every last breath.

"Christ, you're not in labor." Nicole scratches her arms. "Jesus, how could we have blown this? He's counting on us."

I stand up and throw the cup into a dented trashcan. "Let's go. It's dark, and we have to get to him. I don't know how many blocks it'll take to get to him. I don't know—" I cough and hold my throat.

We pull ourselves up and half jog down Irene Street until we see some familiar buildings. We're getting closer, I can feel it. I recognize things. Then we see the Hollywood Market. We run into a group of teenagers standing on a corner just outside. The streetlight is almost totally burned out, a yellow glow hugging them. I can see the glow of a cigarette being passed around. The sun is gone and the moon rises.

We approach them. I clear my throat. "We're, um, looking for a park. Near here. Can you help us?"

One girl looks up—honey-colored eyes with long, long lashes. She turns back to the group she's with. Nobody says anything.

"Please," I say. "We're looking for someone. We, um, lost someone. And need help. Please."

"Depends on who you are and who you're looking for," the girl says. She takes a long drag and holds in the smoke, then releases it, billowing, into the air. I almost choke on it.

"Jesus, Bambi," one guys complains. "You're sucking like a vacuum. It's supposed to be for all of us. Take it easy."

They turn away from us. Bambi smiles over the haze of pot.

"C'mon. They don't know shit." Nicole tugs on my arm and tries to pull me away.

I watch as the last of their marijuana gets smoked. Light comes from the trickle of cars that drive down the street—yellow headlights reflect off newly sided homes. When we turn to go, Bambi says, "Word is there's a corpsicle on the streets."

"Corpsicle?" I ask.

Bambi rolls her eyes. "Yeah. A frozen kid. Out in the ball park."

"He's not anywhere near a baseball field," Nicole says. I feel a wave of relief.

Bambi flicks a cigarette on the street. "Fucking morons. Ball park is where everybody goes to get laid. Behind some old historic buildings nobody's bothered to repair yet." She points. "Follow this road ten or twelve blocks, then turn left. You can't miss it."

"No," I whisper. The acid from my stomach burns my esophagus, nose, and mouth.

Nicole grabs my arm. "Get it together. We need to go."

The moon rises higher, and the night is a little brighter. We stumble down the street—a street that looks like every other street. We turn and see the spare park— the swing set looks like some kind of rusty relic—the cement tube a black shadow in the moonlight. "That's it," I whisper. "Klondike!" I try to shout, my voice nothing but a raspy whisper.

He doesn't respond.

"Klondike!" Nicole hollers. We run to the park and look in the cement tube, but he isn't there.

Please, I think. Please have been picked up by police. Or somebody. Please.

We rush into the trees following Klondike's path in the bright snow.

Klondike sits, leaning against a tree, gripping my box in his cold hands, green eyes staring straight ahead.

CHAPTER FORTY

"Klon?" Nicole bends down beside him. "Klon. Wake up."

My throat tightens. "Klondike?"

Moonlight filters through bare branches lighting Klondike's face—the smooth side. The creek bubbles downstream, a thin layer of ice on the top. I rub my chapped hands together.

"He's not moving." Nicole shakes Klondike's shoulders. "Klon. Please wake up."

I lean in and put my ear to his lips. Nothing. "Klon?" My stomach knots. "Klon, are you okay?" I ask.

Nicole shakes him harder. "Please, please wake up. Please," she says.

I move my hand to his wrist. Icy. No pulse. I try to lay

him down, but his body is stiff and I can't put him down straight. I finally get him into a position where I can do CPR. I pull off his coat and push hard on his chest. But when I do compressions, I feel the snap of his brittle ribs under my palms. "Oh God," I say. "Oh God."

I breathe into his mouth, but nothing happens. He doesn't move. He doesn't breathe. His heart doesn't beat. I can smell feces and urine and gag on the smell of death.

Nicole rocks on her heels. "Oh fuck."

I turn to her. "We could've gotten help. Hours ago. He would've been alive, but— Oh God," I whisper. I hold his hand in mine. "Please, Klon."

We sit huddled next to him, not talking, just listening to the night. I close my eyes and wonder what death feels like. Maybe there won't be any more cold. Maybe Klon's scars will go away. Maybe Nicole is right. Death is better. But then I remember the million-star hotel and the Devil gettin' married.

Nicole throws Klon's coat over my shoulders and I shrug it off.

"Don't be stupid," she says. "He's dead. He doesn't need—" She chokes on her words. I slip the coat back on and am assaulted by his smell. I throw up—the burn coating my stomach and esophagus. I dry heave until my head feels like it will float away.

This is our fault—my fault. I could've gotten help but didn't. And now Klon is dead. We shiver, sitting next to him, waiting for night to go away, hoping to wake up from this. Morning light creeps across the purple sky in streaks of oranges and yellows until splinters of light shine through the trees. I stare at Klon's face. He looks so peaceful. No tics. No twitches.

Bambi and her friends walk by. "Tough break," says Bambi. "That's two stiffs this week with Limp—'scuse the pun."

Nobody laughs.

She has an annoying thing about flicking her nails— her pinky nail especially long. "This one was just plain dumb, though. Somebody told him to come take cover before nightfall, and he refused to move. Just repeated, 'Stay here. Don't move. Stay here,' over and again." Bambi shrugs. "Fucking weirdo if you ask me."

Nicole wipes tears from her eyes. Her hands tremble. I hold on to Klon's hand even tighter.

Bambi tilts her head to the side. "Boo-hoo. So he's expired." Her black eyes are ice cold. "We're all gonna fuckin' die sooner or later. And with that face, it's probably better he did sooner."

Nicole turns to her. "Fuck off," she says. "Who asked you?"

My stomach clenches. "Go away," I say. "This isn't a show. This isn't okay. It's not okay that this happened."

Bambi shrugs. "Fucking saps. Oughta start a greeting card company or something. Shit." The group laughs. But it isn't real laughter. It's just this dead sound that hangs in the morning air.

Nicole turns to me and I look away. I want to blame her for everything, but I can't. I didn't go get help. I knew better. I never had Nicole's life. I have no excuse. But the anger I feel. I can't even look at her because—because Nicole needed me to be strong and I wasn't. I hold my breath, hoping to hear a croak, cough . . . anything. But he doesn't move. I sit next to him and hold his hand in mine. I try to remember a prayer. Any prayer.

Nicole sits on his other side and says, "I don't know if I believe in you. I don't think so. But if you're there like everybody says you are, you better take care of Klon. He didn't deserve this." She swallows. "He's just a kid." She looks up at me expectantly.

"Happy birthday" is all I can think to say. "Yesterday was your birthday."

Nicole takes out the marshmallows and places them on his lap.

"We'll stay with him. Until—" I can't speak through my own tears.

Nicole nods. She understands that he didn't want to be left alone.

We lay Klondike's body in piles of damp leaves. "So he'll be comfortable," Nicole says.

I push his eyelids down, and we crouch behind some trees. Then we wait. Nicole holds Klon's hand. Tears brim in her eyes and spill down her cheeks. "You were all I had left," she says. She cries softly, leaning her head against the tree, its bark biting into her cheek.

What about me? I want to ask. I pull my legs to my chest and lean my head on my knees, trying to keep from breathing his smell.

I'm wearing a dead person's coat.

I want to shout. I want to stomp and pound and stop things. I want everything to be different. I want time travel to be true.

And I want to hate Nicole.

But I can't do any of that. Because all of this is my fault. All of it.

My burning eyes droop shut. I drift in and out of sleep. Nicole and I stay with him all day. We don't talk. No more Mafia stories or science facts.

Klon is dead.

The second night falls and we huddle together. In my dreams, I stare down at Mom's coffin, listening to the frozen earth pound the wood. I shiver and curl into a ball, waiting for the earth to swallow me up.

Sometime late morning, a scream jerks me awake from my fevered dreams. A boy chased a runaway basketball to Klondike.

"They found him," I manage to say through the pain in my throat. "He won't be alone now." I turn to Nicole, but she's gone. Her plastic bag of postcards lies next to Klon's body. I pick it up and hold it to my chest.

She's gone.

CHAPTER
FORTY-ONE

wait, hugging the bag tighter, afraid to go through it.

No heat comes from the sun. A bitter chill settles in.

I wait.

An ambulance arrives. The EMT wears thick gloves and a hat. He takes his hat off for a second and whispers something under his breath, making the sign of the cross, then gently cradles Klon in his arms, laying him on the gurney.

The other EMT, a woman, touches Klon's forehead and sighs, shaking her head.

I feel better knowing they care. Klon isn't just another statistic to them. He's a kid. I want to go to them. Maybe they can help me, give me something for this throat. Maybe they'll help me find Nicole.

But I know they can't. I'll be swept away to some shelter, pumped with medication, and given a bed to sleep in. And I'll sleep. For days. They'll tell me they're looking for Nicole, but they won't find her. Because she's a runaway. She's invisible. And she wants to die. All she's got is me.

They drive away, siren and blinking lights off. No hurry now.

I stare at the pile of leaves where we laid Klon, shaped around where his small body lay. Klon's gone. Nicole's gone.

I finally open Nicole's bag and flip through her notebook. On the last page it says: "Chicago—Yerington; San Francisco—Yer; New York—Yer; Honolulu—Yer; Detroit—Yer. No famly. Lies."

The eyeglasses I stole for her are shattered next to the notebook. Everything in her life has been a lie. And I'm no different from anybody else, because I didn't have the guts to tell her the truth. I didn't have the guts to stand up to her and get help for Klon. I took the easy way out, the path of least resistance.

And now . . .

I hold the postcards and notebook in my trembling hands.

I dump everything on the ground and search through it.

They're gone.

She took Plan B with her—the pills.

No, I shake my head. She wouldn't. She'll be back. She probably went to sell them, get money. We should've sold them long ago. Maybe that's her Plan B, because she has to come back. Rule number three: We stick together. Nicole doesn't break her own rules.

But then mobsters don't lie to one another.

I lied.

I huddle up, clutching Nicole's worry dolls. She took the money. But I have my box. My stupid box of dumb photos and letters of people who are dead—of people who don't matter. I take off the locket and stare at the picture in the gray light. Another whole day has passed.

"There's no place like home," I whisper. But I don't even know what home is.

Tears burn my eyes. Night returns.

Nicole doesn't.

She's gone.

I go through the postcards and notebook again. Something else is missing.

Her stupid Mafia, glory death, ace of spades garbage.

I can't believe I'm irritated. But I am.

And I am alone.

I walk the streets until I find a group of teens. I recognize Bambi. Her eyes are glazed over; she's too high to hold her head up. "I need to find Rhodes," I say.

One points down the street. "Twenty blocks or so."

"How will I know when I get there?" I ask.

"Are you stupid?" he asks.

"No," I say.

"Then you'll know." He ties a dirty rag around his arm, his vein pulsing with pressure. He pulls out a filthy needle and shoves it in the blue, the yellow liquid pumping out. His body jerks, then he smiles. He's gone, too.

I walk the streets—eerily empty. The warm glow of yellow light spills from behind people's curtains. I stop in front of a small brick home with neatly painted green trim, the curtains open. A family sits around a beautifully set table saying grace. A fat turkey lies in the middle of the table—its skin crispy brown.

Happy Thanksgiving.

I stare at them sitting in their fall sweaters, the lovely glow of candles on their faces. A chubby lady wears an apron and passes a big knife to the middle-aged man. The family claps. A rosy-cheeked little girl looks out the window and locks eyes with me. She taps the man sitting next to her, and I leave.

Normal.

That's what normal people do. They sit together around a table on Thanksgiving Day. They eat together. They pray together. They don't spend the holiday in a cheap diner ordering hot turkey sandwiches hoping the latest scam will get them through the holidays. And they definitely don't spend Thanksgiving looking for a friend who's possibly already dead.

Normal people don't let their friends die.

I wonder if Aunt Sarah is normal. Part of me wants to figure out a way to find her. And never turn back.

But I'm done running. I'm done not caring. I'm done with procedures and hypotheses and science. That's what I've done my entire life. I have to make things right. Somehow.

I get to Rhodes before midnight. The scene in front

of me is surreal. Small groups of homeless people huddle together under an overpass. No trees. No grass. Just concrete, asphalt, and chain-link fences. Skateboard paths and jumps. No life.

Boise. Middle America. Benign. Bourgeois. A place where most people would say, "Hey, that's a great place to raise a family." While the normal population sleeps off their turkey overdose, we gather at Rhodes afraid, cold, hungry—alone.

I hate being alone.

I walk through the area, looking for Nicole in the haunted faces, but she isn't there.

"Jeopardy!" I turn and see Charity skipping toward me in a lime-green spandex body suit and platform heels to match. "Jeopardy! We heard."

"Heard what?" I ask. My voice feels so small.

Charity grips my upper arm and pulls me toward him. "Honey, you shouldn't be out here alone. Come with me."

Charity takes me to another abandoned building. But this one seems a lot more organized. He opens the door to an apartment. Hanging blankets divide everything into small compartments. People sleep on soiled mattresses. No matter. People sleep. And I sleep.

I wake up at the first light of day. Cockroaches scurry

across the floor into cracks in the wall, holes in the mattresses, and piles of clothes. One wriggles its way up some guy's shirt. But the guy doesn't move. Nobody does.

Charity snores. His breath smells like a nasty cadaver-putrescence combo. I try to jiggle him awake, but he doesn't even move for another couple of hours. When he finally does, he opens one eye, his false eyelashes sticking to his cheek, and says, "Breakfast?"

I follow him to the kitchen. Filthy dishes are piled in the sink. An old refrigerator hums in the corner—sitting crooked on broken feet. Charity opens it up. I cover my nose and concentrate on holding down anything my stomach might have in it. Charity pulls out a couple slices of cheese. He hands them to me. They're covered with green mold and white fuzz. Then he guides me through the living area until we get to his corner.

Everything smells musty and fishy.

He yawns, wiping the mold off his pieces of cheese before putting them in his mouth. That would explain the halitosis. He looks at me, "Ah, honey. You get used to it." He eyes my cheese.

I hand it over to him and tap my throat. "Too sore," I manage to say.

"Long night. Goddamn religious fanatics. Always

wanting to do freak things." He shrugs. "I'm all for whatever, but they gotta pay, right?"

I nod.

"We heard about the little one," he says. "Sorry. Cool kid—obscene little shit—but okay." He shakes his head. "You looking for your friend?"

I nod.

"Where do you think she went?" he asks.

I clear my throat and try to keep my voice steady. "To die. I need to find that place. The place where we go to die."

Charity shakes his head. "No way, honey. Nohow. I don't do the mass graveyards gig."

I try to control the ache that burns my stomach and pricks at my eyes. Don't cry, I think. She might not be dead. Not yet.

I can't help but picture Mom's empty prescription bottle next to her whiskey. Her languid body looking so peaceful.

But the smell. The smell of death is sickly sweet.

I have to get to Nicole on time. "I thought you didn't believe in that stuff," I finally say. "Please," I whisper.

"You ever been to Hell, baby?" he asks.

I shake my head.

"It's right next to Heaven. Just one wrong step, and 'Bye-bye.'"

I try to swallow but my throat is too closed to do anything.

He caresses my face. "She worth it?" he asks.

The tears finally spill down my cheeks. "Yes," I whisper.

FORTY-TWO

"May I ask who's calling?"

"Maya. Maya Aguirre," I say trying to control my breathing.

"Dancing Queen." Again.

"Baby, is that you?" His voice sounds strong. Like I remember. I can picture his smile and the way he looks before he thinks up a new scheme. I kind of think he likes doing what he does just to see if he can pull it off.

But he didn't pull off his latest scheme. And Klon is dead and Nicole . . . And I am standing in a phone booth in Garden City, Idaho, with a drag queen getting ready to go find my friend. My family. The only person who matters right now. I lean my head against the booth, cooling my forehead on the glass.

"Maya? Maya, I love you so much."

The words get caught in my throat and swell too big to come out. Words. They stay stuck. Deep down inside. They hurt.

"It's okay. You don't have to talk. Are you okay?"

No. No I'm not okay. And I don't know what to do.

"I'm just happy to know you're there, baby. I'm just so relieved. I've been so worried." He pauses. "You're strong, baby. I know that. But it's okay to need help. It's okay to ask for help."

Who could I ask?

I'm so scared. Would he understand that?

"I never taught you that. It was stupid of me." I listen as he talks until the minutes run out. Then I listen to the dial tone, clutching the phone to my ear.

"Hey, honey, you gonna stand and hump that phone all day?" Charity asks. "Christ, it's too Goddamned cold to stand out here." Charity taps the phone booth with his chipped nails.

It's taken us a few hours to walk here. Every minute counts, I know, but I'm so so tired and my body just hurts everywhere.

I follow him to what looks like the outside of a factory building. Music thunders. Smoke pours out from the doorway. Streams of teens walk inside.

It's early afternoon, and the place booms with music. "A rave? We're going to a rave?" I ask.

Charity shakes his head. "I need cash for a ride back. You can't imagine how much these boots chafe. And you, darling, you are on your own."

"Where?" I ask.

Charity is distracted by a guy in tight jeans. "Nice nut huggers," he says.

"Where?" I say again.

He points toward the river. "The Garden. It's all yours."

I walk past some state fairgrounds and find my way to the river, its icy waters churning. It's late afternoon, and the sun has that orange-sherbet color, like its rays are melting all across the sky. Misty rain starts to drizzle from the sky, turning it a gray blue, blotting out the light.

I sit at the river edge, relieved. I imagined it would be covered in corpses—like some kind of morgue. But it's actually really peaceful. I find a broken Coke bottle on the ground and pick it up, tucking it in my pocket. Find a garbage can. That's normal procedure, not: Find dead friend.

I walk downstream past groups of kids getting stoned. Then I see her jacket. I run toward her, and when she turns around, she's a he. I barrel into him, breathless. "Where'd you get that?" I gasp and grab his shoulders. "Where did you get that jacket?"

"Whoa, psycho chick. Lay your hands the fuck off." He pushes me away. His friends laugh, and he gets braver. "You lookin' to party?"

"Where'd you get the jacket?" I ask. My voice sounds so small in the wind.

He taps his groin. "Nothing's for free around here." Some of his friends circle me, and he takes a step forward.

The Coke bottle pushes against my hip bone. I stand up as tall as I can. Being five feet three inches doesn't help. But I stand, my hands trembling, and take out the Coke bottle, cutting my hand on the jagged edge. "You don't know who this has cut. You don't know what incurable communicable disease I've got." My hand doesn't tremble when I hold it in front of me. I can almost feel what it would be like to sink it into his thigh and grind it around while he screams in pain. "One step closer, you better hope to pull off agamogenesis, because the closest you'll come to sexual reproduction will be internet porn."

"Huh?"

"Mycrobacterium leprae. Leprometous strain. Your dick *will* fall off."

"What the fuck is she talking about?" one says.

It figures Nicole wouldn't be around for my prime obscenity hour.

They all back off. I must be too crazy for them to waste their time. "Where," I repeat, "did you get that coat?"

The guy points toward a clump of trees that juts out into the river. "Jesus, it's not like dead kids need coats, you freak bitch."

I have to catch my breath. It can't be. I push past him and run through the woods, twigs snapping on my face. I stumble and rocks get embedded in my hands. When I get to the river, there's a path of stones in the shallow river edge out to a big boulder, and I see her. Rain pours on her limp body.

I stumble through the icy waters and scramble onto the boulder. Her eyes are closed. I stare for a moment. And wait for that subtle up and down, up and down movement in her chest but see nothing.

Her lips are blue.

She holds the pill bottle in her hands, some pills scattered on the boulder.

She's dead.

I'm too late.

Again.

I collapse to my knees and start to shake her. "Please," I whisper. "Please. Please." I can't hold my hands still enough to find a pulse, and can't see through my tears to see if her chest is moving, so I pull her up and shake her rag-doll shoulders. "Wake up. Please. I'm here. Please. Just. Wake. Up."

Nicole coughs, her eyes fluttering open. She slurs her words. "Hey, Jeops."

"Oh God," I say pulling her to me and putting my arms around her. "Oh God."

Nicole closes her eyes.

I hit her. Hard.

She jolts awake. "What?" she says. "Where's Klon?" she asks.

"He's okay now, Nicole."

"Cappy," she whispers.

"Cappy," I say.

"So thirsty." She burns with fever.

I open her palm, pills stuck to it.

"Couldn't swallow," she mutters. "No water. Just wanted

403

to sleep; not feel anything anymore."

I sigh. "C'mon." We slide down the boulder into the water, and I lean her on my shoulder. "I've got you."

When we get across the river, I put my coat on her. We walk through the dark streets, Nicole slumped on my shoulder. The only thing I can think about is finding a way to help her. I can't let her die, too. It's like everybody who means something to me—

I stop the thoughts that crash through my brain.

She will live.

I just have to find a way to get help.

I look for police cars, ambulances, clinics—nothing. The green neon sign of an all-night drugstore catches my eye. We pass it and walk another block until I find a bench where Nicole can lie down. A couple sits on the bench. They stare at us. They cover their noses with their hands.

Fuck you, I want to say. I was there, too. Where you are sitting on that bench. Was it five weeks ago? Six weeks ago? "Move over," I say. "She needs to lie down."

The couple moves away, hunched together to escape what they don't want to see.

I wait outside the drugstore until I see a middle-aged couple go inside and walk in with them. The man holds a prescription in his hand and walks back to the pharmacist. The pharmacist stares at me and half listens as the man goes on about his colonoscopy and polyps and needing the extra fiber in his diet.

Way too much information.

When they walk by, I bump into the lady and slip some boxes into her purse, hoping she'll set off the sensors.

Bingo!

When the alarms go off, the pharmacist runs to the front of the store and grabs the couple, surprised to see I'm not the one who set off the alarm. They all begin to argue, the man talking about how stress certainly isn't going to help his stool soften, the lady gasping when the pharmacist pulls out the Ex-Lax boxes from her pocket.

Nice touch, I think.

I slip around the metal sensor, leaving the store. I sit Nicole up and crush ten pills of aspirin into a bottle of Gatorade, holding it to her mouth.

"Drink," I whisper. "Just drink this. One sip at a time."

She falls asleep, and I shake her awake. "We need to find help. Put your arm around my shoulder." We walk until the moon hangs high in the sky.

Then I see the sign to the same shelter the police officer

had told us about that first morning in the alley. The Path of Light Home for Women and Children.

I look up at the stars bright in the obsidian sky. The clouds have cleared. "Thank you," I say. I reread the name of the shelter and pound on the door. "Help us," I say. "Please." Nicole slumps to the ground and I sit next to her, leaning my head back, closing my eyes.

The door opens and a man takes Nicole from my arms. They pull on latex gloves, strip her down, and wrap her in blankets, head to toe. Then they do the same to me. Three people come in and ask us what has happened. Nicole is slipping in and out of consciousness, and I force myself to stay awake—stay awake for her.

"I got first shift," I say, and hold on to her hand.

She smiles. "Don't fall asleep."

They race us to a clinic, social services in tow. Billie—a psychologist working on her doctorate at the local college—has been assigned our case. "You have names?"

I nod. "Jeopardy and Capone."

"Okay," she says. "Where'd you come from?" she asks.

"The Garden," I say, and stare out the van window at the city; the buildings blur, and I bite my lip, trying to swallow back my sadness, trying to stop trembling. It's like the cold won't go away. Nicole's head rests on my lap and I lay my hand on her chest, feeling the soft thud of her heart, barely there.

We drive up to the emergency entrance, and nurses, doctors, who-knows-who-else come out with rickety gurneys and lift us onto them. Glaring fluorescent lights shine above. I close my eyes listening to the soft hum of the lights, the ring of telephones, and murmur of muffled voices behind glass windows and closed doors. I hold Nicole's bag of lies in one hand and reach for her with the other, but she's ahead of me.

They shove a needle into a thin blue vein on the top of my hand, hanging a bag above me. Our area is crammed with people buzzing around us carrying machines, tubes, IV drips. "Help her," I say, and clutch Nicole's bag tighter.

But they don't hear me.

And I don't know if I even speak or if everything's in my head.

"You got a pulse? You got a pulse?" I watch as they plug Nicole into some machine and stare at a green straight line that starts to blur. "Damn it, we're losing her."

They pull the curtain closed, and I scream.

Or I think I scream.

CHAPTER
FORTY-THREE

Afternoon sunlight seeps through the blinds. I rub my eyes and hope that when I open them, I'll be back in Reno. I listen to the noises around me: the beeps of machines and rustle of paper gowns and doctors' masks. I breathe deep and smell floor wax and pee. Somebody says a prayer. Somebody breathes heavy. Somebody mumbles.

I open my eyes to a curtained cubby and know that none of it has been a dream.

And I know that Klon is dead. And Nicole—Nicole! I sit up, and my head feels like it's been filled with exploding nanotubes.

"Take it easy, honey. You're gonna need to take it one breath at a time. Your body's been pretty hammered."

Black pinpoints dot my vision and I lie back down until my world stops spinning. When I open my eyes again, I see Billie—the social worker.

"Where—" I start to ask.

"Garden City Community Clinic."

"How long?" I ask, my voice hoarse but throat feeling better.

"Two days."

"My friend—is she . . . ?" I can't finish the question.

"She's alive. She started to go into organ failure and has slipped into a coma."

I try to digest her words. "Will she—"

Billie sips on a cup of coffee and clears her throat. "I'm not going to sugarcoat this, okay? You look like you're too smart for that."

I nod.

"She might not make it."

"She'll make it," I say. "She's strong."

Billie nods. She doesn't believe me. She's seen Nicole's scars. She knows this isn't the first time. But it's different now. Things will be different.

I rub my head. They've cut my hair, and I scratch at the short curls.

"They had to cut your hair. Lice."

I shrug. I was looking like a chia plant with dreads, anyway. "Our things," I say.

Billie takes the box and Nicole's bag of things out of a locked drawer and hands them to me with the keys. I hug them to my chest, turning away from Billie. "Why are you here?"

Billie smiles. "I was worried. I'm just glad I was here when you woke up."

"Who are we to you?" I bite my tongue before I say more. I'm starting to sound like Nicole—jaded.

"You got to her just in time. You saved her."

What did I save her from?

"Was she at the Garden?"

I turn away from her and nod.

"Do you want to talk about it?" Billie asks.

"I wouldn't know where to begin," I say.

"What about the box? What's in there?"

I stare at the crushed box. "I'm not sure anymore."

We're quiet, listening to the sounds of other patients. "Where is she?" I ask. "Where's Nicole? Can I see her?"

I slip and say her name. Nicole would kill me. Rule

number two. Or was it rule number three? I get them all mixed up.

Billie nods. "She's at St. Andrew's. Only family's allowed to visit a minor. Do you know about any family?" she asks.

I hold Nicole's plastic bag in my hands. Seven years of postcards from a crackhead mom trying to give her daughter some hope. Lies. "Yeah," I say. "Me. I'm it."

Billie says, "We would like to know your full names, where you're from."

I turn away.

She follows my gaze and stands in front of me. "You have somewhere to go?"

"I'm not sure."

"A mother? A father looking for you? Someone?"

I shake my head. "No one's looking for me. But—" I sigh and close my eyes. I don't know what to say to anyone anymore. Can I trust her? "I have an aunt who I'm trying to find."

Billie sips her coffee. "Where does she live?"

"If I knew that, I don't think I'd be in this mess, okay?" I say.

We're quiet. She opens her mouth to say something, then closes it. "There's a shelter. The one you found the other night. It's better than the streets. A bed. Food. A safe place to be. For now. Until you find—"

Why do I always feel like people think I've invented Aunt Sarah?

"Is it far from St. Andrew's?" I ask.

She shakes her head. "You can take a crosstown bus."

"Okay."

"So you'll come?" she asks.

"I'll come."

Billie checks me out of the clinic. I can hardly walk, I'm so weak. I clamber into the van, and we pull up to the shelter.

Home sweet home, I think.

CHAPTER FORTY-FOUR

When I open my eyes, I notice for the first time there's a security guard sitting behind a window, staring at me like I'm in some kind of aquarium. I sit up and stretch—the only one in the room. The other beds are stripped of their sheets and blankets.

I creep out to the front desk. The same guy is there who helped Nicole and me the other night. A sign about God's light and salvation hangs in the window. Stacks of pamphlets are piled on a wobbly card table. Family violence, paternity rights, drug abuse, sexual assault, stalking—the pamphlets each have a little cross on the upper right-hand corner that says "Find your way by following His light."

"Hove I slept long?" I ask. My voice is hoarse but my

throat is feeling much better.

"Since yesterday afternoon." He looks at the clock. "About eighteen hours."

"Eighteen hours?" How is it possible after having slept two days at the clinic? That's gotta be a record. Maybe Nicole's right and I have a sleeping disorder. I better get that checked.

"And my friend?" I ask.

"Alive," he says.

I sigh.

"First things first." He hands me a fresh pair of underwear, sweats, a towel, generic shampoo and soap, a toothbrush, and toothpaste. "Go wash up and come back out here. I'll give you the rules to the shelter."

The steaming water pours over my body, and I lather myself everywhere. I get out and wipe away the steam to see myself in the mirror but turn away from the gaunt face that stares back at me. I run my finger across the layers of grime that cover my teeth and brush for about twenty minutes.

I still can't believe I forgot to pack a toothbrush.

Like that matters anymore.

I go back out to the front desk.

"I'm Jim. You need to eat. And we need to talk." Jim takes me to the kitchen. "This is an exception. There is no eating here outside of assigned hours." He points to the shelter schedule and looks me up and down. "When was the last time you ate?"

"I don't remember."

He hands me a cup of broth. "Start with this. At dinner, maybe you can have toast, too. Five o'clock."

I sip the broth.

"No weapons; if you want to stay, you're going to have to enroll in the community volunteer program; and a kid your age needs to be studying to get her GED; no smoking, drugs, or alcohol are tolerated; curfew's at eight o'clock at night; during meals, you get your own food and you clean up your mess. We have circle time with the psychologist after dinner. You don't have to talk, but you're expected to be there. Any questions?"

"Do you, um, have to report me—" I start to ask.

"We're here to keep kids like you off the streets. If we report you, you won't come. We don't report. You're off the streets. You might be smart enough to get a diploma and get the hell out of this mess you're in. Got it?"

I nod, and he serves me another bowl of broth—this

time with some noodles in it. "My friend?" I ask.

"At St. Andrew's. That's all I know."

We sit in silence at the table until I eat everything. He serves me a third bowl. "Take it easy."

I slurp it down. It tastes like heaven.

"Are you planning on staying?" he asks.

I nod.

He hands me a folder. "You can get a job at these places. They work with us. It's more like an internship. They pay transportation and give you a meal. In return for volunteering your services, you get to stay here. Off. The. Streets."

Nothing could be better, I think. I browse through the pages and find Boise Public Library. "I'd like to work here."

He nods. He goes and gets a letter. "You plan on telling them your real name?"

I smile. He doesn't realize that I have about twenty. "Sure," I say.

"Sure," he says.

The librarian at the reception desk smiles and says, "I'm Miss Foley. We'd love to have you here," then goes into a spiel about being responsible, on time, respecting library property, blah blah blah. But she's nice. Real nice. And she sends me to work in the computer lab the first day. She comes back after a while. "I can tell you know what you're doing," she says. She pauses. "You're different from most of our volunteers. I don't get why you're here."

"I think there are lots like me out there," I finally say. "Too many."

She stares at me. She sees me. It's like somebody really sees me for the first time in months.

We set it up so I work in the afternoons, study in the evenings, and spend my mornings outside Nicole's window, crouched in some twig bushes. The days get shorter, colder—the nights longer. Billie always wants to hear my story: Why I ran away, what happened on the streets, blah blah blah. I don't really want to tell it. She's not pushy. I guess she's used to finding broken kids and not knowing how to piece them back together.

After a week of volunteering at the library, I bring the box. "Miss Foley, I have to find somebody. Do you think I can come in early to do some research?"

Miss Foley looks at the letters in the box. "Absolutely."

Then she leaves me alone. She always gives me space. It's a good job.

Today I stand outside Nicole's window and put my hand against the pane, hoping she'll know that she's not alone. It's weird. I haven't done a procedure or hypothesis since, well, for a long time.

And I feel better. No more plans or procedures—just living day-by-day, waiting for things to come. Because that's all I can do now. Wait. Wait for her to wake up.

I clap my hands against my thighs. The clothes from the shelter aren't nearly as warm as I wish they were. The doctors and Billie say I'll warm up when I gain weight.

"She knows you're here, you know."

I stand up from the bushes. "Oh. Um sorry. I wasn't doing anything. Just . . . sorry."

"You're here every day." The woman wraps a scarf around her neck and zips her coat up.

"Yeah. I—" I turn to leave.

"Don't go. She needs you."

I stare at her. She has kind eyes.

"Tomorrow my shift starts at six o'clock in the morning. She could use a friend. Maybe you can go and talk to her."

"I'd like that," I say.

"You okay?" she asks.

I'm getting a little tired of people asking me that. But I nod. I'm going to see my family.

CHAPTER FORTY-FIVE

I get to the hospital before six o'clock and wait. She pulls up in a hybrid and shuffles down the frozen walk toward the doors. She looks my way and waves me over. I follow her.

"I'm Catalina." She pulls back her long black hair into a ponytail and slips on a white coat.

"'Tis the season, Dr. Ramirez," a man says, passing Catalina in the hallway, handing her a bunch of charts. "Curtain one, alcohol poisoning. Curtain two, salmonella—dumb bastards made homemade eggnog. Every Goddamn year," he whispers.

Catalina shrugs.

"Curtain six"—the man looks at the chart—"you

don't even wanna know."

"Ho-ho-ho," Catalina says dryly and flips through the patients' charts. "Ewww," she says.

"Yep. Told you so. See you tomorrow." He winks. "Happy Rounds to you, Ramirez."

Catalina hands me a hot chocolate.

"Thank you," I say.

"Follow me." She turns on her heel. We push past the chaos of the emergency room and walk down a quiet hallway. "Technically only family is allowed in. So you're family, okay?" she says.

"Yes," I say. I don't even hesitate.

She leads me down the hall. "She can hear, you know."

"Will she get better?" I ask.

She looks at the chart. "She's emerging. She's starting to respond to things we say and physical touch. We hope it's today or tomorrow. The sooner she wakes up, the better."

"After that?" I ask. "Where does she go?"

"All the kids . . ." Her voice trails off. "All the kids they find in the Garden are taken to Willow Springs on suicide watch. These cases are pretty sad," she says. "She has no family to contact."

I hold Nicole's postcards in my hand.

"Come on." Catalina leads me to Nicole's bedside and then leaves me there.

"Hey, Nicole."

She looks like she's just in a deep sleep. I look at the window and can see where my nose and fingers left prints on the pane.

I lay my head on Nicole's bed and close my eyes, pretending I'm her—stuck in silence. I listen to the sounds of the hospital: footsteps patter in a distant hallway, machines beep, telephones ring, somebody breathes heavily, somebody says a prayer.

The room smells like ammonia and cinnamon spice incense. Some carolers jingle-bell down the hallways. I don't think anybody should allow carolers into a hospital at Christmastime. It's pretty depressing.

"Hi," I say. "I wasn't around for the first few days because I fell asleep. Big surprise, right? You'd think I have some weird sleep disorder."

The carolers stand in the doorway and belt out "God Rest Ye Merry, Gentlemen," jingling bells and wearing stupid Santa hats. When they finish, the other patients offer them quiet applause.

"You know, Christmas was probably in September,

not December. In the year seven B.C.—the year most people think Jesus was born—Saturn and Jupiter moved to within a degree of each other when he was born. It's only ever happened three times in the history of the world. I mean, it's probably happened a lot more, but only three times since man has started counting. Anyway, if we take all the facts, it looks like Christmas was mid-September."

Silence.

"I'm volunteering at the library. In the afternoons." I sigh. "I kinda needed access to computers and stuff."

Silence.

"I'm studying at this alternative ed high school. The shelter doesn't give us much of a choice. We've got to volunteer and study to stay. So my classmates are mostly pregnant teens, ex-felons, and runaways. Probably the only place I'd have a real shot at homecoming queen. Funny. I don't miss high school. And at this school, everybody's pretty laid-back. It's kinda nice to be anonymous. It's nice to be Jeopardy.

"I think I got on some homeschoolers' list, though, by accident. Last week, the Boise homeschooler association invited me and my 'guardian' to an ice-cream social. They want to make sure the homeschooled kids don't come out all socially retarded or something. As if high school did wonders for my social skills, right?"

I pull Nicole's blankets up and take her hand in mine. "Please," I say. "Please wake up."

Her hand remains limp. Lifeless.

I clear my throat. "About the postcards." I pull out her plastic bag. "I'm sorry I lied. I just didn't want—" What? I didn't want her to know everything she believed in was a lie? She was bound to find out sometime. Why did I lie?

"It's just. It's just sometimes lies aren't all that bad. And maybe your mom does that to give you hope." I clear my throat. "Maybe she's trying to make up for something. So she created a dream. Kind of like my dad with the box of stuff."

I sit with her in silence. There's nothing to say. Not really. "I miss you," I finally say. "I miss your stories." I lay my head back down on her bed and close my eyes. I listen to the evenness of her breathing and try to think back to where everything went so wrong.

Genesis, I think. It was all wrong from the beginning.

"It's time to go." Catalina taps my shoulder. "You can

come back tomorrow—I have a six A.M. shift again."

I squeeze Nicole's hand and say, "It wasn't your fault, you know. That he died.

"I'm trying to find where he is. So he just doesn't become a John Doe, you know?" I get up to go. "It wasn't your fault. It was mine."

CHAPTER
FORTY-SIX

"I've been to a synagogue, Lutheran and Methodist churches, even a Mormon temple. But they wouldn't let me in the temple, so I sat outside and looked at it," I say.

Nicole stares out the window. The hospital called the shelter to tell us she has woken up. And they let me skip class and volunteer work to come see her. Billie even gave me a ride.

"And the Catholic church. It's pretty nice with its stained-glass windows." I went to mass at St. Mary's. People shuffled into the pews wearing elegant clothes. I tried to pray.

"I go in those places, though, and don't feel it. I don't feel this holy presence or like I'm more protected or loved there. I wish I could have Klon's faith."

426

Nicole pulls the blanket up, shivering. Her silence is deafening—louder than any of her nonstop monologues. I want to shake the words out of her—the stories, the mob facts, anything.

"You know I've come every day for the last couple of weeks. If your coma brain could remember as well as your conscious brain, you'd already know all about the rise and fall of monarchies. Sorry I bored you with social studies homework. They're going to send you to Willow Springs—some kind of institution. When you get out of here." I sigh. "You can't just give up."

It's like Nicole's still in a coma—her bloodshot eyes scanning the room. She looks disappointed, like she wishes she had died.

And I'm afraid for her—afraid that being stuck in a room between four white walls, she'll give up. She'll die.

I read Aunt Sarah's letters to Nicole. "I know there's something we're missing here. Something we haven't seen." I carefully pick at the return address label under the lip of the box, but it's stuck, and I'm afraid of messing it up. "Something's here. Something obvious," I say.

When I leave, I say, "We'll get there, okay?"

But she just turns her back to me.

I go to the library with my box of things. I reread the

letters from Aunt Sarah to Mom. Then I pull out a dried flower, staring at it. A piece of her home. I run my fingers across the faded petals and pull down a book on state symbols.

And I find it. Indian paintbrush—the state flower of Wyoming.

I borrow a magnifying glass and look at the return address stuck under the rim of the box and can make out "J—s-n —le, W-."

Jackson Hole, Wyoming.

The phone rings. And rings. On the sixth ring I'm going to hang up when she answers. "Hello?" she says, out of breath.

My throat closes up again.

"Hello?" she repeats.

"Hi," I rasp. "Um, can I please speak to Sarah Jones?"

"Speaking."

My hand trembles as it cradles the receiver. "Are you, um, Michelle's sister?"

"Who is this?"

"My name is Maya. Maya Aguirre," I say.

I listen as she gasps and drops the telephone, then

scrambles to pick it up. The seconds tick by.

"Hello? Maya?" she says just as my money runs out. How irritating. She probably doesn't know how hard it is to get the cash to call.

I have found her. Auntie Em. I think about my purpose, hypothesis, procedure.

Purpose: Find Aunt Sarah

Hypothesis: If I call back collect, will she answer? I'm afraid to find out.

I realize I don't care about making hypotheses or procedures anymore. I can't predict what people will do, but I can control what I do. So I cradle the phone in my hand and call back collect.

"Will you accept the charges?"

"Yes," I hear her voice. I wish I could say it sounds like Mom. But I hardly remember anything about Mom. And I realize now that I want somebody to fill in the blanks.

"Um, it's expensive. Collect calls," I say.

"You're not calling from Papua New Guinea, are you?" she asks.

"Nah," I say. "Just Boise, Idaho."

"Then I think I can foot the bill."

And we talk.

I go to the hospital and sit by Nicole. When it's time to go, I say, "Nicole, they're going to release you later this week."

She turns to me and looks me in the eyes.

"They're going to send you to Willow Springs. Instead of being property of Nevada, you now belong to Idaho. Do you really want that?" I ask. "So what if he's not real? You can still go to all these places." I pull out her postcards. "We can go. Together."

The hospital has forced Nicole to wear gloves because she's bitten her fingernails so low they bleed all the time. Since they have her on suicide watch, she's not even allowed to eat her food with a fork. But she hardly eats. It's as if she has decided to stop; stop eating; stop speaking; stop being.

I pause. "You know, I have a plan." And I do.

The plastic bag of postcards slips from Nicole's fingers and thunks on the floor. She stares down at it, then turns her back to me. "Nothing has ever been real," she says, "except for these." She points to her scars.

I pick up the postcards and throw them on her bedside table. I want to shake her. She can't be like the rest

430

of them. She can't give up.

"I've found her," I say. "She's real. There's more than those." I motion to her scars.

Nicole turns to me, eyes blazing.

I unclasp my chain and place the locket in her hand. "Good exists, Nicole. It does. It has to." I think about Klon and who he was. I have to find him. I have to find his mom, too. She has to know.

Good. There would be no balance if there were no good. The universe wouldn't make sense if there were no good. "Klon was good. He was the best."

Nicole stares at the necklace in the palm of her hand, studying the faces in the faded photograph. She shakes her head. "You'd never get it—not ever."

"Maybe not," I say. "But I want to try."

She turns back into the Nicole I knew in Kids Place. She has shut off. "Fuck off," she finally says. "I'm not your social-studies humanitarian project anymore. Go find someone else to save." She throws the necklace down, the locket flipping open. We both look at the faded photograph. Auntie Em.

Aunt Sarah.

Would she take both of us?

CHAPTER FORTY-SEVEN

One hundred and eleven dollars. From Boise to Jackson Hole. Each. And it goes about three hundred miles out of the way because it's some kind of weird B route. I sigh. Where am I going to get the money to pay for the trip? And I don't think Aunt Sarah would just fork out two hundred–plus dollars for bus tickets. I wouldn't— especially knowing where I'm coming from.

I slip back into my scientific mind so I can find a purpose—a way to get the money. And I actually have a good plan. A plan that's easy enough to execute but will pretty much screw over, I calculate, about twenty high schoolers. And then I will be a con. I will be my dad.

I think about him. What would he do? Anything to

keep me off the streets. Anything to keep me safe.

What will I do?

"May I ask who's calling?"

"Maya," I say, and wait for "Dancing Queen." This time, though, "Chiquitica" floods the phone line. I wonder if the Nevada prison system gets a discount on ABBA elevator music.

"Maya?"

"Dad?"

"Maya, baby." He sighs. I picture him with a white-knuckled grip on the telephone. He chokes out the words, "How are you? Where are you? Oh my God. Are you okay? They've looked. And I thought I'd lost—" He can't talk fast enough.

"I'm okay," I say. "Kind of." I hold on to the phone and wish I could be with him.

"Okay."

Silence. We've never been big on long conversations.

"You know, Dad, there's this South American bird that seems like a real MRSA."

"Mersah?" he asks.

"Yeah. Flesh-eating bacteria." Does nobody know what that is?

"Of course." Dad laughs.

"Anyway, he has like two to twelve wives in his harem. Just kind of messing around on the South American pampas."

"Ouch," Dad says. "More loony than anything, I'd say."

I smile. It's good to hear his voice. "Anyway, it seems like he sucks at being a dad. I mean with all those wives and breeding and stuff. But he's actually the one who incubates the eggs after his wives leave him high and dry. And then he raises the birds. All alone."

Silence.

"I guess," I finally say, "I guess sometimes you've just got to look beyond the surface."

Silence.

I have to breathe in deep so I won't lose it.

"We okay?" Dad asks.

"Yeah," I say.

"What are you going to do?" he asks.

I pause. "Give Aunt Sarah a try."

"You found her?"

"Yeah."

"Thank God," he says. "Thank God."

We're quiet and I finally say, "It's okay."

He whispers into the phone. "That's my girl."

Then the line goes dead.

It takes me a few days to get the nerve up to call and ask her.

"Can I pick you up?" she asks. "I mean I can take a bus to meet you. We both can. Mike just had LASIK eye surgery, so he can't drive. And they, uh, well I can't drive for a while until I finish my community service. It's not as bad as you think." She sounds nervous. "I honestly didn't see the mayor's cat or mailbox or, well, I spilled my Jivin' Juice cranberry smoothie. But normally I'm a good driver. Really good."

I laugh.

So does she.

I didn't expect that. That she'd come all the way to Boise and pick me up. With her husband. And then we'll be stuck in a bus for who knows how many hours not knowing how to fill the silence.

But I have so many questions. And it doesn't sound like she's the quiet type.

"Um. Okay," I say. "But I don't think I'll be alone. My

friend, she um—" I don't finish the sentence because I don't know how.

After a silence she says, "Your friend is welcome here."

I can hear that there's more to that sentence that she's not saying. I want to say we're a package deal, but that would probably freak her out. It's good to ease into these things.

"Where are you staying?" she finally asks. "We can leave this afternoon—evening. We can be there in a day. Or less. I've gotta get the bus schedule. I have to call Mike. We can get this organized and done today. Today. If"—she pauses—"if that's okay?"

There's a pause.

"I—we," she corrects, "look forward to having you here. I've missed you." I can hear the urgency in her voice, like she doesn't expect to see me at all. Maybe she's worried I'm like Dad. Maybe she's afraid I'll slip away.

"Okay," I say. "If it's no trouble."

"Not at all!" I half expect her to jump through the phone. "When can we come?"

"What day is it?" I ask.

"December twenty-first."

"Maybe the twenty-third. I've got some things to

arrange. We can meet at the bus terminal." I think it's better she doesn't see the shelter and where I am now. It's better to start off with a clean slate in neutral territory.

"Anytime. Anywhere," she says.

I walk down the white corridor, my footsteps echoing in the hallway. Willow Springs Mental Hospital for Adolescents isn't far from the shelter. There's a yellow waiting room, but the rest of the place is white. Sanitarium white.

Well, better than mint green, I guess.

When I walk in the door, it takes me a second to get used to the pine smell that's supposed to cover up the odd mix of urine and cigarette smoke. There's a sickly looking Christmas tree in the lobby with homemade ornaments and clumps of cheap tinsel.

Nicole sits in her room, staring out the window. She's become a shell. She hasn't said anything to me since they transferred her. Or to anyone.

I sit down and start to read aloud from my history book—for one of my homework assignments. I'm working hard to finish the second quarter of tenth grade.

"Nic," I say. "Christmas is almost here."

Silence.

"You know, I'm not too big on the whole holiday, but I don't want to . . ." I sigh. "I don't want to be alone. I used to think that I liked alone, but I don't. And you've just kinda checked out."

Silence.

"I miss you," I say. "Things are going to be okay now. I know they will."

Nicole shrugs.

"You don't deserve what happened to you. You didn't deserve those cigarette burns and bad families."

Nicole pulls out a folded-up picture and shows it to me—the one Klon took from the book at the restaurant.

I've wondered where that picture went. She looks at it and crumples it up, throwing it in the trash.

I pick it up and iron out the creases. "Stop this. Just stop it."

Nicole turns her back to me.

"You deserve better, Nic. Klon wasn't your fault. Neither was your sister."

Nicole turns to me and shakes her head and rubs her skinny arms with gloved hands. She looks more skeletal every day.

"It wasn't your fault. And Klon—it was mine. I was

438

supposed to be the strong one that day. I was supposed to stand up to you, and I didn't because I was scared. I was scared that what happened to you in the system would happen to me. That's why I didn't go to the police; that's why I didn't fight with you about it."

Nicole unravels a string from her bedspread, curling the dirty white thread around her finger.

"I've told Billie at the shelter about Klondike. They found his body at the morgue and are trying to find his mom. I don't think it'll be too hard."

Nicole raises an eyebrow.

I nod. "They have this thing called CODIS—Combined DNA Index System—and Nevada has lots of data. They take DNA samples from the families of missing persons and put them into a database. Then they just have to take a sample from Klon and get a match. It's a good thing. We'll find his mom."

Nicole turns to me. "He's not a fucking science experiment."

I swallow. "I know. But this is the way he can go back home."

"Where they threw him out like trash," Nicole hisses.

"But I wrote her a letter, see. I wrote about how good he

was. About Tourette's. About how wrong she was." I sigh. "I know where he comes from doesn't matter. His real name. Where he was born. How old he was. We knew him, Nicole. We knew who he was. And he was good. He was *real*. But it meant something to him—to be where he could find his family, his God." I sigh. "I'm just trying to make things right for him. Because I don't know what else to do."

Nicole sits on her bed and folds her legs up to her chest. Her hospital-issue sweat suit looks more like a tent. Some kid walks by and says, "Hey, Helen Keller. You gonna come to session?"

Nicole doesn't even flip him off. She just sits, staring out the square of a window.

She gnaws on her lower lip. "Well, you got what you needed. You found your family—your precious aunt Sarah."

I shake my head. "She's not the family I found. Okay? We have to do this together."

Silence.

"Theme of the day," I say. "Your pick."

Nicole looks at me with her bloodshot eyes. She shakes her head.

"Your turn," I urge. After a long silence, I finally say,

"Okay. What's the place you've wanted to go to most? For as long as you can remember?"

Nicole taps her gloved fingers on the windowsill. "Home," she whispers.

"Home," I repeat. "Let's go."

But she doesn't say anything. Nothing. She stares out the window and I sit in the crushing silence of her white room. After a while, she takes out a crumpled piece of paper—smudged with words. My words.

"I can't read it," she says. "I can't see worth shit."

It's the paper from her prescription bottle at Kids Place. I've dreamed of saying those words my whole life—to make a difference. And now I'm afraid they're just smudges on a page. Meaningless.

I breathe in deep. "It's this stupid Einstein quote I read a few years ago. And I wrote it to you because I wished I could've written it to my mom. I, um. It's—" I hand the paper back to her and say the words that have danced around my head all these years. "'There are two ways to live your life—one is as though nothing is a miracle, the other is as though everything is a miracle.'"

Nicole turns away.

"I think," I say, "I think that's what Klon meant when he

talked about people doing what they should—the everyday stuff."

"Klon's miracles," Nicole whispers.

"They could be ours, too," I say.

"Group time." Some guy with wire-rimmed glasses pokes his head in Nicole's door. "Sorry," he says to me. "Visiting hours are over."

I zip my coat up. "I'll be back tomorrow."

She has already turned away.

CHAPTER FORTY-EIGHT

illie motions me into her small office while she finishes talking to some guy on the phone and points to the chair.

The wooden seat digs into my thighs and I clasp my fingers around the edge, holding my breath.

"Do you know anything about her?" Billie asks. "This aunt who's coming to pick you up?"

I shrug. About as much as I know about my mom and dad. It's funny how little we know about the people we're supposed to know the best.

"Why didn't you tell the people in Nevada? The people at social services?"

"I didn't think they'd listen," I say. "Credibility issues

with the family." And if I had listened and they had listened, I wouldn't have had Nicole or Klon. And they were worth all this, I think.

"I'm glad for you. That you found a place. And Nicole—"

"She's coming, too," I interrupt. "I mean that's what I hope."

"Let's get real here, Jeopardy. She's already gone. I've seen her before—in hundreds of other faces. Statistically speaking, she's gonna be one of the ones who pull it off. Suicide is the third leading cause of death for kids your age. She—"

My ears ring with Billie's words. They all blend into a monotone beep. Then when she stops talking, the room fills with silence until the walls look like they're bulging with the words she won't say.

"What do you expect from me?" she says after a pause.

I swallow. "You could be different. You could see past her scars. I did."

Billie looks at me with tired eyes. "What do you expect from her?"

"Just one of Klon's miracles." I stand up to leave. "It's not too much to expect," I say.

I throw a card key on Nicole's bedside stand—one I stole from the day cleaning staff. "I leave tomorrow. Wednesday, December twenty-third. She's coming to get us. Ten thirty in the morning."

Nicole glances at the key.

"I could use the company. I don't even know her," I say. "But she's coming by bus—all the way from Jackson Hole—for both of us. She'll have tickets for both of us."

Nicole turns away.

"The tickets are open. You can come anytime." I looked up the ticket rules on the Internet. "Well, within the next six months. Either way, when you're better. Or now. Anytime. But decide what you want to do. Live or die. Don't hang out in this limbo land." My stomach knots. I know I'm giving her the key to leave—the choice to die. Nobody on the street will make her wear gloves. Nobody will force her to eat. Nobody will care what she does. She'll just become invisible again.

She looks up at me with dead eyes.

"You made a choice to come with me before. Make the same choice again," I say. "This time we'll get there. We'll go home. I'll get you there."

Nicole turns away.

"You're just as guilty, you know." I clear my throat. "You've let them make you become part of the system. You were five years old. That's all. And you didn't call because you were afraid. Not calling probably saved your life, okay? He could've killed you, too. And your life is worth saving."

I take out the brittle flower and place it on her nightstand. "Come home," I say, and walk away.

CHAPTER FORTY-NINE

"Thanks for the ride." I climb out of Billie's car.

"You want me to hang around?" she asks. "Let me rephrase that. I'm going to hang around until I see this aunt of yours."

I nod. It feels kinda good to have somebody watching out for me; somebody to make sure Aunt Sarah isn't an ogre and Uncle Mike a troll. Uncle Mike. I have an uncle, too.

I look around the terminal and don't see her anywhere. "Can you hold this a sec?" I pass the backpack to Billie— the one the shelter has given me with a change of clothes and snacks for the trip. "Let me take one last look just to make sure she's not here."

"She's not here." Billie holds my backpack.

I pause and nod but take a walk around the bus terminal anyway. Just to be sure. When I come back, Billie's bought us a couple of vending-machine hot chocolates and Danish rolls. They're not half bad.

Between bites, Billie says, "She's too weak to get out of bed most of the time. I think they're going to put in a feeding tube."

I swallow and look away, wiping the tears.

"I'm sorry," she says.

"Thanks for seeing," I say, "past all the scars. She needs glasses, you know. And maybe you could visit her. Be there for her." I clear my throat. "And my aunt. I think she'll have a ticket for her—one of those open-ended ones. Can you make sure she gets it?"

"I can do that."

We fall into a strained silence, both eager to see who's going to come off the bus and through the doors.

People stream on and off the buses. I look at the time: ten fifty-three. She's twenty minutes late. Maybe she changed her mind. Billie asks about the bus from Jackson Hole, but there's no bus from Jackson Hole. And we don't know her route. She just said ten thirty in Boise. So we wait. Billie reaches out to hold my hand, and this time I don't pull it away. This is my last plan—last procedure. If this doesn't work . . .

I can't come up with a hypothesis because the pain in my chest is too sharp.

Groups of people huddle together in the cold morning air. I don't recognize anybody. I guess I hoped there would be some kind of genetic pull that would lead me straight to Aunt Sarah. Like I'd know she was in the room.

So I sit down facing where people get off the buses and wait.

Three, four, five more buses arrive, and people spill into the lobby—a mess of heavy winter coats, Wellington boots, muddy floors, and welcomes.

Eleven forty.

No Aunt Sarah.

I can tell Billie's getting frazzled. She's successfully torn and divided her hot chocolate cup into even pieces and created a mini checkers game. She's probably wracking her mind trying to figure out how she'll cope with a fifteen-year-old's meltdown. I don't figure they cover devastating loss in her psychology classes.

My last chance is gone. It's over. I'm going to Don and Cherry's—back to where I began. Klon died for nothing. And Nicole . . .

Then I see her.

A small woman with short, brown curls approaches me. Her cheeks are red and chapped. She looks flustered, nervous. But behind Coke-bottle glasses she has warm eyes. Gray eyes. Like mine. Behind her stands a man who's at least six feet five or taller. His hands are clasped in front of him, thick eyebrows furrowed.

I put out my hand to shake hers and she pulls me into her thick arms.

And I feel like I could melt. Though I know that's scientifically impossible.

CHAPTER FIFTY

The door beeps when I open it. I pound my boots on the welcome mat and step inside.

A lady looks over her horn-rimmed glasses at me. "You're the spitting image of her," she says.

"Um, who?" I ask.

"You must be Sarah's niece. Maya, isn't it? Just passing through, are you?" she asks.

She's one of those asking people. I can imagine her keeping a tally of people's lives in her small shop.

"No." I clear my throat. "This is home." I wander up and down the aisles of the store. "Do you have any postcards?"

"Right here, darling."

Figures. Right next to her at the counter.

"Thanks." I look through some sepia-toned cards and pick one that has a picture of a sign propped against an old saloon that says "Elk head drop off." I laugh. "This is great."

She rings it up. "Postcards. Not so popular nowadays."

"Hmmm," I mumble while writing the note—a long one with big letters, lots of detail. I wonder if they got her glasses yet. I glance at the clock. I have just enough time to get to the post office and send it off. I double-check the address, pay her for the card, slip my coat on, and head to the door.

"You got a sweetheart? Some clandestine romance?" She raises her eyebrows.

Well, at least she gets straight to the point. I shake my head.

"So? Who's that special person?" she asks again, winking and smirking.

"Family," I say. I walk to the door and shrug on my coat, bracing myself for gale winds. One thing's for sure here in Jackson Hole. It's cold.

"Hey, Maya!" the lady calls out to me.

I turn around.

"Welcome home," she says.

ACKNOWLEDGMENTS

Many thanks to Alexis Erwin, Katrena Kalleres, and Corey LeMay for their expertise. And always my rocks, Carrie and Cesar; my cheering squad, Rick, Syd, and Kyra; my writing family, the Slingers; and my amazing editor and my agent, Jill Santopolo and Stephen Barbara.